THE KINGS OF *Vegas*

Also by Karen Mack and Jennifer Kaufman

Freud's Mistress

A Version of the Truth

Literacy and Longing in L.A.

THE KINGS OF *Vegas*

A NOVEL

KAREN MACK *and*
JENNIFER KAUFMAN

WILLIAM MORROW
An Imprint of HarperCollins*Publishers*

 For information, address HarperCollins Publishers, 195 Broadway, New York, NY 10007. In Europe, HarperCollins Publishers, Macken House, 39/40 Mayor Street Upper, Dublin 1, D01 C9W8, Ireland.

HarperCollins books may be purchased for educational, business, or sales promotional use. For information, please email the Special Markets Department at SPsales@harpercollins.com.

hc.com

FIRST EDITION

Designed by Nancy Singer
Sparkle © Fendy/stock.adobe.com

Library of Congress Cataloging-in-Publication Data

Names: Mack, Karen author | Kaufman, Jennifer author
Title: The Kings of Vegas : a novel / Karen Mack and Jennifer Kaufman.
Description: First edition. | New York : William Morrow, 2026.
Identifiers: LCCN 2025010073 | ISBN 9780063435612 hardcover | ISBN 9780063435629 ebook
Subjects: LCGFT: Novels
Classification: LCC PS3613.A272548 K56 2025 | DDC 813/.6—dc23/eng/20250506
LC record available at https://lccn.loc.gov/2025010073

ISBN 978-0-06-343561-2

26 27 28 29 30 LBC 5 4 3 2 1

For Nate Mack, Joyce and Jerry Mack, and Parry Thomas—
Nevada visionaries who moved to a dusty desert town
and turned it into that glittering City on the Hill.

THE KINGS OF *Vegas*

Chapter 1

Josie King couldn't think of one reason why she ended up in this man's bed. She didn't even know his name. Maybe the prospect of facing her family had sent her over the edge. Bad behavior was somehow appealing when she got into one of these hollow moods. That's what last night was all about. The bigger and redder the line, the more temptation there was to cross it. Maybe it's human nature, but in her case, she feared it was genetic.

She'd spent the day driving the desert road from LA to Vegas, which she had done so many times before. Most people found the landscape barren and monotonous but she loved this drive, the highway bordered with rows of cholla cacti, red boulders, Mojave sage and towering ponderosa pines. Halfway there, she slowed down and looked around at the stark beauty and silence of the desert. There were remnants of decaying structures and shreds of blown-out tires lying next to the abandoned wilderness. She was tempted to pull off an exit and roam around one of the ghost towns that remained in the area—examples of the region's savage history. These were once booming outposts that went bust, people fleeing to other places with their high-powered rifles and stolen horses.

She would be staying at the ranch where she had spent the first seventeen years of her life. But coming home this time was different. Her father's funeral was scheduled for the end of the week, and his sudden death had left her stunned. Her family was gathering there now. It had been a long time since they all got together.

At one point on the drive, loneliness hit her almost like a bout of homesickness. Except she wasn't yearning to go home. She was dreading it. It was at that point she decided to take a detour. What the hell. Nostalgia was overrated.

Chapter 2

Josie decided to jump off the I-15 and take the old Route 66 between Victorville and Barstow. She pulled into Buffalo Bill's, a local casino twenty-five miles south of Vegas, located at the California/Nevada state line. She parked her serious-looking black Mercedes sedan in the free lot behind Denny's, next to the F-150s, mid-range Chevys, Silverados and beat-up hatchbacks. Her family never owned black cars because they always looked dusty and absorbed the sun, so, naturally, the first thing she did when she moved to LA was buy a black car.

Josie looked in the rearview mirror, put on red lipstick and combed her long auburn hair. The sky was brutally blue and the sun beat down on the car's roof. It was so hot that her skirt stuck to her thighs, and her white silk blouse was wet with sweat. At nearly 5 p.m. the place was crowded with locals who had just gotten off work. Just past the roulette wheels and the video poker machines was the Wild Bill Bar, which overlooked the packed buffalo-shaped pool. Josie ordered a shot of tequila and sat at a nearby blackjack table with its smooth green felt and ivory chips. All around her, the slots were insanely ringing—a cacophony of brain-numbing noises from the floor.

Despite the subzero air-conditioning, Josie still felt hot. She took in the adrenaline-charged crowd, the barrage of blinking lights and clanging bells. Drinking, smoking, livid neon colors—the gambler's version of an amphetamine-fed euphoria. It amused her to watch people in their ritualistic attempts to beat the house. A woman said a prayer, crossed herself and threw the dice on the table. A group of Texas tourists moved to a new table because the old one was "cold." An Asian woman bet only on red because it was the symbol of prosperity and good fortune.

In spite of herself, Josie got caught up in the frenzy. It reminded her of when she was a teenager; she had lived for the excitement of her father's casino. Back then it was all she could do to hide the momentary exhilaration of knowing that she could win. And win again. Josie was a blackjack prodigy, or as her brother Sam called her, "a fucking genius with numbers." And that's when her troubles always began.

An older dealer with puffy bags under his eyes stood behind the horseshoe-shaped table and gave her a condescending smile, his teeth shockingly white against his dark tan. He opened six fresh decks of cards and then shuffled, cut, and dealt them. The new cards felt like satin in her hands.

As the game began, Josie kept her cool, hardly looking at the cards and trying to seem as disinterested as possible. She placed mostly low bets on the table, as if it were totally random. She wanted to look like a beginner—and it worked. She won with a pair of tens, but never doubled down. She enjoyed being underestimated. It gave her an advantage.

At some point she realized she could count cards right in front of him and he'd never suspect a thing. It had been a long time since she had played, and her confidence came roaring back. She gave the dealer a blank stare, pushed a stack of chips on the table and started betting and winning. She didn't want to be noticed so she never bet more than twenty dollars. She wouldn't rack up big winnings here. It was enough for her to know that she could. The cocktail waitress came by to offer her a drink—on the house. She ordered a shot of tequila and then another.

A tall, handsome man in faded blue shorts and T-shirt sat down next to her. He had thick dark hair and wore navy leather deck shoes. "Nice playing," he said. She was up over $500.

"I like to win," she said, smiling.

"Doesn't everyone?" he responded indulgently.

She noticed the way he was looking at her. She had never randomly hooked up with a total stranger before, but the thought of one night of mindless sex, acted out with someone she would never see again, suddenly appealed to her. She wanted him. It was reckless but she didn't care. Everything around her was reckless. What harm would it do? A gorgeous, willing man was sitting right next to her and she knew what he was thinking.

"Feeling lucky?" he asked.

"I am now," she answered, almost touching her Patrón-tinged lips to his ear.

She wasn't about to pretend she was unaware of what might happen. He smiled and studied her. She was unaccustomed to flirting codes of conduct but this seemed to work. He leaned over and kissed her on the neck. He smelled clean, like a bar of Ivory soap, and his eyes were grayish green—the kind of eyes that change color depending on one's mood.

When she said, "Let's go to your room," he didn't seem surprised.

"Do you always get what you want?" he asked, clearly amused by her proposition.

"Not always," she said, carefully laying her hand on his thigh, her fingertips pressing in slightly.

He nodded to the dealer, then wrapped his arm around her waist as if he had known her more than ten minutes and guided her to an elevator. The moment the door closed, she leaned into him as his fingers lifted the back of her skirt and he slid his hand between her legs, touching her slowly. Her mouth was slightly open. She was tumbling off an invisible cliff and she could feel the heat of his body. "I'd like to take you right here," he whispered, and she would have let him if another couple hadn't entered the elevator.

"Don't look so disappointed, sweetheart," he said, laughing lightly.

They walked into an empty hotel suite and fell against each other with no hesitation or dialogue. She had never felt so desirable and so completely in control. Skin to skin, they wrestled their clothes off and he pulled out a condom. It didn't escape her notice that she was with someone who just happened to have a condom in his wallet. They fucked for what seemed like hours. Then they lay naked on the floor.

"How was it?" he asked.

"Good," she murmured. He stood up and led her to a bedroom, where he nestled his head between her legs and they fell asleep.

Josie tried to remember the last time she had felt pure lust. The touch of someone's hands, the swallowing of a body, a person who was a stranger, a kiss that didn't make sense except how it felt. Discovering that corner of her that had been hidden for years. She thought this was all behind her and then it descended with a titanic rush, this holy roller revival of her lost libido.

At 2 a.m., she opened her eyes and looked around. Reality set in. Here she was at a hotel on the outskirts of Vegas, her clothes thrown in a tangled mess on the floor. All she could think about was leaving. She gently pushed away the covers and got dressed in the bathroom. She was in no condition to drive but she had to get out. Just as she was headed for the door, the man stirred, and then leaned on his elbows.

"Where are you going?" he asked, his eyes half-closed, watching her.

"I have to leave."

"Are you sure?" He sat on the edge of the bed for a moment, smiled languidly and walked over to her. He rubbed his thumb along her swollen lower lip and then softly moved his hands under her blouse. Body heat was coming off him in waves. He lifted her up and carried her back to bed.

Josie had always heard about these three-four-times-in-a-night kind of nights. But she had never experienced one.

"I really do need to go," she said early the next morning.

"Okay. See you around . . . ?"

"Josie."

"See you around, Josie. I'm Bobby." He flashed a smile.

She considered getting a cup of coffee from the bar before she drove home but was nervous Bobby would appear. That would be awkward. It had been years since she'd been in one of these down-home, local casinos and Josie was surprised how garish it looked in broad daylight. Last night there was an almost magical buzz in the air: a trip through a universe of red and green uppers and downers, quarts of tequila, vodka, whiskey, beer—everything you needed to push it over the line and get roaring high. This morning, the world was flat. There were a few people playing blackjack, the craps tables half-empty, older women with sun-damaged chests and cotton candy hair clutching their buckets of quarters, slot zombies mesmerized by the hypnotic effect of the machines.

Josie got back to her car, threw her purse on the passenger seat and sat there for a while, appalled by her behavior. She wasn't some crazy tourist, after all. Or a veteran of one-night stands. She had to stop thinking about it. She tried to bury the memory of his warm skin and focus on the day ahead. Still, it had been a long time since she had been kissed like that.

Chapter 3

Josie followed the familiar route she had traveled so many times as a child. The dry desert air seared the land to a crisp as she cruised along, past billboards advertising casinos, strip clubs or housing developments. She noticed half-built tract homes that looked abandoned, a semi on the shoulder of the highway with a sleeping driver, heat waves rising from bubbling blacktop. Across the road, there was a stand of glorious Joshua trees. Mormon settlers renamed them after the biblical saint who led the Israelites across the Jordan to the Promised Land. The distinctive branches reached to the sky with outstretched arms, as if in prayer.

She turned off Route 93 on King Road toward Sunrise Mountain. If she looked slightly to the east, she could just make out the blue waters of Lake Mead, a glistening oasis surrounded by deep rock canyons.

Her cell rang and she heard her brother's voice over the car's speakers.

"Where the hell are you?" Sam asked. He sounded impatient and annoyed.

"Somewhere."

"Oh. That's nice. Somewhere. I'm at the ranch but I'm not going in until you get here."

"What's up?"

"Frank's being an asshole. The twisted heir apparent."

"It should have been you." Josie knew this was what he wanted to hear. And in many respects, it was true.

"That's bullshit," Sam scoffed.

"The favorite's the favorite."

"Dad was a prick and was playing everyone."

"Well, there it is. God, Sam. Give it a rest," Josie said, wishing she had a drink.

"Fine. Fuck it. Just get home, okay?" Sam shot back, slightly slurring his words.

Josie spent the rest of the drive on autopilot. Coming home was never quite how one imagined. When she closed her eyes, everything looked different, as if she were at the wrong table playing with strangers and she didn't know the rules. She had fled Vegas seventeen years ago. Memories of senior year in high school still haunted her.

When Josie finally pulled up to the ranch, she stopped the car for a moment and took a breath. As the youngest child, she had spent so many hours roaming this desert, and while the landscape was the same, the ranch was almost unrecognizable. As she approached the security guard, he smiled and waved her through the gatehouse.

In the last year, her father had overseen major renovations that transformed the ranch into a palatial estate. Most of the familiar landmarks were gone. There was a big, new gate with the word "King" in black wrought iron, and a life-size bronze sculpture of a rearing stallion off to the side. The dusty driveway was now paved with small pebbles and lined with olive trees, and the duck pond had vanished completely. In its place was an Olympic-size infinity swimming pool, complete with waterfalls and rock formations.

Her father's twin-engine, six-passenger Eurocopter, with custom audio and calf leather banquettes, rested on a large helipad next to the stables. Her older sister, Sunny, had told Josie that she was "going crazy" because their father was taking flying lessons and had been commuting solo to the office. He'd said he'd had it with the long car rides. It was ironic that with everything her father was involved in, he had dropped dead from a heart attack at his desk—next best thing to dying in your sleep.

Josie parked her car next to a row of Range Rovers and late-model

BMWs. Her brother Frank and sister, Sunny, had already arrived. Josie wished she could take a shower to wash away last night—but there was obviously no time for that.

She got out of the car and steeled herself for what was to come. A security guard, who was standing outside the front door, escorted her into the house. Josie noticed several new oil paintings in the entry. One was a Pissarro landscape, and the others were Warhol portraits of Geronimo and Sitting Bull. A row of chandeliers blazed light from the ceiling, the crystals tingling slightly in the blessed, air-conditioned breeze.

Her father had come a long way from the kid who grew up dirt-poor in Boulder City, a dusty old town an hour's drive from Las Vegas. Roy King was a small-time operator who came to this town with nothing but an idea and rode that vision straight into the American Dream. He created a place where it was always Saturday night, where the quest for the hot hand was a sacred rite and where the motto was "It's Your Lucky Day." It was a place fit not for a king but for the regular Joe looking for a cheap deal and lots of action. The Jackpot became one of the most profitable casinos in history.

Josie always knew she was Vegas royalty, but she never felt privileged, not by a long shot. If she'd led a normal teenage life with best friends and worries about being popular, maybe she would have been happier. There should be rules about how much freedom to give a kid. But her family had no boundaries. None.

Chapter 4

The living room was unusually quiet. Josie didn't hear voices so at first she thought her family might be gathered somewhere else in the house. But when she stepped into the room, all her siblings were there: Frank, the eldest, and his wife, Sue; Sunny, her older sister, and her husband, Trent. Everyone except Sam. The men stood up briefly when she appeared. Frank was dressed in a suit, string tie and cowboy boots. His gun was holstered under his jacket. Trent, who still had the athletic build of a college rower, was wearing his usual khaki pants and a pink Lacoste polo shirt.

Frank gave Josie an awkward half hug, and Sunny greeted her with tears and a kiss on the cheek. Something wasn't right. Josie could feel it.

"Sam's not here yet," Frank said, unsmiling. "Probably off getting stoned somewhere. He doesn't give a shit that we're all sitting around waiting for him."

Frank and Sam were still at it, apparently. No one could remember when the discord between the two brothers began, but by the time they got to high school, the brothers had little in common, and eventually, they moved to opposite corners, and stayed there. Sam was tall, rangy, with a handsome face and sandy hair. He was easygoing and affable—one of those people who always felt good about themselves. Like everyone else, Josie adored her older brother Sam. He'd go out most weekends, party, and then bring pretty girls back to the ranch late at night. They'd swim naked in the duck pond, while Frank stayed in his room with the light on.

Frank was rarely included in the social scene. It was the classic problem of the movie star's brother. There was a strong family resemblance, but Frank's looks were a pale version of Sam's—similar, but without the same appeal. Since Frank was two years older than Sam it was even more awkward if he tagged along, so he seldom did. The tragedy of sibling rivalry is that it never ends, Josie thought. People said they'd grown out of it, but had they really?

"Has anyone called Sam?" Josie asked.

"What's the point?" Frank threw up his hands. "Most of the time he doesn't answer."

"And hello to you too." Sam appeared at the door as though on cue.

"You good?" Frank asked.

"Yeah."

"You sure you're good?" Frank pressed, trying to peer into Sam's face.

"You need to ask twice? I'm fifteen fucking minutes late."

Josie could tell Sam was high. He had that glazed look in his eyes and his voice sounded a little raspy. In the past few years, she had heard that Sam's "problem" had gotten worse. A lot worse. He started out on pot, then moved to blow and now God knows what.

Sam winked at Josie, flashed a wide grin and enveloped her in a bear hug. His dog, Rex, a shepherd mix, plopped down next to him. Frank frowned as Sam grabbed a crystal lowball glass from the bar, filled it with water and set it on the floor. Rex lapped it up gratefully.

"Can we get started?" Frank asked, mopping his brow. God, Josie thought, he looked whipped. His dark hair was thinning at the crown, and he'd gained a lot of weight in the last few years. So had his wife, Sue. When Frank first married her she favored "hot date" outfits and modeled for local car commercials, but over time she had transformed into her version of a respectable matron. She was wearing a pantsuit in a jarring shade of fuchsia, and her hair was now streaked with gray.

"Theo Goldman just left and we're all a little shell-shocked here," Frank said, referring to the family lawyer.

"You know Goldman's running for mayor," Sue interrupted. "I told him I'd chair an anti-radiation committee to consider building a huge wall around the test site."

Sue loved to talk politics, thought Josie, but she always came off sounding like a nutjob.

Sam was only half listening, as if everything she said was gibberish.

"Does this have to do with Dad's will?" Josie asked carefully. "I thought we were meeting tomorrow at the law office."

Sam was drinking bourbon from an open bottle of Van Winkle Reserve. Josie watched as he helped himself to a canapé from a silver platter, then tossed another to the dog. Good ole Sam. He never changed. He took another swig from the bottle and some liquid trickled down his chin. Sue looked at him and winced.

"Show a little class, Sam. For Christ's sake, we're trying to have a serious meeting here!"

"No problem," he answered, but the bottle slipped from his fingers and shattered on the ground. Everyone watched as a stream of brown liquid ran like sewage over the wood floor. The smell of bourbon filled the room.

"Oops," Sam said sheepishly as a housekeeper rushed in to mop it up.

Frank shook his head in disgust. He waited until the staff left and then planted himself in the center of the room, as if he were taking the floor at a board meeting.

"Excuse me," he said in an authoritarian voice. "I'd like your attention."

"Well, yes, sir!" Sam rolled his eyes. Rex trotted over to Frank and shoved his snout into Frank's crotch. Frank pushed him away but the dog was insistent.

"Tell your dog to fuck off," Frank said.

Sam smiled, grabbed Rex's collar and pulled him back to the sofa. Rex laid his head on Sam's knee and gazed up at him adoringly.

"Okay. Here's the deal. I asked Goldman to come to the ranch," he said, clearly relishing his role as head of the family. "After all, we're his biggest clients."

"We *were*." Sunny sulked. "When we had money."

"What? What's going on?" Josie asked. When they *had* money?

Sunny's eyes were red, puffy and filled with tears.

"We all get nothing for three years," Sunny said, sniffing the air as if she could smell the impending disaster. "*Nothing*. Nada. How am I supposed to live?"

"All those distributions you've gotten, that's how," Frank said. "Did you piss them all away on fillies with names like Giddy Fucking Up?" Frank chuckled and looked around the room. No one smiled.

After Sunny and Trent were married, she suddenly became passionate about the equestrian world, and all the competitions and expensive paraphernalia that went with it. She upgraded from a perfectly nice, two-story house to a sprawling horse ranch outside of town, which she called a "farm." There were no western saddles or lassos. Just hunters and jumpers with riders wearing black velvet helmets and jodhpurs in the desert heat.

The grand indoor arena where their horses were trained had air-conditioning and an elaborate wrought-iron chandelier. Josie remembered that her father used to say that Sunny and her "pretentious dick of a do-nothing husband" sure got one thing right—they knew how to spend money.

Sunny still had her figure, though, and looked put together wearing a dark, fitted suit with her hair pinned down in a low bun. She made it her job to be well-groomed, like her horses.

"Maybe spending a half million dollars on a mare wasn't such a good idea," Frank needled her.

"Not helpful, Frank," Sunny retorted.

"I agree with Sunny," Trent added, warily watching Frank.

"You agree with Sunny?" Frank mocked, a dangerous glint in his eye.

"Let's just focus on the business at hand." Trent's voice was loud but he avoided Frank's eyes.

"Well, thank you, Mr. 'I went to school in New Haven.' You think anyone in Nevada gives a shit?"

"Jesus, Frank. Lay off, will you?" Sunny snapped. "Keep your criticisms to yourself."

"Actually, I'm not criticizing you. I'm criticizing your deadbeat husband, who hasn't earned a dime since he married you. What *do* you do all day with that fancy degree, Trent?" Frank asked, spoiling for a fight.

"Kiss my ass, Frank. I've had about enough of this!" Trent spat back.

"That's a lot of attitude for someone who's got a free fucking ride," Frank said, unable to mask his contempt.

Why doesn't Trent just punch Frank in the face and get it over with, Josie thought. Everyone in the family felt like doing that at one time or another. She watched Trent's cheeks redden, then he slammed his drink on the coffee table and abruptly stood up, his chair crashing behind him.

"I'm leaving! Coming, Sunny?"

"You go on ahead," Sunny said, shaking her head in exasperation. "I want to talk to my sister."

Trent shot her a hard look and stormed down the hall. All the black Range Rovers and Mercedes with Nevada plates were lined up in the driveway. Josie hoped nobody was blocking Trent in, or he'd have to return after his grand exit.

"Dad would be so mad you treated my husband this way."

"No, he wouldn't." Frank smiled. "Dad didn't like him either."

Chapter 5

Who were these people? Josie thought back to the last time her family was close. They were children then. Now they were adults, with adult problems and complicated lives.

"Here's the deal," Frank said, all business. "First of all—the ranch. It goes to Sam and Josie for life, and when they decide to sell, profits are split four ways."

"That doesn't seem fair," Sunny said, peeved.

"Well, I guess Dad thought they were the only ones without a place to live."

"Why should we be punished because we took care of ourselves and acquired big estates?"

"How should I know? Go out to Palm Mortuary and yell at Dad. Second. Listen up. In order to receive the inheritance, you must be a Nevada resident and live in Las Vegas."

"What?" Josie asked, stunned.

"You can look at it two ways," Frank said, cutting Josie off. "It's a trap Dad set for us or a fucking great offer. You choose."

"This is one hundred percent not going to happen. He can't dictate where I live."

"Oh yes, he can. *And* where you work. You know that dead-end accounting job you have?"

"I'm taking some time off," Josie said, ignoring his insult.

She had recently given up a mundane job at an accounting firm in the San Fernando Valley where she dealt with tax deductions, IRAs, small trust accounts and other money matters so routine, they were almost bookkeeping.

"So you're doing nothing, right?"

"Right. I'm doing nothing." Josie shrugged. Frank was always so dismissive about her job. But she liked the work, the predictable routine, the comfort of numbers. It was an attempt at a normal life after the chaos of their childhood.

"Well, that's convenient, because each of us has to work full-time at the Jackpot for three years for the money to vest."

"Dude, as much as I'd like to be your bitch, no can do," Sam said. His tone was casual, as though his inheritance wasn't hanging in the balance.

"Dad knew that . . ." Frank responded coolly.

Last year, Sam's gambling license was suspended by the gaming board, and he was banned from the casino for eighteen months. He was caught offering drugs and prostitutes to undercover officers as if they were a hotel amenity, like a mint on your pillow. After cops found a few grams of cocaine in his pocket, he was lucky his license wasn't rescinded for life. Their father ended up paying a million-dollar fine to clean up the mess.

"Anyhow, in six months, you'll be reinstated, and you'll be eligible for your inheritance, which, by the way, you don't deserve," Frank continued.

"Everyone knows the gaming board was trying to screw me," Sam said at the same time.

Sam was an expert with excuses. Barely out of high school he started working in the casino part-time. He did a great job too. He glowed with potential. Unfortunately, as the years went by, age didn't diminish his wild and volatile behavior. He liked partying with sleazy guys, ex-cons, lawyers with mob ties, trash peddlers and bleached blondes who weren't quite talented enough for the chorus line.

"Oh, c'mon. Let's not pretend," Sam said to Frank. "You probably maneuvered this whole deal just to screw the rest of us."

"Oh, right, like I personally wrote Dad's will. If you were ever fucking sober and showed up more than once a week, you'd know that was impossible."

Frank paused and looked at Sam with disgust. "You were the golden boy. How do you just piss it all away?"

"Hey, look on the bright side." Sam fixed him with a stare. "I'm not killing anyone—except maybe myself. Which is more than I can say for you."

Frank's mouth dropped open, and then snapped closed. "Shut the fuck up."

"I know," Sam said, standing up, squaring off with Frank. "Why don't we count bodies? Kind of like Monopoly but with corpses."

"Sit down," Frank ordered, pushing Sam away, at which point Rex bared his teeth and latched onto Frank's trousers.

"Shit," Frank shouted, kicking the dog off his leg. "Get him off me!"

"Good dog!" Sam said, pulling Rex's collar.

"Stop it!" Josie yelled in alarm. They both turned and stared at her. Her brothers were careening dangerously close to the forbidden topic of her family's homicidal history—a history that had traumatized all of them. None of them had ever talked about it in the open, and now, she thought, was not the time. "Can we just cool down and deal with what's important? Seriously?"

Sam backed off, grabbed Rex and sat back down on the couch.

"Chill," he said to Rex, who was still growling.

Frank brushed off his pants, which were wet with dog drool. "Son of a bitch," he murmured.

"Are you two done? Because I have some serious questions. Like—is this even legal? Making me move here? My daughter will be devastated." Josie couldn't even begin to imagine the battle she would have with her ex, Stuart, over custody of her twelve-year-old.

"I asked that very question," Frank said, fully recovered and sounding pleased with himself. "It's all perfectly legal. If you don't want to meet the terms, you can do whatever you want. No one's putting a gun to your head."

Sunny poured herself another drink. "We should hire a team of lawyers and contest the will."

"That would only work if we could prove diminished capacity or fraud. Which we can't. There is also an 'in terrorem' clause. Anyone who challenges the will gets nothing." Frank looked down briefly at his hands, examining his buffed nails. "Instead of bitching and moaning like some spoiled losers who've pissed away millions, why don't you look at this as a father's desire to do what's best for his family?"

"O-kay! This is fucking bullshit." Sam headed for the door, Rex trotting after him.

Josie's gambler's instincts kicked in. There was something else going on here. Frank was in too good a mood. That was his tell.

"Thanks for the pep talk. Why so happy?" Josie fixed him with a stare.

"Well, I'm not thrilled. Three years is a long time to wait for the cash." Then he grinned. "But, on the bright side, I'm finally CEO. Now you all work for me."

Chapter 6

After everyone went home, Josie and Sam sat outside by the pool. It had been a scorcher of a day. The thermometer outside the back door read 110, and one could actually see the air trembling on the horizon.

The sun turned red from a distant sandstorm and the oppressive heat lifted. It was deadly quiet except for the wing beats of the red-tailed hawks circling their prey. They screeched like a coven of witches as they swooped down on an escaping diamondback and spiked it with their powerful talons. According to a local legend, if you see a hawk carrying a snake, it's a warning of danger ahead.

Josie always hated September. It was brutally hot, and everything was brown, black or dead. Huge ravens hulked around on power lines and squabbled over roadkill. Gnats and deer flies swarmed the backyard. She took off her heels and dangled her bare legs in the pool.

"You okay?" Sam asked, taking a hit of coke and wiping his nose with his thumb.

"Not really. Completely blindsided," she said as she watched him do another bump. "You have to do that now?"

"Absolutely. Need fortification to watch Frank's 'I'm finally in charge, fuck you' blaze of glory. The only thing that's gonna stop him is embalming fluid."

"Sam, enough! I have my own problems. I'm supposed to uproot Billie and move her here? And get Stuart to agree?" Josie's heart raced at the thought.

"My whole fucking universe is exploding and what do they care? Sunny's horses are *her* kids and Frank's son is in prep school and never comes home, even for holidays," Josie added.

"Well, would *you* if Frank was your father?" Sam said with a smile. "Anyhow. What's the big deal? Hire a good lawyer and fuck over your ex. He certainly deserves it."

Josie nodded and looked at him darkly. "I don't understand why Dad didn't consult us."

"You can handle it. Listen to Frank's bullshit, then do whatever you want."

"Easy for you to say."

"Yeah, well, I'm fucked too." Sam sighed and rummaged through his pockets, pulling out an empty coke vial . . .

There was a deep double boom off in the distance, almost like a mortar bomb, and they looked up to see a formation of Thunderbirds from Nellis Air Force Base streaking across the sky.

"Fucking hot dog Thunderbirds," Sam said, squinting his eyes at the sky. "Let's get out of here. Go get a drink or something."

"Well, there's an idea," Josie said. She watched Sam pull out his phone and dial a number.

"I just have to meet someone at the gate . . . I'll bring the truck around in thirty."

They exchanged a glance and Josie knew exactly who he was meeting but now was not the time to make an issue of it.

She took her suitcase upstairs to her old bedroom. Nothing much had changed since she was a teenager. Her classic Breyer quarter-horse collection still sat on the bookcase and her favorite handmade quilt with its tiny meticulous stitches was still folded at the end of the bed. The closet was pretty much empty except for a few things she kept here for when she came home to visit. There was a faint smell of mothballs so she closed the closet door.

She flopped on the bed and thought back to all those lonely nights she had spent here growing up with only her old Mormon housekeeper,

Mrs. Porter, to keep her company. Her mother, Dorothy, had died when she was six. And by the time she was twelve, Sunny, who was six years older than Josie, was away at Vassar, where she eventually met Trent. Frank and Sam had enrolled locally at UNLV's hotel management school and worked nights at the casino with their father. Casino families were much like the families of firemen, policemen and the military. Sons followed fathers into the family business. The Strip was filled with hometown joints run by grandfathers, fathers and sons, and Josie's family was no different. Many nights, they didn't come home at all.

To make things worse, her life at school was a different version of other young girls'. She attended the public junior high school, six blocks from the Strip. The ranch was a forty-five-minute drive from the school. During the week, she instructed her driver to drop her several blocks away so no one would see the shiny black Cadillac, and she never stayed for after-school activities. Most of her classmates lived in the neighborhood, and their parents worked nights as dealers, cocktail waitresses, musicians and bartenders. The rest of her class consisted of army brats from Nellis Air Force Base, who knew how to get along anywhere because they always came from somewhere else.

But that wasn't her. She wasn't even sure where she fit in and what she was supposed to say or do. It didn't help that she looked like a ranch hand, with only the elderly Mrs. Porter to advise her. Her uniform in those days was baggy jeans and a T-shirt, and she wore her long auburn hair in a tight braid.

The saving grace was that she excelled in math. It came easily to her and there was comfort in something so quantifiable. Numbers had a harmonious simplicity that no other part of her life did. A complex set of equations was merely a challenge, a game. She loved the thrill of sailing through a tough problem to one simple solution. There was power in being able to analyze the world around her.

The monotony of school and homework was broken up by Sam, who was often around in the early evening, playing blackjack with a few of his friends before he went to the casino. Josie liked the action, and she'd often stand behind her brother and watch. The point was to get twenty-one, her brother's age exactly. That's all she knew. The guys would usually play outside on the patio after dinner, when it was still light and the sky was just beginning to darken and then burst into flames. Sam's half-smoked cigarettes filled the ashtray, and lukewarm bottles of beer sweated on the table.

"Blackjack, you fuckheads," Sam said, slamming his cards down. He flashed a wide smile at his three friends.

"Shit!" His friend, Jake, was scraping for a hit but got an eight. "Busted. I'm done."

"This deck is colder than fucking Alaska. I'm out too." Nick pushed his chair away from the table.

The group hung around for a few more minutes, then drifted off to their cars.

"I have a question," Josie said to Sam as he absently shuffled the deck.

"Sure."

"Okay." She sat down next to him. "I noticed in the first game, Jake was holding a ten and a five and then hit, and got a queen and he was out. But before that, he had a jack and a six and he didn't hit, but he lost anyways, so what should he have done? In the same hand, Nick had a nine and a three and then got an eight, and he was out. Then the fat kid, Hootie, had a seven and a queen, and stuck, which doesn't seem like such a strong hand either, and then the dealer had two face cards, but one was an ace and what's with that? Is an ace a one or an eleven? Are you following me here?"

"Yes. It's either," Sam said.

"Okay. In the next hand, Nick got a six and a three and then hits and gets a queen, and Hootie was dealt a king and a six, but stuck, and why would he do that with just sixteen?"

Josie went on to describe each play for the entire evening.

"Jesus! Did you memorize all the hands?"

"I guess. Yes." Josie shrugged.

"How did you do that?"

"I'm good with numbers," Josie said proudly.

"No shit," Sam blurted, barely containing his surprise.

"So can you tell me the rules?"

"Seems like you already know a lot." But he fanned the cards out and explained them to her in detail.

"How do you know when to hit and when to stay?"

"Most people stick at seventeen, but it's not a good hand. Chances are you'll go over if you hit."

"Sounds pretty easy."

"The rules are simple, but the strategy is tricky," Sam warned.

"So what's the best way to win? Or is it all luck?"

Sam thought for a minute, and then dealt them two hands.

"Well, it's not *all* luck. It's skill. And the best way to win is by counting cards."

"What's that?" she asked, picking up a hand.

"Basically, card counters memorize the number of high cards left in the deck—the tens and face cards. Those are the 'good cards.' They also keep a count of the 'bad cards'—threes to sixes. The more high cards left in the deck, the better their chances of winning."

"So you just have to remember what cards have been played?"

"Yep. You have to use your brain to keep a running count of good cards to bad. It's all about ratios and probability and statistics."

"Like math," Josie said, slowly realizing with a wave of enthusiasm that this was something she could do.

"Yeah, like math. I can't really do it myself but I know guys who can."

"So it's okay to do it?"

"It's not illegal, if that's what you're asking, but it changes the odds. Dad neutralizes anyone he thinks might be counting."

"Neutralizes?" Josie looked at him blankly.

"Sweeps them, dumps them, recalibrates their location. Get it?"

"Oh." Josie knew better than to follow that line of inquiry. "But only if he catches them?"

"Right." Sam smiled. "Only if he catches them."

"Teach me," Josie said, placing the shuffled deck between them.

"Okay, kiddo," he said, turning his back to her and lighting up. The air was suddenly pungent with Sam's weed. "Start out with one deck. And try to keep track. You need to remember the cards already drawn and those about to come up. Play out sample hands to yourself. In the end, it's a plus-or-minus situation. Favorable or not."

"Let's play," Josie said, her face flushed as she eyed her cards.

Sam took another toke and then picked up his hand.

"Okay, one game, then practice on your own. That's how you learn, plus watching us play. The guys who are good at it practice day and night. Don't write anything down. Don't whisper to yourself."

"No problem. It's just basic math."

"And everyone loses eventually," he warned.

I won't, she thought.

For the next several months, Josie spent her evenings alone, sitting on her bed with a stack of cards. It was almost a ritual. Mrs. Porter left her dinner on the kitchen table and Josie put it on a tray and took it up to her room, then she changed into sweats and pulled out the decks from her night table. The sessions lasted deep into the night, hand after hand, deal after deal, constantly shuffling. Using a plus-and-minus system, she would calculate the high cards remaining—ten and over—and adjust the strategy. She started out with one deck and worked her way up to six.

"Fourteen face cards, two aces, six lows," she murmured to herself.

"Eighteen face cards, one ace, ten lows."

"Six face cards, one ace, ten lows."

Over and over. She shuffled, split the deck, cut the cards, and began again. As time went by, she hardly looked at the cards. One glance and her running tally told her what she needed to know. And if she watched very carefully, she could calculate the count even right after the shuffle. She could track a group of high cards through a six-deck shoe. She could figure out where the low cards were and when the high cards would come up. All of it based on simple math—probabilities, ratios and strategy. The world disappeared into a land of red and black numbers, aces, face cards and all the possibilities open to her.

Chapter 7

Josie changed into a mid-calf, boatneck black dress and low heels—the modest outfit she'd packed for her father's funeral. She hadn't planned on going anywhere else, so it would have to do. Her hair was still windblown from the drive, so she brushed it back behind her ears. Then she looked at her face. It was pale and drawn. The corners of her mouth were turned down. She dug in her purse for some lip gloss and blush and tried to tamp down the fury of today's revelation.

The ride to the casino took about a half hour. They turned right on historic Fremont Street, one of the most famous gambling centers in the world. It was lined with glittery casinos and flashing lights, including a towering, neon cowboy nicknamed Vegas Vic, who waved his arm welcoming visitors to the city. Fremont had been a place for serious drag racing in her younger days.

The area was called Glitter Gulch for good reason. Josie noticed that it hadn't changed much in the seventeen years since she moved to LA. They passed the Golden Nugget, the Mint, the Four Queens, the Horseshoe club and that little dive where everyone used to get fake IDs. Then they turned into the Jackpot executive parking. As Sam headed inside the building, Josie stopped him.

"Wait a minute. Didn't the gaming board ban you from our casino?"

"You think they have spies to monitor my every move?"

"Maybe," she said, blocking Sam from the entrance.

"You think I'm being funny?"

"Hilarious," Josie retorted. "You should do stand-up."

Sam shrugged and turned on his heel. "Never mind. Let's go across the street to McCarthy's place. Better crowd."

Sam was referring to Desperados, the casino run by Rob McCarthy. He was one of the youngest and most successful casino owners in Vegas. Initially, Sam had judged McCarthy's cool casualness and jet-set lifestyle as that of just another playboy trying to run a casino. But over time he'd been forced to admit that the guy was a brilliant businessman and a canny marketer who knew how to attract customers.

Josie looked at the modern glass-and-steel casino, which was packed. To the side was a long line of people waiting behind velvet ropes. A bouncer stood guard checking IDs and reservations for Mardi Gras night at the rooftop private club. Josie followed Sam to the front of the line, where the bouncer greeted him with a big smile and waved them through. Sam glanced over at Josie.

"Stop looking like some cursed princess. Your outfit is bad enough."

The scene upstairs was the exact opposite of the tense living room drama at the ranch. From black and white to psychedelic neon. Rob World, as people called it, was a fantasy place where the music was blasting, the liquor flowed (at $500 a bottle) and moral boundaries were tested every night. There was a rooftop infinity swimming pool, complete with two-story cabanas and soft, white sand. Starting at 11 p.m., Skinny Dip night began with dance contests and $10,000 prizes. Circling overhead were topless erotic acrobats. A single table was $5,000, but from the way people lined up, you'd think he was giving them away.

A six-foot-tall blond hostess planted a kiss on Sam's cheek and escorted them to a VIP booth of pale aqua leather where they could see the action. It was impossible to talk without shouting, even in the booth. Just as they were about to sit down, Sam waved to a man across the room who walked over to them.

"Hey, man, good to see you." Sam turned to his sister. "Josie, meet Rob McCarthy."

McCarthy was in his early forties—tall, with an athletic build and impeccable taste in clothes. His navy silk suit looked custom-made, and his starched-collar shirt had the initials "RM" embroidered on the cuff. He wore a heavy, steel Breitling watch with a glowing, multiple-time-zone face, and his gold cuff links were etched with what looked like a family crest. His face was long and angular. A man who was used to being the center of attention and was nonchalant about his effect on people. And the man Josie slept with last night.

Chapter 8

Josie knew the two most important things in gambling are knowledge of the game and self-control. Odds are, destructive behavior comes back to bite you in the ass. She wouldn't call it karma exactly, more like serious bad luck.

Josie and Rob looked at each other for one agonizing moment. *Guilty*, Josie thought. Unchecked libido. No sharp, witty retort came to mind. Only a slow-moving revelation of a humiliating discovery.

"Nice meeting you." Rob smiled, not betraying any recognition. He casually admired her tall, slim silhouette, her wavy, auburn hair and her long legs. Who knew Roy King's younger daughter was such a knockout? And what were the chances that she was in his bed this morning? At least a million to one.

He turned back to Sam. "Sorry to hear about your father. What can I get you? You're my guests tonight," he added.

"We aren't staying . . ." Josie said, trying to keep her tone light and even.

"I sure as hell could use something," Sam said. "It's been a shitty day. How about bourbon, rocks? And bring her one too."

Rob put a casual hand on Josie's waist and guided her into the booth.

"Move over, I'll join you. So—Josie, is it?" he asked, clearly amused.

"Yes." Josie's tone was curt as she studied the cocktail menu. She found it hard to concentrate. He knows my damn name, she thought, with a sting of embarrassment. He slid into the booth next to her, nonchalantly slinging his arm across the back of the booth so that his hand touched her shoulder.

"Didn't realize Sam had another sister," he said, pressing his thigh against her leg. She felt a rush as she thought about his body next to hers, the thrill of the illicit encounter. I fucked someone I shouldn't have and now, my luck, here he is, she thought. For a moment she couldn't hear the conversation around her. God! This was mortifying. Busted and by Sir Fucking Galahad, no less.

"When did you get to town?" McCarthy asked innocently.

"This morning," Sam said. "She drove in from LA. Almost missed our meeting," he added. "I told her to get here last night . . ."

"I'm sure Rob isn't interested in my schedule," Josie interrupted. "And to tell you the truth, I'm exhausted. It's been a long day. Ready?" she asked, nodding at Sam. She moved as if to slide out of the booth, but Rob wasn't budging.

"Jesus, Josie. Let's at least finish our drinks," Sam said as the waiter set the bourbon on the table. "What's the matter with you?"

"Excuse me," Josie said to Rob. "I'd like to go to the ladies' room."

"Of course. I'll show you where it is."

"No need," she replied quickly, still not looking at him as she hitched her purse over her shoulder.

Rob slid out of the booth, ignoring her, and then followed her out the restaurant door. As soon as they were out of Sam's line of vision, Josie turned on him.

"Bobby? Your name's Bobby? Hanging out in a T-shirt and shorts like you're the pool boy?" she spat.

"I don't remember you asking a lot of questions." He grinned broadly.

"I thought I'd never see you again!"

"How about we never see each other again tomorrow night?"

So suave, so annoyingly self-confident, Josie thought, trying to push aside the memory of his hand sliding down the inside of her thigh.

"Look. You're our competitor. I'm not 'seeing' you again. Or whatever you want to call it."

"I'd call it great sex."

"It wasn't that great," Josie lied. He looked at her with one raised eyebrow, clearly not believing a word. "And frankly, I'm not even sure how the whole thing happened."

"As I recall, 'Let's go to your room' was the second thing you said to me."

"I was in a state. I was drunk," Josie said defensively.

"You weren't that drunk." He laughed. "Tell me, was it just sex or do you want to see me again?"

She closed her eyes, ignoring his question. She knew he was toying with her.

"What were you doing there anyway?" Josie asked. "Slumming?"

"Buffalo Bill's was my first casino." She didn't miss the note of pride in his voice.

"You still own it?" Josie looked around her—the low-rent Buffalo Bill's couldn't be more different from the gleaming Desperados.

"I'm a sentimental guy. And it's quite profitable."

"So you keep an empty hotel suite in case you get lucky?" she asked, narrowing her eyes.

"I'm not going to say it doesn't come in handy," he admitted with a smile.

"I'll bet."

"Poor Josie," he said, giving her the same look he gave her last night. "Are you disappointed I'm not some tourist you picked up?"

"You slept with me under false pretenses. That's like lying."

"I don't remember you dropping your name either, Josie King. Daughter of Roy King."

"Look," Josie whispered. "I don't really want my whole family to know . . ."

"Of course you don't," he said agreeably. He loves this shit, she thought. "Relax. I'm the Master of Secrets," he added. "Come sit back down."

They walked back to the table and Josie slid in without comment, pulling a cigarette from her purse. Rob casually took a gold Cartier lighter out of his pocket, flipped the lid and leaned in, looking her straight in the eye. He hesitated a moment, keeping his eyes on hers as the flame burned the end of the cigarette. Josie felt her cheeks redden as Rob began conversing easily with her brother about the changes taking place in Vegas.

"So, you in town for a while?" Rob asked Josie, as if making small talk with a new acquaintance.

"Just a few days." Josie gulped down the last of her drink and gathered her things to leave.

"That's too bad," he said sincerely.

Sam looked sharply at both of them. He knew Rob would sometimes fuck with people on purpose, just to test them. But this seemed like something else. There was an attraction that disturbed the currents of air around them, like waves of heat coming off the desert. Josie's face revealed nothing, but Sam had the same gambler's instincts she did, and he wasn't fooled.

Chapter 9

For every action there is a reaction. People forget that little law of physics. For instance, Josie thought, when you shoot a gun, there's always a kickback. Anticipating it separates the novices from the seasoned shooters. When the bullet leaves the chamber, you have to be prepared for the recoil. And Josie wasn't. Her one one-night stand was Rob McCarthy. What the hell, she fumed.

On the drive back to the ranch, Sam glanced at Josie sideways. Her eyes were closed and her head was leaning against the window.

"So. What's up with you and Rob?" Sam asked casually.

"What do you mean?" Josie didn't even open her eyes.

"Something's going on there." It wasn't a question.

"Nothing's going on. Shut up."

"You are so fucked-up," Sam said with a laugh.

"Well, you're fucked-up and you were my role model."

Sam gave her that half-smile, the one that said he knew he was a disappointment.

"I know you wish I was different, Josie. Do the twelve-step AA program and find God! Get sober in a mansion overlooking the ocean that costs thirty grand a week!"

"Maybe. But honestly, I don't know how to help you anymore."

He sighed. "I don't want to be saved. If I did, I could do it myself."

"That's what all the addicts say." Josie shook her head. Sam could sense her frustration.

"I appreciate your love and concern, I do." His voice softened as he reached over to squeeze her hand.

"Thank you, but that's small comfort when everything is falling apart."

Josie looked down the dark highway and then closed her eyes again. She had grown up in the desert about thirty miles from Las Vegas, past Durango, two miles north of the Horse exit at the base of Sunrise Mountain. There was one long, meandering road in and out, covered in loose gravel that blew dirt and silt on car windows, and caked the tires with knee-deep mud whenever it rained.

When she and Sam were kids her family had owned about a hundred and forty acres, including a stable of American quarter horses bred for rodeo, a riding corral, along with a pack of dogs, blackbuck antelope and white-tailed deer. The main house always reminded her of a grand lodge in a national park, with giant logs and stone fireplaces. There was a carved stone fountain in front and a thirty-foot-deep well in back that pumped pure artesian water. Next to the main house was a six-thousand-square-foot pavilion that housed her father's million-dollar classic car collection, and an underground vault where her father stored his silver bricks, ammunition and God knows what else.

Sam parked in front of the fountain and they headed to the kitchen. Josie wasn't hungry and neither was he, but they raided the refrigerator anyway. Slim pickings—leftover hors d'oeuvres from this afternoon. The chef hadn't planned on feeding anyone that night.

Sam gave her a bear hug. "Chin up, kiddo. Sleep tight."

When Josie reached the staircase, she automatically glanced upstairs at her mother's bedroom door and her heart ached. She used to count the steps from her bedroom to her mother's bedside. She still remembered. Twenty-two. The memory of her childhood days was suddenly vivid, unrealistically golden—she could almost smell her mother's perfume.

There were a few framed photos in the hallway, including one of the family's annual Christmas card. She must have been around ten at the time.

She remembered that year clearly. It was early December and a photographer had come to the ranch to shoot the holiday card. He was frisked before he entered the house, his camera bags emptied out on the driveway. She and her sister were dressed in red-and-green velvet dresses with lace collars and the boys were in bright embroidered cowboy shirts. Behind them were two giant wreaths wired on the barn doors. All and all, it looked like a Norman Rockwell painting. No one would ever suspect that the barn was wired with a security system to rival CIA headquarters in Langley, and an escape tunnel ran from the house to the barn. Every casino owner was afraid of kidnappings and Josie's dad was no exception. With the family's easy access to piles of cash, casino kids were perfect targets. At that time, her father was so paranoid, he built the house so the only access to the children's wing was through the master bedroom.

Beautiful and fragile, her mother died of cancer when Josie was six. She remembered lining up her dolls on the edge of the hospital bed and her mother's soft, faint smile. Toward the end of her illness, Josie would lie down on her mother's bed like a dog curled up at her feet.

After it was over, her father seemed spent, and listless. He had lost the love of his life. According to Sam, who confided in Josie on rare occasions, their mother was quite possibly the only person in Roy King's universe who he never crossed. In his mind, he had married up. Way up.

Josie's mother, Dorothy, was different from the other casino wives. She was born into a Philadelphia Main Line family and met Roy King on a college trip to Vegas with her Vassar classmates. He was struck by her elegance, refinement and beauty—a tall, willowy blonde with classic features that she passed on to both her daughters. She was the anchor of the family, the emotional support, and it all disappeared the day she died. Of all the children, Josie, the youngest, suffered the most. In a sense, she lost both her mother and her father that day.

After her mother died, Roy King would often get home from the casino at all hours of the night, his heavy footsteps clumping on the wood floors, checking each bedroom. No bedtime stories, no recounting the day's adventures, no family dinners or outings. None of the parental tenderness that most children take for granted.

As the years passed, the children got wilder. Especially Sam, who had been so close to his mother. He was suspended from school several times for drinking on campus and Josie disappeared in the desert for hours on end. She was adrift and restless, unsupervised. Wandering alone in the desert was Josie's escape, and she reveled in the freedom of lacing up her hiking boots before sunrise and heading for the canyon. People sometimes think the desert is dangerous and hostile, but for Josie it was her salvation.

Chapter 10

Ashes to ashes. Dust to dust. The world was not black and white. According to Josie's father, there was a gray area. He was a good guy. He was a bad guy. She loved him. She hated him. She loved him. Her relationship with him was complicated, but when all was said and done, she would give anything to have him back. Even though she had moved away, somehow she thought he would always be there. When she first heard the news of his death, she was devastated. Filled with numb disbelief. One thing she never doubted: his love for her. And she knew that no one would ever look at her that way again.

The funeral was almost surreal. At least her father would have liked the ceremony, Josie told herself. The whole town showed up, crowded into Grace Presbyterian, many dressed in cowboy clothes, boots and hats. A shiny black hearse led the way to the cemetery, followed by Hall of Fame rodeo riders handling four white stallions prancing like showgirls. It was something else, Josie thought. Senators, politicians, judges, cops and fine, law-abiding citizens all paying tribute to her father.

Josie had noticed a few of her father's old girlfriends sitting in the back, the ones he never brought to the house—the ones the kids pretended didn't exist. In the last few years, Josie couldn't keep track of his mistresses. None of them lasted very long. Except for Corinne, the blond former showgirl, who was conspicuously absent. She came the closest to getting the ring. But in the end, Josie's father moved on. She often wondered whether Sam's roving eye was modeled after his father's behavior.

A more sympathetic way to look at it was that Roy never got over the loss of his beloved wife. And neither did the rest of the family.

But who was Roy King really? As a young girl, it was hard to pretend that Josie didn't know about the violence that seemed to be a routine part of his business. She learned early on that when security took people into the back room, they were beaten, usually with a club or some brass knuckles, the punches' force concentrated where it would do the most damage. Her father kept cheaters in line, made an example of them. You do it right, he told his children, the word spreads and the problems disappear. He was ruthless and relentless. Those who knew him recognized his undisputed power to handle whatever or whoever was needed in any given situation.

And then there was the Carl Taylor incident. It happened in the summer of her twelfth year. Josie had been out in the desert, as usual. Because of the heat, she set out before seven, and by ten she was parched but victorious. She had found a glorious desert tortoise and was carefully carrying him home. Moses she named him—a wanderer in the desert, like herself. Tortoises are native to the Mojave, and can live up to eighty years. They spend most of their time under rock shelters, so it was rare to actually find one. This guy had a beautiful, dome-shaped shell, and his sharp, clawlike scales dug into her arm. She was headed to the fenced-in part of her backyard to dig a burrow for him, when she spotted her dad's Cadillac in the driveway along with another car. That was odd.

It was the middle of the afternoon. Roy King was never home at this hour. Josie stood outside in the searing heat, trying to decide what to do as she shielded the tortoise with her T-shirt. Sweat glistened on her neck and soaked her back.

"Okay," she said to herself, almost in defiance of her doubts. She walked in the kitchen to find Sunny and Sam seated at the breakfast table. The chef was pretending to be busy, chopping vegetables by the sink. Frank was standing guard, leaning against the wall with his arms crossed, and he blocked her from going into the hall. A vicious argument was taking place in her father's office, and the loud, angry voices reverberated throughout the house.

"I want to go to my room," Josie said, placing Moses on the table, holding her hands over her ears. She got a glass of water from the sink and poured it on the tortoise to cool him. The water dripped off the shell and all over the floor.

"Jesus, Josie! Get that thing away from me. And stay here," Frank ordered.

"No! I want to go upstairs," Josie said, desperate to block out the noise.

"Sit down and shut up!" he barked, pushing her toward the chair.

They had all learned not to violate the laws of their father's world. None of them moved. There was a long, still moment. Then a crash.

"Fuck this, I'm going in!" Sam said, jumping out of his seat and shoving Frank aside.

"Goddamn it! Wait a minute!" Frank shouted.

"Shut up, you chickenshit." Sam rushed into the hallway.

They all followed, just in time to see Carl Taylor, an old friend of the family, slamming out the front door. He avoided their eyes, stumbling down the front steps. Their father stood for a moment in the doorway of his office, and then walked stiffly into the hallway. Normally, he was an intimidating presence, a man just shy of six feet, with broad shoulders and a prominent jaw—a western icon, with his snakeskin cowboy boots and his sterling silver, custom-made belt buckle given to him by the National Finals Rodeo champion after he forgave the guy's ten-grand loss at the tables.

His thick, dark hair was always immaculately slicked back behind his ears, and once a week, his barber, Joey D, would come to the office, trim the stray ends and throw in a shave. Everything about him was controlled and his deep, authoritative voice accentuated this trait.

And then there were his unusual hazel eyes, changing from green to blue to gray, like a chameleon. Josie's brothers rarely looked at him straight on. Roy King could size them up in an instant.

But now he wobbled a bit, holding the side of his head. They could see an angry bruise forming on his forehead. Blood streamed out of his left ear and soaked the collar of his white linen shirt.

"Daddy, you're bleeding!" Josie said in alarm, still holding the tortoise.

"Jesus Christ!" Sam said as he ran for the door. "I'm gonna get that fucker!"

"Sam! Stay here. I'm fine. Frank, get me some ice." Their father's voice projected a sense of calm but his mouth was drawn tight and his twitching fingers betrayed the true state of his emotions.

Sunny dabbed his neck with a tissue, while Sam just stood there, stone-faced, a little muscle in his cheek ticking with rage. Josie felt sick to her stomach as she watched her dad hold ice on his head, his hair damp with sweat. His eyes drifted to the tortoise and he smiled with a combination of affection, amusement and something darker. She couldn't tell what it was.

Her father wouldn't talk about what happened, even though Frank pushed. Finally, her father rose and motioned for Sam to follow him back into his office.

Bloody tissues littered the kitchen table and floor. Frank looked lost. He stood frozen in the hallway, and then, without a word, disappeared into his room. Sunny, playing the older sister, took Josie's hand and offered to help her build a burrow for the tortoise. They all might have been able to move on if not for what happened next.

A few days later, the *Las Vegas Sun* reported that well-known real estate developer Carl Taylor had been found dead. The story flooded the news media. Photographs of the crime scene with lurid descriptions of the victim's body were everywhere. Taylor's body was found in a shallow grave nearly a hundred miles outside of town, off 160 North near Death Valley Junction. There were multiple shots to the head from a .22-caliber automatic pistol, the mob's preferred execution method. Different theories of who had committed this vicious crime monopolized the news media for days. Police never found the killers, but the kids all knew. For them, it was the Big Secret.

As the years went by, Josie watched her father beam while

strolling through the crowds at his casino, shaking hands with regulars and slapping others on the back. He seemed to know everybody who worked for him, and showed genuine concern about their lives. He touched them, pinched their cheeks, slung his arm around them. Roy King was everybody's Big Daddy, the King of Glitter Gulch. These moments filled her with pride but Josie knew that this world was not really what she was seeing—bright lights, green cash, happy faces and a magnanimous ruler.

As the funeral service concluded, the choir sang a powerful gospel version of "Amazing Grace." With the light from the stained glass windows filtering down on her father's coffin, bathing his portrait in a heavenly glow, Josie almost forgot the dead body in the desert.

Chapter 11

The reception at the ranch dragged on for hours, with people arriving to pay their respects until late in the night. Upstanding citizens mingled with a gathering of gangsters and gamblers. There was Ice-Pick Willie with his son, Billy, who had just joined the Marines, Dave "The Man" Berman, Sam Giancana and Jimmy "Striker" Costello. The entire Factor family arrived, including Jake "The Barber," who had imported the topless Lido de Paris to his Stardust Hotel. And the jittery little Morrie Sedway, looking over his shoulder the whole time.

"My God. Roy's daughter! I haven't seen you since you were a teenager." Mel Davis clasped Josie's hands in his and smiled benevolently. The distinguished-looking gentleman had been a longtime friend of her father's, and if the town had a kingmaker, Davis was it. His silver hair was slicked back and his dark, custom-made suit was Italian.

Mel Davis and Josie's father had started out in Vegas together. Originally from New Jersey, Davis was a small-town numbers guy under the protection of the New York syndicate. He had been a decorated officer in the navy, and after the war, he moved to Vegas to operate one of the Strip hotels. Davis eventually controlled at least three other casinos, and then branched out into a slew of legitimate businesses.

As far as Josie could tell, Mel Davis had spent the last thirty years, like her father had, trying to make the transformation from gangster to respected businessman and philanthropist. At this point, Davis's vast financial empire included commercial real estate, theaters, shopping malls and housing developments. He was a driving force in Nevada politics, responsible for the careers of senators, county commissioners, mayors and one congressman. No one crossed Mel Davis. Not even the feds.

Josie remembered Davis's visits to the ranch when she was a child. People always compared him to Roy King—two aging lions who had survived decades beyond their infamous past. Unlike her father, however, Davis was a quiet, unassuming man known in the old days for his ability to negotiate settlements. He kept the peace in Vegas at a time when each casino was run by a different family organization.

He nodded as his bodyguard approached him and whispered something in his ear. "Give us a minute," he said, quietly, as he turned back to Josie.

"You know what? You're the spitting image of your mother. Now *that* was a beautiful woman. I remember, I met with your dad once—you couldn't have been more than ten. We were sitting right out there on the patio," he said, pointing to the picture window that overlooked the vast acreage of the ranch. "I saw you running in the desert and I thought, this one, she's like a wild horse. She likes her freedom. So, how've you been, sweetheart?"

"Oh, well." Josie hesitated. "Not great. But I remember you. Dad used to say that you were the one."

"The one what?"

"I don't know. The one he admired? The one nobody could touch?"

"Yeah, yeah." Davis laid his hand over his heart. "So, if you ever need anything—well, you know."

He turned back to his bodyguard.

"Give her my private number," he said.

As she watched Mel Davis walk back toward the bar, two men approached him with manila envelopes. Doing business even at a fucking funeral, she thought.

At a certain point, Josie couldn't manage one more sweaty hand or whispered "Sorry for your loss." She needed to be alone. She grabbed a bottle of bourbon from the bar, walked down the hall to her father's study, locked the door and collapsed into his worn leather desk chair.

She took in all of Roy King's civic awards and commendations displayed in the heavy mahogany bookcase. There were framed newspaper clippings and photos of him with famous politicians, celebrities and distinguished members of society. Despite ample evidence to the contrary, Roy King actually believed he was a virtuous man, even when he did bad things. Josie listened to people milling around outside—big voices laughing, chatting, drinking liquor, scarfing down food. She didn't know how long she had been sitting there when she heard a knock on the door.

"Josie, you here? Open up. What are you doing?" Sam asked.

She got up and unlocked the door.

"I'm fine. I just needed a break."

"It's pretty intense out there." He shoved a hand in his pants pocket and produced a small, clear envelope filled with white powder. He trickled a line down his index finger and inhaled deeply.

"You want a hit?" Sam closed his eyes and savored the high.

"No, thanks. Now isn't the time."

"Oh, Josie, for God's sake." Sam laughed. "Sometimes you need to just let it go. How about something to eat? We have turkey, beef, ham, Chinese food, deli platters and twenty different kinds of herring floating in white sauce."

"Disgusting. Who ordered all this?"

"Sunny, obviously. I feel like I'm being held hostage in our all-you-can-eat buffet."

Just then Josie noticed Frank and his wife, Sue, headed toward them. Frank was holding Sue's hand and they both wore solemn expressions. They had looked like that all day and it was getting on Josie's nerves. Sue was wiping her nose with a ragged Kleenex.

"You two are annoying as fuck," Sam said, trickling another line of coke on his finger.

"Jesus! It's your father's funeral," Sue admonished. She slapped Sam's hand and the white powder on his finger dissolved in the air like dust. "You're an embarrassment!"

"Fuck you, Stepford wife," Sam snapped. "Talk about embarrassment."

There was a nasty silence. Sue eyed him with venom.

Frank grabbed Sam's collar. "You're a disgrace to this family," he hissed, "and if you insult my wife again I'll fucking shoot you."

Sam wrestled out of Frank's grip. "Go ahead, pussy. You don't have the balls. And you owe me two hundred for the coke," he said. "Lucky for you my dealer and his kids are in the living room."

"We're done here," Frank growled. He hustled Sue out of the office. Sam rolled his eyes at Josie and headed in the opposite direction.

Josie closed the office door again. She sat at her father's desk, downed a full glass of bourbon and dropped her head in her hands. How did normal families grieve, anyway?

After a while, she sat up and rifled through a few desk drawers. She pulled out a pile of parking tickets and a couple of warrants. Her father usually tore those up. There were a bunch of keys to who knows where and some old correspondence with a New York lawyer. Then another knock on the door.

"Who is it?" Josie asked, annoyed.

She realized she'd forgotten to lock the door when Rob McCarthy appeared in a black silk suit. Perfect funeral attire, down to the somber gray Brioni tie.

"Sam told me you were here," he said, stepping into the office and closing the door behind him. "I came by to pay my respects."

"That's nice," she said, following him with her eyes. She got up from her father's chair.

Rob planted his hands on her shoulders and leaned in to give her a kiss on the cheek. Then it happened. Josie pulled him close and kissed him with a long, lingering intensity. After a moment of hesitation—or maybe surprise—he slid his hand into her hair and kissed her back. Josie was stunned by how much she wanted him.

"This is a mistake. I'm sorry," she said, not sounding sorry at all.

"No need for apologies." His voice turned husky. "Are you okay?"

"Not really," she said. "I want this party to be over. I want a bolt of lightning to strike Frank and my holier-than-thou sister-in-law. I want Sam to get his shit together."

She began unbuttoning his crisp white shirt. "I want to get drunk and do everything I shouldn't," she whispered, guiding his hand under her dress.

He caressed the inside of her thigh, moving his hand higher until she moaned out loud. "Oh God." Josie felt lust and heat rush through her. She clasped her hands around his neck. His skin was warm and she breathed in deeply until she closed her eyes and cried out. Rob smiled, put one hand over her mouth, whispering "shhh . . ." as Josie wrapped her legs around his waist. Without saying another word, he undid his pants, pushed himself inside her and fucked her against her dead father's desk. She had just left her father's funeral. His friends and family were right outside the door and the thought of someone walking in on them turned her on more than she could imagine. When it was over, she stood up, pulled her dress down and took a swig of the bourbon. Then she combed her hair with her fingers.

"I think I'm starting to like you," Rob said lightly, as if this wasn't a completely unhinged encounter.

"Well, we have so much in common, don't we?" she replied sarcastically.

"So are we going to have a thing or is this it?" he asked, stroking the side of her neck.

"This is it," she said definitively. "But thanks for the condolence call."

When Josie was young, she had watched a snake try to swallow a rabbit twice its size. Curiously, it ended well for the snake. Every now and then, something thrilling and inappropriate can be exactly what you need.

Chapter 12

TWO MONTHS LATER

How do you move from one life to another? That was the dilemma Josie faced on a daily basis. Uprooting herself from LA had been traumatic for both Josie and her daughter, Billie. She briefly wondered if she should have abided by her father's will or ignored it? But in the end, there was really no choice. And truthfully, she never liked LA in the first place.

"LA isn't a place you're supposed to end up. It was meant to be temporary. If you remember, you didn't even want to go. Vegas is your home," her father had reminded her when she chose to stay there after college. For once Roy King had actually sounded like a normal parent.

"The old days are gone," he added. "If that's what's stopping you. Things are different now."

Josie hadn't been so sure at the time. She did miss Las Vegas. She was a desert rat. It was part of her DNA. She often longed for those days spent hiking on a trail, following a creek in a dense thicket bordered by heavy boulders. Once in a while, she'd catch a glimpse of an eagle soaring over the limestone crags or a mountain lion disappearing in the rocky slopes.

And always, there was the casino. Josie's father started taking his children into the casino when they were kids and teaching them the nuances of the business. She learned how the casinos rate gamblers and who qualified for comps—everything from a free show to full RFB (room, food and beverage)—all the way to the whales, the casino's biggest gamblers. Whales were the prize and for them the casinos pulled out all the stops. Jets, suites, any kind of entertainment they wanted. It was a world that fascinated Josie. An Education. In the back of her mind, she always thought she would return someday.

And then there was the money. Lots of it. The Jackpot profits were over $200 million a year. Her yearly take would be close to 5 percent. Ten million dollars. When her father was alive, he distributed enough for each of them to maintain their lavish lifestyle.

Even though Josie was getting the same distributions as her siblings, she made the decision early on that she wanted a normal suburban life for Billie. While Sunny spent her distributions on horses and a free-loader husband, Sam blew his on a daily routine of drugs, booze and women. Frank was very secretive about how he spent his money, although he poured a ton into his Grecian mansion for his social-climbing wife. The bulk of Josie's distributions, on the other hand, were invested in securities accounts of stocks and bonds at City National Bank, which she monitored closely.

But now everything would be dictated by the will. And who would give up $10 million? Her father won even from the grave.

Rob was another complication. He had sent her a lavish flower arrangement, the kind that someone sends when they're making amends—or trying to impress you. Josie brooded over her behavior, which defied any twist of logic. But Rob seemed to have an amused tolerance and a strange affection for her impulsive lust fucks. He had called her several times, "checking in." He was obviously interested, despite her cool dismissal of him. In truth, she hardly knew him.

Maybe the problem was, she just wasn't any good at relationships. After her divorce, she had a series of boyfriends who all got tired of her failure to commit. She didn't want to get married again and she couldn't see herself starting another family, not when she had Billie.

But underneath it all, she was bored with the lot of them—they were safe, and predictable. There was no *wow* factor. Maybe that's why she was such a bad girl with Rob. He brought back the pizzazz.

Josie had considered all the options, then decided Billie would move to Vegas in January at the end of the semester and finish the school year here with her. Billie was miserable during the weeks she lived with her father and his new family—that much was apparent. Josie couldn't leave her there until the summer.

But that wasn't going to be easy. Since the divorce, Stuart had been impossible. It was one of those classic situations where you looked back and wondered what you ever saw in that person. When Josie was the innocent twenty-something associate at the accounting firm, falling for the good-looking, sophisticated older mentor, she felt like she had won the prize. She was the one he chose. But once the ring was on her finger, Stuart showed his true colors. Now he had money problems to boot. Although that could work in her favor. And it would be worth every cent.

Chapter 13

Josie drove to the Jackpot with a certain amount of trepidation. Today was the first day of work and she still had no idea what Frank had in mind for her, only that he was obviously thrilled to be in charge. She pulled into the executive parking lot behind the casino and an armed guard waved her through and opened the metal gate. The garage was loaded with cameras from every angle. She found her reserved parking place down the row from Frank's spot. His silver S-Class Mercedes sedan was immaculate, with a personalized license plate that read "Jackpot 2." Her father's plate had read "Jackpot 1."

She entered the casino with the ID card that had been delivered to her the day before. There were closed-circuit monitoring devices throughout the entire casino, and armed security personnel at each point of entry. Much more high-tech security now than when she was last here. Her father was old-school about it all, with trusted security guards at the entrances, on the casino floor and in the parking garages. Now with video surveillance, the catwalks and one-way glass seemed outdated. But Josie assumed her father's cardinal rule was still in effect: no drama in front of the customers.

Josie walked through the casino floor, where, even at this hour, the tables were beginning to see some action with a few of last night's holdovers—men with unshaven faces, smoking and nursing drinks. There was quiet conversation, and a few cocktail waitresses walking around refilling glasses. At the slots, older women in wrinkled flowered blouses rationed out quarters from their cardboard buckets. Josie spotted a lot of new construction and a row of upscale shops selling designer eyeglasses and expensive shoes.

The reception area of the executive suite was not at all what she remembered. Instead of her father's preferred Old West style, it had been redone in modern white leather furniture with a glass-and-chrome coffee table. There were vintage silver dollars in a Lucite display on one of the side tables, and on the wall was a huge framed collage of different currencies from around the world. A Roy Lichtenstein lithograph called *Ten Dollar Bill* hung on another wall along with Andy Warhol's silk-screen print *200 One Dollar Bills*. Money, money, money seemed to be the new theme here. Josie noticed there were security cameras lining the hallways that hadn't been there before. Cindy, her father's longtime assistant, greeted her with a hug and a big smile.

"Things just aren't the same around here," Cindy said, glancing toward Josie's father's office. She was in her mid-fifties, dressed in a conservative navy pinstripe suit. Cindy had been with her father for thirty years. She was a member of the Paiute tribe but had never lived on the reservation.

"Your brother is waiting for you."

Frank had moved—lock, stock and barrel—into Roy King's office and made himself at home almost immediately. Something about the sight of him sitting in a place where she had been with her father so many times felt invasive, like someone breaking into her house and rifling through her personal possessions. It wasn't as if she wanted the office herself; it was just that she hadn't pictured Frank slithering in so quickly. But he was now CEO and she worked for him.

Frank had gotten rid of her father's worn leather couches and chairs but kept his massive antique mahogany desk. The walls were covered with western art, original oils that her father had collected—Remingtons, Russells and, surprisingly, a gorgeous Georgia O'Keeffe sunset. In the corner, on a stand, was a crocodile saddle given to her father years ago by a Malaysian prince who had won $1 million over a weekend.

"The prodigal daughter returns!" Frank stood up from behind his desk. He was wearing an expensive charcoal suit with a pale blue button-down shirt and a red silk tie with little horseshoes on it. She also noticed his black snakeskin cowboy boots, the same distinctive style her father used to wear.

"So how does it feel to be back?" he asked.

"I'm not sure." Josie looked around the room. "So . . . where did all this art come from? At the ranch and now here? Did Dad buy all this?"

"Dad bought the paintings at the ranch. The art here is owned by the casino. We rotate it around. Except for the O'Keeffe. I acquired that myself."

"No kidding. How much did *that* cost?" Josie asked, wondering how much Frank was paying himself.

"I got a good deal . . ." He waved his hand vaguely.

Josie suddenly noticed a taxidermic desert tortoise sitting on the bookshelf. When she moved closer, she realized, to her horror, it was her beloved pet tortoise, Moses. Josie looked at Frank, outraged.

"That's Moses! What the fuck, Frank!" she said.

"Jesus, Josie! Calm down. It's a fucking reptile! He died after you moved away. We could have left him for the coyotes but Dad knew how you felt about him."

"I thought he wandered off!"

Josie looked at the tortoise's greenish-brown dome-shaped shell and his sharp-clawed feet. She should have left him in the rock shelter where she first saw him. Goddamn it! What a mistake! He might have survived if she had only let him be.

"Put him away," she said, turning toward the ten-foot-high windows and their view of the glittering lights of Fremont Street. "I can't stand to look at him like this."

"Such a delicate flower," Frank said, picking up the reptile by his neck and putting him in the closet. "You get the card key? Security's a little tighter than before, but you can come and go whenever."

"Got it," Josie said tightly. She decided to tamp down her anger and move on.

"Okay then, let's talk about your new role here," he said, changing the subject. "I've given some thought to it. You know, Sunny has taken over the dress shop."

"So am I in charge of the souvenir stands or what?" Josie asked, unsmiling. "And by the way, what's happening downstairs? The all-you-can-eat buffet is gone?"

"Putting in a showroom. It's gonna be Showgirl Shangri-la. I'm tired of the over-the-hill lounge singers in the lobby bar."

"And all the new shops?"

"Upgrading the place. No more tacky T-shirt stores."

"But those are our customers . . ." Josie was surprised. Her father had built the Jackpot as a casino for the middle class. Despite the whales who played in the private suites, their main business had always been families on vacation and local working people.

"We'll find some new customers. Listen, I have something much more important." Frank handed her an overstuffed accordion file. "I want you to take this off my hands."

Josie looked at the cover sheet with surprise. "Union negotiations?"

"Al Burns from the Culinary Union wants another meeting. He's a cutthroat operator who's been firing up his members and making my life hell. What's worse, the maids, cocktail waitresses and bartenders all think he walks on water. They have no idea what a self-serving son of a bitch he is."

Josie had been around her father long enough to know that you don't pick a fight with the labor unions. Vegas Local 226 was as powerful an organization as any in the state—over fifty thousand waitresses, bartenders, cooks, laundry workers, housekeepers, bellmen, basically everyone who kept hotels and casinos operating. Roy King never wanted them mobilized in front of his casino.

"Remember the hotel they targeted on the Strip a few years ago?" Josie asked. "Six months of pickets and zero business. Dad told me he didn't know how they'd fucking survive. This strike stuff is serious, Frank."

"Which is why I'm getting you involved," he said. "You were always the numbers girl. You can add up what this bullshit will cost us."

"Dad was always able to keep the unions happy."

"Dad's dead and times have changed," Frank said, cutting her off. "Profits are down. We're drowning in debt."

"What do you mean we're drowning in debt?"

"I'll take you through it later. Let's deal with the union first."

"So what do you want me to do?" Josie had a queasy feeling in her gut. What was Frank not telling her?

"Read their demands, figure out what this is going to cost us and then let's talk."

Josie heard a throat clear behind her. Cindy was at the door with a tall, heavyset man. He had a large head, a thick, muscular neck, pale skin and lips so thin they looked like a slash in his face. He reminded Josie of a dangerous predator, the kind who ate their prey before they were even dead. He was wearing an ill-fitted suit with an open-necked sports shirt and a gold chain.

"Hey, Lionel, have you met my sister?" Frank asked, trying to sound upbeat.

"I believe I have," Lionel said, but Josie knew for sure she had never met him.

"I don't think so," she responded coolly.

"Lionel took over Moe's job after Dad died," Frank said quickly, his eyes darting past Josie. "Head of security."

Nothing seemed to add up. Moe Thompson had been her dad's right-hand man for as long as she could remember. Josie swallowed her misgivings and walked to the door, carrying the bulging union file under her arm.

"Welcome to Vegas," Lionel said as he shut the door behind her.

But it didn't sound like a welcome.

Chapter 14

Frank closed the door and sighed. Josie wasn't even here an hour, and she already made him nervous. Lionel lit a cigar and sat down on the couch, the leather crumpling beneath his weight. He had huge hands with prominent knuckles and he was flipping a silver dollar between his fingers. Heads. Tails. Heads. Tails. They both sat in silence as they heard Josie's heels clicking down the hall.

"So what do you have her doing?" Lionel asked, blowing a puff of smoke in Frank's direction.

"I threw the union stuff at her. That'll keep her busy."

"How much does she know?"

"Nothing." He answered abruptly.

"Let's keep it that way."

Lionel snuffed out his cigar and stood up slowly, then helped himself to a drink from the monogrammed crystal decanter set on the credenza. "Did what's-his-name start yet? The new in-house counsel?"

"You mean Trotter? Next Friday. The funeral for Bowden is this weekend. We have to be respectful," Frank said. "I don't want to play the bleeding heart here but I still don't think you had to get rid of him. He wasn't talking."

"Cry me a river. You want to call New York and tell them?"

"Your guys were listening twenty-four/seven. Bowden couldn't take a piss without us knowing about it."

"My sources thought otherwise. The guy was singing. Why else would the FBI be sniffing around?"

"I think they jumped the gun," Frank insisted.

"You're getting a lot of money not to think," Lionel told him darkly. "Anyhow, we got the bugs out of his house, so you can relax. Nothing leads back to us."

Frank looked at the motherfucker's face. This prick making him kneel. He remembered how these guys had treated his father. But Lionel, for all his homicidal tendencies, served a purpose. His father had put up with this shit and so would Frank. But not much longer. He'd pay up and tell them all to fuck off.

"What about Sam?" Lionel asked.

"What about him? The gaming board's so far up his ass they're coming out his eyeballs."

"And Josie? I hear she used to be some kind of math genius or something?"

"If counting cards makes her a math genius, I guess so. That's what she did as a kid. Anyhow, she flew the coop years ago. She's got no clue as to what goes on here."

"I checked her out, you know. She was a forensic accountant for Christ's sake. I don't like it. She's not a bored housewife like your other sister."

"I told you. My hands are tied. It's in the will." Frank held up his hands as if surrendering. "Sunny's out to lunch and Josie can do a fucking CT scan of the books and she won't find anything. I'll see to it."

"You do that. I'm sending out the next deposit in a few days. The auctions are coming up and Gambassi has his eye on a Manette."

"Manet," Frank corrected.

"Whatever."

Chapter 15

In poker, when something was off, Josie could always spot the tell. The best players can catch it. A hand brushes across a forehead. A knee shakes. Something wasn't right. Josie couldn't put her finger on it. But her gut never lied. It reminded her of when she was a forensic accountant. When records were manipulated, she could smell it. She liked solving puzzles and narrowing down possible perpetrators. There were always new and interesting ways people embezzled and defrauded—bribery, corruption, kickbacks and extortion. She'd seen it all in her nondescript office on Ventura Boulevard. Lionel was right to be suspect.

She reviewed documents until 7 p.m. and tried not to resent the piece-of-shit office Frank had given her. It was a third the size of Frank's corner suite and at the end of the hall. There was a small window that looked out on Fremont Street.

The place had pretty much cleared out and she was the only one still around. She was on her way out when she decided to get a few things from the supply room, which she assumed was behind the door at the end of the hall. As she tried to turn the knob, a security light came on and a camera lit up her face.

"Can I help you?" a deep voice echoed from an overhead speaker.

"I need some legal pads," Josie said, startled.

"The supply closet is down the hall on the right," the voice said abruptly.

"Excuse me, but who are you?" she asked, keeping her voice even and neutral.

"Security, ma'am."

"Security. For what, office supplies?" She didn't even try to mask her incredulity. "Who's in charge here?"

"We work for Lionel Barrick, head of security."

"Is he the only one with a key?"

"He's the only one with access. You'd better speak to him."

Josie glanced up and stood to the side, avoiding the camera's field of vision. Jesus, she thought. What was so damned private that it needed guards 24/7?

She went back to her office, gathered papers in her briefcase and walked to the elevator. She didn't notice the beefy man in a gray sports coat and sneakers at the end of the hall. As she made her way through the casino, she also didn't notice the young guy in scuffed cowboy boots hovering near a craps table but not playing.

Josie turned into the new, brightly lit Gallery of Shops—a faux-fancy name that Frank had given the mirrored corridor off the casino. The biggest draw was a classic red Ferrari F40, rotating provocatively on a raised platform. A sign boasted that the car was personally approved by Enzo Ferrari himself and could hit 200 miles per hour in eight seconds. It was priced fully loaded at $1 million. Standing next to the rail, talking into a radio earpiece, was the same man in the gray sports coat from the hallway. This time Josie did notice him. His face was pitted with acne scars.

Her thoughts drifted back to her father, the stories that floated around him and the chronic undertow of questions that were never answered. Some things never change. Josie had more questions than ever.

Chapter 16

Day two. Nine a.m. Josie woke up in a fog, hoping for some clarity. She never did well with uncertainty. Whatever the fuck was going on, it wasn't good; she knew that much. It struck her that her ordinary suburban accountant life was over. Not that those years in LA were great, but at least they were safe, predictable. Now she was facing the unknown.

She wanted more than anything to go back to bed but she pulled herself together and threw on one of her old work suits. She glanced at herself in the small mirror behind the closet door. In LA, she had a walk-in closet the size of this bedroom and a freestanding bathtub you could have sex in, not that she ever did. This place would take some getting used to, she thought.

Her new home was a rental in Green Valley, an older suburban neighborhood on the edge of town near the Boulevard Mall. It was a temporary solution to Josie's predicament, never intended to be a permanent residence. The ranch was too far out of town for Billie, and the thought of sharing the place with Sam, considering his lifestyle, was not at all appealing.

This house had been recently renovated with all new appliances, but still, the ceilings were low, the plank floors were fake and the closets were way too small. Sunny hated it, of course. The heir with despair, she teased. Poor Josie. Sunny stepped in and hired a moving company called Cross It Off Your List. Five days and $25,000 later,

Josie was fully moved in but couldn't find a goddamn thing. But here she was. The LA house sold in a week and everything that wasn't moved here was in storage, which she would get to on the twelfth of never. Meanwhile, Sunny had also hired a local broker to look for a nicer house for Josie in Summerlin, an upscale neighborhood near Sunny's ranch.

Outside, the day was sunny and dry. By the end of the month, there would be biting winds and nighttime temperature drops of over twenty degrees. November was always the calm before the storm. Josie pulled her Mercedes out of the garage and headed toward Fremont Street. Everything had changed, and nothing had changed. The signs still beckoned with promises of sex; this was Vegas after all—"totally nude" dancers, escort services, hotel rentals by the hour and local bars still vying for the title of "Best Strip Club in the West." In addition, all-you-can-eat buffets, Lions Club Gun Shows and casinos offering the largest slots payout "in history." The American Dream in action, Josie thought.

She swept her security card in the gate barrier system and noticed the Jackpot executive parking lot was nearly empty. Most of the top brass started at around 11 a.m. because they routinely worked until after midnight. Frank's car was already there. Josie decided to corner her brother. She pasted a nonchalant expression on her face and walked into his office without knocking. Frank was shuffling through some papers, which he carefully placed face down when he saw her. After some small talk about her move here, he smiled indulgently, although his eyes darted to the door behind her.

"So, what's up?" he asked. "Any questions?"

"For starters, what's with all the fancy security and the locked door at the end of the hall?"

Frank hesitated for a moment and gave her an unconvincing blank look.

"Which door?"

"What do you mean 'which door'? The one down the hall."

"Oh, right. Just some storage and back-office people," he said, swiveling his chair away from her.

"If it's just storage and back office, why so much security?" she pressed.

"If you haven't noticed, I've stepped up security around the whole hotel. Lionel revamped everything."

"He revamped the security in the storage closet? C'mon, Frank. And speaking of Lionel, where did that goon come from? Why'd you fire Moe?"

"Jesus, Josie," Frank huffed. "What is this? A fucking interrogation? Moe was old-school, a dinosaur."

"He was Dad's guy, you know? I talked to Sam last night and he said you fucked Moe over."

"Sam's washed-up and does nothing but blow. You're actually listening to him?"

"Should I be listening instead to the fucking Frankenstein you hired to replace Moe?" Josie asked.

Frank shut his eyes and rubbed his forehead with his fingertips. Then he stood up.

"Excuse me if I'm actually trying to run this place instead of coddling our lunatic brother. This isn't a rehab center for entitled fuckups. Tell you what. Next time you want to see me, knock."

"Sure I will. And I'll kiss your ring while I'm at it," Josie snapped.

Josie started to walk out the door, then turned around. "And give me back my fucking turtle."

Chapter 17

Josie carefully carried Moses to her office and put him on a shelf in her closet. Poor Moses. The next time she was at the ranch, she would find a shady spot to bury him.

She spent most of the afternoon and early evening dealing with the reams of union documents Frank had dumped in her lap. She was shocked to learn that this dispute had been going on for months. There were at least four hundred pages of memos and grievances, but it looked as though Frank had done virtually nothing to respond to them. At 7 p.m. she packed up her briefcase, but instead of going home, she decided to take a look at Sunny's dress shop.

The place had undergone a serious face lift. The tasteful ivory walls were lined with gilt-framed photos of French bombshells in Saint-Tropez. Oversize potted palms sat next to faux French Provençal furniture. The carpeting was a subtle shell pink, a big difference from the garish gold-and-red patterns of the casino floor.

Sunny appeared in a tight black dress and spike heels, fully made up. The seductive sounds of Charles Aznavour floated through the air. She gave Josie an air-kiss and sang out, "Bonjour!"

"Back at you. Got any tequila? I've had a shit day. And I'm way beyond Chablis," said Josie.

"I get it. Problems with the firstborn? Don't fuck around. Just punch him in the face."

"Didn't they used to say, kids are like waffles? You should throw the first one out."

"Welcome to Vegas. I'm still fuming about the way he talked to Trent. Frank's such an asshole. Trent wanted to deck him right there in the living room but he has too much class."

"Frank hasn't apologized, I gather," said Josie, a little sheepishly. She secretly agreed with Frank about Trent. Sunny didn't get it. Trent was a deadbeat. He didn't even pay for his own toothpaste.

"No apology, and no one in the family defended me either. Everyone just sat there, including you. You all think I'm just the dumb sister with lousy judgment in men."

Josie didn't take the bait. After all, her choice of husband didn't stand up to close scrutiny either. "Well, the good news is, you've got an ironclad prenup."

"You don't understand," Sunny insisted. "Trent is loyal, reliable, he adores me and we have a wonderful life together."

Josie bit her tongue. This "wonderful" life burned up a fortune—between the Hermès saddles, the horses and the whole entourage that accompanied them. She had learned over the years not to pry too deeply into Sunny's life. Her sister was touchy and easily offended. Truthfully, it had been a long time since they had actually talked about anything meaningful.

"So, what do you think about all the changes going on here?" Josie asked to distract her.

"I don't really care." Sunny considered the racks of designer frocks. "If Frank wants to upgrade, it's fine with me."

"You don't think it's going to turn off our customers? You know as well as I do, they're grind players: Twenty is a big bet for them."

"Well, maybe we should get some new customers, premium players," Sunny said. She held up a cocktail dress with little *G*'s all over it. "What do you think?"

"Very nice, if your initials are *G*." Josie looked out at the slots, where a hefty, middle-aged woman wearing a long T-shirt and leggings robotically pulled the lever. "You really think our customers are going to fork over two grand for a dress like this?"

"They will if they win," Sunny said. "You ever heard of impulse shopping?"

"What did Dad think about all this?"

"Well, *you* wouldn't know this because you weren't here," Sunny answered pointedly, "but the last couple years, Dad really backed off. It was all about his cars and his horses. He gave Frank a lot of leeway." She hung the dress back on the rack. "You know, I'm not his biggest fan, but Frank's working hard."

Josie remembered what her father used to say when someone would try to defend an employee by saying he worked hard: "A horse works hard. Fire his ass."

"Anyhow," Sunny continued. "I bought you a new pair of Gucci loafers. Those flats you always wear are tragic. They're on my desk in the back. You're welcome."

Josie dodged a few rows of stacked boxes, sat down at Sunny's desk and slipped on the shoes. She had to admit, they were chic, the leather luxuriously soft. She headed back into the showroom in time to see Eddie, one of the longtime pit bosses, walk in holding an unlit cigar. The man had the muscular build of a former D1 athlete and wafted a sweet, musky scent of aftershave. He was wearing a dark jacket with a purple silk tie, probably Armani. Eddie greeted Sunny and then noticed Josie.

"Oh. Hello, Ms. King. Nice to see you again," he said warmly, slipping the cigar back in his pocket. "Trying to quit. Don't ever start." He smiled. "By the way, Sunny. Keep an eye out for Mrs. Reynolds. I just sent her over. One of the whales—from Dallas. Big spender."

"Thanks for the tip," Sunny said, blushing slightly.

"Happy to help. You two ladies have a nice evening, now." He gave Sunny a wink and headed back to the casino.

Josie watched him leave. She arched an eyebrow and gave Sunny an amused smile.

"So, you're fucking him, right?"

Chapter 18

Growing up, there were plenty of things that Sunny didn't tell Josie. By the time Sunny was in high school, the sisters led separate lives. Six years apart didn't seem like a lot now, but when Josie was ten and Sunny was sixteen, it was almost as though she was from a different generation. In addition, Sunny never went where she said she was going. She never came home when she said she would. Sleepovers and birthday parties were conveniently invented to cover up her covert activities. At times, she even printed fake invitations to show their father.

They had grown up in a world where everyone turned a blind eye to the lying and cheating that went on around them. Duplicity had seeped into Sunny's bones.

To be fair, the allure of Eddie the pit boss was not lost on Josie. Pit bosses were one of the "suits" on the floor, responsible for some of the vast sums of money that flowed through the casino. It was their job to be coolheaded and charming enough to defuse tense situations but also to turn on a dime and strong-arm anyone who got out of line. They were the exact opposite of Trent.

Josie didn't care a whit about Sunny's husband, but there were the obvious titillating questions regarding the affair: When did the secret lovers meet? Did they have nooners? Late nights "working" at the shop? Meeting an old friend for a drink? And where? As Josie knew well, hotel owners notoriously kept suites for this purpose, but Sunny wouldn't have had access to one. Or would she? Maybe the head of housekeeping, who was one of Sunny's high school friends, would accommodate her.

"How long has that been going on?" Josie ventured, well aware that Sunny was on her guard.

"Not that long." Sunny shrugged. "A few weeks." Josie didn't believe a word of it. But she pressed on, thinking Sunny just might confide in her.

"Is he married?"

"Separated."

"Sure he is. Does Trent know?"

"Trent wouldn't notice a red flag if it was sticking out of his ass. I *do* love him but it's complicated. You know how it is."

"Actually, I don't," Josie said. "I got divorced when it got complicated. But I stupidly didn't have a prenup, so it's a good thing I got out early."

The two sisters looked at each other in silence. Then Sunny turned away, began riffling through one of the dress racks and produced a Valentino sheath in a rich shade of green.

"At least wear something decent." She thrust the dress at Josie. "That suit looks like crap."

"Fine." Josie gave in and went to the dressing room. "Throw in some sexy underwear and I'll go fuck the bellman."

Chapter 19

The union crisis continued to ramp up. Josie arrived at the office before sunrise and left after nine at night. She fueled up with sandwiches from the casino kitchen, which arrived at regular intervals throughout the day. Now the halls were dark and empty again, with the musty smell of stale coffee lingering in the air. She liked being the only person there, no sounds of secretaries chatting or phones ringing. One night when she was prepping for an early meeting, her phone rang.

"Hey Josie, this is Rob." She could hear the throbbing base of electronic dance music and loud voices in the background. She looked at her watch. It was nearly ten.

"Hey," Josie said.

"Sam told me you were back in town."

"News travels fast."

"Good news does. How about meeting me for a drink?"

"I'm working."

"Say fifteen minutes?"

"I'm really slammed. Sorry."

"Consider it community service."

Josie laughed in spite of herself. "Maybe some other time."

"I wasn't offering some other time."

"I was being polite," Josie said, not missing a beat. There was a pause. Was he really used to calling women on a fifteen-minute turnaround?

"Well, if you change your mind . . ."

"I won't." Fifteen minutes, was he kidding?

She silenced her phone and returned to the paperwork. Earlier that evening, Cindy had warned her in a motherly tone that she'd better not "burn the candle at both ends." Their former house counsel, Steve Bowden, had been working around the clock on this union thing before her father had died. Cindy had found him asleep at his desk several mornings.

"He was driving home when he got into the accident. Terrible," Cindy said, shaking her head. "He must have fallen asleep at the wheel."

Josie had heard that Bowden had driven his car into a telephone pole and died instantly.

He was only forty years old with young kids.

It was after midnight when Josie wearily got in her car and headed home. She decided to drive down the Strip, knowing there was enough stimulus there to keep an armadillo awake. She watched the crowds of people walking the streets, tourists following guides with little flags on sticks, cabbies weaving in and out of traffic. Restaurant and casino doors were wide open and wedding chapels had cars lined up for a quickie drive-through ceremony—even at two in the morning. You could pick up your dry cleaning, go to the gym, buy a car or pawn your mother's diamond ring any time of day or night. Las Vegas was the land of the twenty-four-hour day.

Her shoulders ached and her head felt heavy. She opened the windows to get some fresh air and then, without thinking, closed her eyes. The car lurched sickeningly toward the curb and she abruptly opened her eyes and turned the steering wheel back on the road. Her heart was pounding and her stomach tightened. Jesus, she needed to go home, take a shower and get some sleep. She thought about their former house counsel who fell asleep at the wheel. She didn't want to end up like him.

Chapter 20

Three weeks before Christmas, the union went on strike. Frank had dug in his heels and refused to negotiate, so all hell broke loose. The employees took to the sidewalks, blocking every entrance to the casino and holding up yuletide-red signs with white block letters that read "Shame on You" and "No Contract. Merry Christmas."

As Josie pulled into executive parking, she passed a man holding a sign that said, "Fuck you King family." He was wearing a black hoodie and he aggressively stared her down as she drove into the lot.

Frank was in crisis mode, overwhelmed by running the day-to-day casino operation and bringing in replacement workers to cross the picket lines. He raged on and on with a bunker mentality that was almost delusional, even joking about hiring "some guys who shoot people for money."

"Jesus, Frank," Josie fumed. "You act like these people are your enemies. Some of them have worked here over twenty years. Dad treated them like family."

"Here we go again," Frank groaned, his voice rising. "The loyalty of the workers. Same fucking story from the union pricks. They're loyal until they're not. And this whole family thing! Employees aren't family. You can't fire your family. Although sometimes I'd like to. Dad bought into this whole charade."

"It wasn't a charade for Dad," Josie interrupted. "He really felt that way."

"And look how appreciative they are. It's not family. It's business and we can't afford it. We're in a goddamn mess here."

"The casino? It's makes a couple hundred mill a year."

"*Made* a couple hundred mill a year."

"You keep saying that. I don't understand . . ."

"The market's changed." Frank shrugged, looking at Josie with distain. "We're like an aging showgirl. No one wants to fuck her anymore. Just hold the line. Got it?"

"Yeah. I got it," Josie said, frustrated and angry.

"And you didn't fucking knock again," he added.

To make things worse, Rob McCarthy was getting glowing publicity for supporting the union workers. His hotel had struck a deal with them the year before, and now he wanted to cement his place in the good graces of the maids, bartenders, cocktail waitresses and food servers who were camped out in front of the Jackpot.

Every day at noon he would march across the street with an army of staff—all union members themselves—and pass out roast beef sandwiches, tubs of chicken salad, coleslaw, ice-cold drinks and Christmas cookies. Sometimes he'd show up in the morning with doughnuts, sweet rolls, coffee and hot chocolate in big cardboard boxes.

Obviously, McCarthy knew how to take advantage of a situation.

Josie decided it would probably be a good idea to pay him a visit. He hadn't called her since they last spoke. She felt her stomach flip as she asked Cindy to set up a meeting. This is why you don't fuck the competition, she reminded herself.

Cindy set up the meeting for 3 p.m. that afternoon. Before Josie left her office, she combed her hair and freshened her makeup with more care than usual. She crossed Fremont Street and entered Rob's casino, Desperados, which was packed, even at this hour. She was directed to the private elevator in the back, which led to the corporate offices. A security guard confirmed her appointment and ushered her up to the third floor.

There was a sharply dressed woman in a tight black suit sitting behind the reception desk. A former state-fair beauty queen, Josie thought. "Mr. McCarthy will see you now," she said.

His office was pure Las Vegas, with plush cinnabar-colored carpets and wall coverings. In China, red is the color of luck, luxury and wealth. Desperados was known to offer all three. There were huge windows across one wall with a spectacular view of the mountains and a small Picasso behind his desk with an art light shining on it. Josie cast an appraising look around the room, taking in the opulent furnishings. For a few seconds, she said nothing, but just stared into the office.

Rob smiled and looked at her inquisitively. She hadn't seen him in a few months and she noticed he had obviously been at some beach resort. He looked relaxed, with a summer tan in December, along with a sunburnt, peeling nose. He seemed younger than he had the last time she saw him. He was wearing a navy blazer with an open crisp white shirt, no tie.

She was about to sit in the minimalist chrome chair opposite his desk when he stood up and gestured vaguely toward the generously scaled club chairs and large credenza/bar in the seating area at the far end of the room.

"Please," he said. There was a fleeting glance between them. "Would you like something to drink? Coffee, tea, vodka?"

"Coffee is fine." She smiled, sitting down. She pushed her hair back from her forehead. The light from the window felt hot on the back of her neck. She crossed her legs and got down to business.

"I see you're taking good care of our strikers," Josie began, her voice cool and casual but with a slight edge. "At this rate, they could stand out there and party 'til Christmas."

"In my opinion," Rob said, cheerfully ignoring her dig, "you should tell your brother to stop being such a hard-ass and make a deal. Every day that goes by you lose more action at the tables."

"Which benefits you, of course," she said, looking directly at him.

"See what a generous person I am to give you advice?"

"Look," Josie said, sighing in frustration. "It's not that easy to deal with my brother. What I need to know is how you successfully negotiated with the union last year. Obviously, we aren't doing a very good job."

"I'd be happy to offer pointers," he responded with a smile. "Let's see, we haven't seen each other since—"

She cut him off, her cheeks burning at the memory of her behavior at the funeral. "I'd like to keep this professional. I mean, we're both adults here," she said.

"I can do that. Can you?" His gaze lingered on her face. "Do you want to talk about it?"

There was an awkward pause as the receptionist set down a tray with two coffees. Josie glanced back at the woman as she walked out.

"Cream or sugar?" he asked, handing her a cup.

"Black. And no, I do not want to talk about it," Josie said, annoyed. "You don't know me at all."

"Well, that's not exactly true . . ." He lifted an eyebrow.

She opened her mouth to respond and then stopped. Their eyes met for a moment as she thought about the heady aftermath of her last two encounters with this man. She was hoping he didn't take this meeting as a flirtation, which was never her intention. But everything he said sounded dirty.

"Listen," he said, noticing her discomfort. "I have a conference starting in fifteen minutes. How about we discuss this over dinner? We haven't tried *that* yet. It'll be in a public place—totally aboveboard."

If she was upset by his continued references to her bold "fuck me now" episodes, her body language didn't reflect it. She wasn't going to be baited into reacting. She agreed to meet him at eight at the Oyster Bar on the top floor of his hotel.

Chapter 21

Josie was lost in thought as she left Desperados and crossed Fremont Street. She passed the picket line keeping her head down and walking straight ahead. Just before she pulled out her security card at the Jackpot's side entrance, she felt a light tap on her shoulder.

"Excuse me, Ms. King? Got a minute?"

Josie turned to see a clean-shaven, stocky man dressed in a casual sweater and slacks. She thought he might be with the union, so she was initially polite, until he pulled out a badge that read "FBI Special Agent Max Gavin." She searched his face to make sure this wasn't some kind of stunt.

"Sorry to bother you like this, but I need to talk to you about something important," he said, handing her his card.

"Here?" Josie asked, looking around at the strikers and thinking this was a hell of a time for him to approach her.

There was a western saloon called the Pioneer next door to the Jackpot. Low-slung and weathered, the Pioneer had been there for nearly fifty years and it showed. The owner consistently refused to sell to the casinos looming over his establishment. It was dark and always full. "A money machine," her father used to say, each time he tried to buy the place.

They walked in and sat at the end of the knotty pine bar. Silver dollars were pressed under the glass of the bar top, and black-and-white photos of old Las Vegas lined the walls. Agent Gavin ordered a beer, as if he was planning on staying awhile. Josie declined.

"So, what's up?" she asked, trying to keep her voice low.

Josie knew her father's relationship with the FBI had been fraught. For years they harassed him mercilessly, always trying to prove he was in business with the Chicago syndicate or the Purple Gang or whatever crime family was moving into Vegas at that time. There were federal grand jury hearings, phone taps and harassment for years. The feds devoted thousands of hours to investigating Roy King, but they could never prove anything—not even tax evasion. In fact, her father had, for a time, provided tips to the FBI on a confidential basis, which the agent in charge said were valuable. Nothing of consequence ever came from the information, and years later, it came out that the FBI agent in charge was on the take . . . and the person suspected of hiring him was, of course, her father.

"I heard you're working with your brother now at the Jackpot. That right?" he asked. A bit of beer foam stuck to his upper lip, and he swiped it away with the back of his hand.

Josie nodded. She knew that he knew. These agents were the opposite of subtle.

"We're *real* interested in what's going on there," Agent Gavin continued.

"What do you mean?" she asked impatiently.

"Well, if you weren't Mr. King's sister, I'd tell you to be careful."

He gulped down the beer, and looked around the place. Josie suddenly felt trapped.

"Could you be more specific?" she asked carefully, watching him order another round.

"Maybe. For one thing, we don't really know what happened to Bowden, but we have an idea."

"Bowden?" she repeated, her stomach sinking.

"Your father's in-house counsel."

"What are you implying?" But she knew the answer.

"We don't have any proof it wasn't an accident, if that's what you're asking. But the whole thing stinks. Your brother has gotten himself involved with some very nasty people."

"So just say it," Josie shot back, her voice rising in anger. "What are you accusing him of?"

"We're not accusing him of anything. Yet," the agent said, in a mildly patronizing tone, which angered Josie even more. "I understand you're an accountant. Any red flags you've noticed? Anything that looks like skimming?"

"Are you joking? You guys harassed my father for years, and now you're coming after my brother? We're done here." Josie stood up and pulled her coat around her.

"Okay. I get it," he said, motioning to the bartender for the check. "But you should know that these guys don't play around. Watch what you say, where you say it and who you say it to. You understand?"

Chapter 22

Josie walked back to the office fuming. Should she or shouldn't she tell Frank? Really, who was she kidding? She couldn't confide in Frank until she knew more. So that left Sam. He was the only one she trusted.

Being told to watch what she said reminded Josie uncomfortably of the old days in Vegas, when everybody was bugging everybody. As a teenager, she would hear a click on the phone line when she tried to call someone, and she knew *they* were listening. FBI wiretaps were rampant. Her father raged that "this was un-American," but there was nothing they could do about it. Even when chatting with her eighth-grade girlfriends about clothes and TV shows, Josie was careful what she said. Sometimes, when she heard the click, she got so mad she would blurt out, "I know you're listening!"

Josie packed up her briefcase and waited until she got into her car to call Sam. She caught him on his way back to the ranch.

"Turn around. It's important," she told him.

"Now?"

"Right now. Remember Operation Pandora?"

"You're joking."

"I'm not." He could tell from her tone that she wasn't.

Operation Pandora was the code name for a huge sting operation that the FBI had initiated in the seventies. It was legendary, before her time, but everyone who grew up here had heard about it. The raid had resulted in a man called the "FBI's most valuable snitch" practically closing down the town. Agents homed in on almost all the casino owners and made their lives a living hell.

Josie had just arrived at her house when she heard Sam pull up behind her in his truck. Rex had half his body out the window and started barking, tail waving, when he saw Josie. She, at least, was his friend. When they walked into the living room, she turned up the music on the stereo, put a finger over her mouth and pointed to the ceiling. She took Sam's hand and led him to the middle of the yard. Rex bounded out the door and then furiously started digging a hole near the fence. Josie quickly described the conversation at the Pioneer.

"So you think your house is bugged?" Sam asked.

"That's what the fed implied. You know what used to go on. You were here for Christ's sake."

"That shit was years ago. You think they still have a hard-on for casino owners?"

"Always. But I don't think it's them doing the bugging this time. Anyway, have you ever come in contact with this FBI agent, Max Gavin?" she asked.

"I can't remember. There's always a few of them nosing around. What does he look like?"

"Like an agent. You know, straight arrow, mid-forties, clean-cut. The point is, he pretty much accused Frank of skimming and even murder. He says Steve Bowden's death wasn't an accident. That's all."

"Murdered?"

"That's what he threw at me. Frank wouldn't really murder anyone, would he?"

"Who knows? I mean, it's not full Bugsy here. No one's firing machine guns in the air, but I wouldn't put it past him."

"What about skimming?" Josie pressed.

"Listen, Dad used to take something off the top. And there were a few 'silent partners,' but he got rid of them years ago. Now? Buckle up. The whole thing's starting to smell." He noticed the dog was still digging by the fence.

"Rex! Stop fucking up the yard," Sam yelled. The dog looked up momentarily and kept digging.

Josie thought about a conversation she had with their father a few years before he died. She was visiting Vegas and had seen an article in a magazine about the Kansas City mob titled "Murder, Inc." There was a picture of her father in it. She cut it out and sat in the living room and waited. When he arrived home, she placed it on his desk in front of him. He glanced at the article, got up from his desk and closed the door.

"Listen, Josie," he had said, looking straight at her. "I'm no angel. I *did* know these people. But I always tried to do the right thing. It wasn't always the *legal* thing, but it was the right thing. You have to believe me, that's not who we are now. And I don't want any of this to ever touch you."

"C'mon, Josie," Sam said, jolting her back to the present, "we should confront Frank. At least warn him the feds are circling."

"Not yet," she said. There was silence. "Didn't you used to have a good friend who worked for the gaming board, the guy who got into all that trouble?"

"Yeah. Scotty Harris."

"Right. I remember. Tell me again—what's his story?"

"Scotty's one of these really smart computer wonks. He got hired by the gaming board to write anti-cheating software. Instead, he figured out how to code the slot machines to hit jackpots when his buddies played the coins in a certain order. He fucked everyone. They won a shitload of cash before they caught him at it. He just got out of the slammer."

"So, I was thinking," Josie said, pausing to give her words more weight. "Would he be able to tell if someone was skimming?"

Sam considered this for a minute. "Scotty's seen it all—that's for sure. When he was with the gaming board, that's what he did. He knows all the tricks. Plus, he has contacts all over the place. We'd have to give him some cash for payoffs or whatever."

"I can get him the cash, but, as you know, there's cameras everywhere in the Jackpot and they'll probably recognize his face. He's going to have to be careful," Josie said. "And in the meantime, I'm going to see what I can find out myself."

"Whole teams of IRS forensic accountants could never catch Dad," Sam said.

"That's because he never wrote anything down. No memos, no calendar, nothing. It was all in his head. Most guys aren't that smart. Most guys always leave a trail."

"Well, good luck," Sam said. "I'm out of here."

He called for Rex, who trotted up with mud caked on his snout. The dog shook dirt all over Josie's shoes and dropped a dead rat at her feet.

Chapter 23

At eight sharp, Josie stood in the doorway of Rob's roof-top restaurant, home of thirty-dollar cocktails, eighty-dollar lobster tails and spicy toro tartare with caviar that was "market priced." The cool, aquatic-themed venue also boasted hip customers who looked like they all had personal trainers and coke dealers on speed dial.

Rob was waiting for Josie at a corner booth with the best view of the Strip, and as soon as she sat down, a waiter appeared. She needed a drink and the dry vodka martini went down easily.

The chef placed a huge tray of shellfish on ice between them—oysters on the half shell, lobster tails flown in from Maine, Alaskan king crab legs and a saucer of Imperial Beluga caviar in the center with X-Acto knife–cut toast points.

Josie's ex used to be resentful of such extravagance. In exasperation, she once accused him of just not liking rich people.

"Nobody likes rich people," Stuart said, bristling.

A tan blonde in a slinky black dress gave Rob a wave. He winked back at her and offered the tray of seafood to Josie.

"Oysters?" he asked.

"Yes. Thank you," she said, delicately picking one up. It was delicious, and even more so because she couldn't remember when she last had something to eat.

"Just to be clear. This is a meeting. Not a date," Josie added.

"Did I say this was a date?"

"Well, no. Not exactly. But it seems like a date."

"It's not a date." He grinned.

"Okay, then. So what do you know that I don't?" Josie asked, sipping a second martini.

"Probably a lot. But if you're referring to the union, we spent hours with our top DC labor lawyers hashing out a deal. It wasn't easy but worth it to avoid a strike."

"I know the deal you got," she said. "It won't work for us. Frank told me we don't have the revenue."

"I have an idea of what your revenue is, and unless there's something I'm missing, there's a deal to be made."

Josie remembered Frank talking about their "load of debt," which Rob probably didn't know about. Or maybe he did. Maybe he already knew what was going on at her place. Her father had always beaten it into them to never carry too much debt. "It's okay when times are good," Roy King was fond of saying, "but the economy *always* turns, and then every shark in town starts circling."

"Would you mind giving me the name of your DC lawyers?" she asked. "No sense reinventing the wheel."

"Of course. Ride our coattails."

Josie finished off her martini and ordered another to give her courage.

"Listen, I'd like to apologize for my behavior at the funeral."

"And the other time too?" he asked, teasing her.

"Yes. Both incidents."

"Incidents, so *that's* what they were. Well, as far as I'm concerned, you have nothing to apologize for."

"That's just not who I am," Josie insisted.

Rob smiled, and then leaned forward and looked her straight in the eye.

"We started this relationship backward. I'd like to get to know you, get your attention and seduce you slowly. The way normal couples do. First there's a look, then a smile, then you touch each other and then . . ."

"I get it. I'll try to pretend I just met you." Josie cracked a crab claw. "So, do you come here often?"

"I'm serious. I mean, usually when an *incident* happens, I suddenly have a six a.m. squash game the next morning, see ya, fuck off. You getting this?"

"Perfectly. That's the way I felt after our first time."

"You did?" Rob looked slightly hurt. "Not me! I thought you were the most beautiful woman I'd ever seen. I didn't want you to leave."

"Now you're just flattering me."

"No. I'm seducing you." He stood up and extended a hand to her. "Let's dance."

He pulled Josie up from her seat and led her to the dance floor. Rob nodded to the DJ and the music turned into a slow jam, silky and romantic. He pulled her close to him. She gave in to the warmth of his skin, his breath on her neck. He had a long back with strong muscles and she could feel herself wanting him. He led her in slow, smooth, gliding movements and she savored the pleasure of feeling weightless and floating above the dance floor. Rob softly pushed her hair back and pressed his lips to her ear. Then he twirled her around until her head was spinning. The martinis were really kicking in.

After a few songs came and went, the security guard walked over and whispered something in Rob's ear.

Josie overheard snippets. Something about a dealer getting harassed and someone "out of control." As the man walked away, Rob turned back to Josie and said, "Sorry for the interruption."

He noticed her face was bright red and she was a little unsteady on her feet.

"Let's sit down," he said, gently escorting her back to the booth.

Josie slid in, adjusting her skirt. Then she rolled into a very long and confusing anecdote concerning a friend of her father's who ended up "floating." "Well, not floating exactly. That's just an expression. He was dumped in the desert."

While she spoke she noticed that Rob was staring at her intensely, smiling as if everything she said made perfect sense. She knew she was slurring her words slightly and had a very nice buzz going.

"Here's a joke," she said. "Two hotel owners walk into a bar at a shitty local casino . . . One says to the other . . . let's get a room—"

"Okay. I know how this ends . . ." Rob said, cutting her off.

"You didn't wait for the punch line . . ." She giggled, fumbling for something in her purse.

"Whoops." She laughed as her lipstick dropped on the ground.

He looked at her for a moment, bent over and picked up her lipstick.

"Don't be offended," he said. "I'm going to get one of my guys to take you home. We'll bring your car back later. And can I give you some advice?"

"That would be great. That's actually what I came for, right? I don't need to know everything."

"Well, you're in no danger of that. You're in way over your head."

A slow burn flushed her cheeks. "Jesus," she murmured. How dare he. Josie stood up with as much dignity as she could summon, just as Rob's security man arrived to escort her downstairs.

"By the way," she said, looking back at him, "do you believe in a hot hand?"

"What do you mean?" He looked baffled.

"A hot hand. Is there such a thing?"

"Of course not," Rob said, going along with it. "A winning streak is a hundred percent random."

"That's what I thought. Blowing on dice, slipping the dealer a hundred. That's all for show. The last deal of the cards has nothing to do with the next, right?"

"Right," Rob agreed, wondering where this was going.

"Okay, then. Good night," Josie said coldly, and followed the security man out of the club.

A half hour later, the same man approached Rob's table.

"What's up?" Rob asked. He was just finishing his dinner, solo.

"It's Ms. King. She asked to play a few hands of blackjack on the way out and she's on a roll. Eye in the Sky says she's counting cards. And she's one of the best they've seen. She's up three hundred grand."

Rob took the elevator down to the casino to find Josie sitting at a fan-shaped blackjack table, chatting it up with two cowboys from Wyoming. A group of tourists wearing baseball caps and T-shirts were surrounding the table, celebrating. "This table is fucking *hot*!" one of them yelled. Rob stared at Josie, taking it all in, then he smiled knowingly.

"Having fun?" he whispered in her ear.

"I'm starting to. I have a *really* hot hand here," Josie said, smiling at the guys next to her. She pushed more chips onto the table. Rob settled his hand on her shoulder. She was momentarily distracted, but then fixed her eyes back on the table.

"I guess I underestimated your abilities," he said.

"People often do," she said, winking at him.

"What's your limit?" Rob asked, referring to the table bet.

"Three martinis and a vodka tonic, maybe two. Without the tonic," she answered, waving over a cocktail waitress and motioning for another drink.

"You sure you want that?"

"*Ab*-so-fucking-lutely," Josie said, throwing down the drink. She leaned over and whispered to him, "Someone once said you can learn a lot about a woman by getting smashed with her."

"I already have," Rob said. "And you've made your point."

"Not even close," she replied. "First of all, there's a whole school of thought that gamblers love the action more than winning. That's why they keep playing until they go bust. That doesn't make sense to me. Because it's not what you win. It's what you take home. And I'm about ready to leave. What's the table max again?"

"Five hundred grand," he told her, although he knew she already knew that.

"That's just perfect. One more hand," she said, swiping her cards on the table. "I'm feeling lucky. You know what that's like, right? You must get lucky all the time."

She was on a roll now, keeping up the patter as her eyes zeroed in on the cards and then moved on. It was almost effortless, this activation of a bilateral network of brain circuits processing numbers and space. Even through the shuffle, she could keep track of the ratio of low cards to high cards. She glanced at the dealer, who had a five showing.

"Splitting nines," she said, noting that plenty of low cards had been dealt, pushing the chances of her winning considerably higher.

She slid a pile of chips into her betting circle. The pit boss looked at Rob. He nodded okay. The dealer flipped over his hole card, a 10, then drew a 5, another 8 and busted. The whole table cheered. Winners all.

"So. What's the count?" Rob asked her.

"Running or true?" No sense denying it. She was putting on a show for his benefit. And it wasn't even hard.

"True."

"Plus eight with seventy-five percent deck penetration. Four aces remaining. You got a problem with that?" Josie was smiling. Anyone would know the odds were entirely in her favor.

"Yep. I do."

"You gonna back room me?"

"Don't be ridiculous," he said, amused but impressed.

"Okay. I'll just take my . . . what is it again?"

"Four hundred grand."

"My four hundred grand and head on home."

She pushed a stack of chips across the table as a tip for the dealer.

"So . . . this has been super fun," she said, kissing him on the cheek and pouring her chips into a bucket.

"On second thought," Rob said, helping her up from the chair and slipping his arm around her waist, "I might be able to give you some more union advice. Why don't you come up to my suite."

Josie reached up, adjusted his tie and patted his shoulder. "Now that would be real neighborly," she said, leaning into him. Then she murmured in his ear, "But you know what they say about leaving while you're ahead."

Chapter 24

When Josie got home, she splashed water on her face, stripped down to her underwear, turned off the lights and crawled into bed. Then her cell rang. She was still feeling the buzz from all the alcohol she had consumed. How many drinks did she have? She couldn't remember. She ignored the phone and fumbled in the drawer of her bedside table for a pack of Marlboros. She slipped one in her mouth and lit up. Her cell rang a second time. She looked at the screen and answered.

"Hello? Josie? It's Rob. You okay?"

"Hey," she said, sitting up and leaning her head against the headboard. She exhaled and waved away a stream of smoke.

"I'm fine. Thanks." She tried to keep her voice cool and even. Then she slumped down under the covers and took another drag.

"Where are you?" he asked, sounding concerned.

"I'm home. In bed."

There was a long pause.

"What are you wearing?"

"Oh. I get it. I don't do phone sex, Rob," she said, inhaling, the end of the cigarette glowing in the dark.

"Are you smoking?"

"Maybe."

"So what do you think about when you're alone in bed, smoking?"

"I'm in no condition to talk right now," Josie said, the cigarette dangling from her mouth like a model on a break.

"What is it you said you're wearing?" he asked, ignoring her response.

She smiled. "Okay, this is the part where I tell you I'm not wearing anything, right?"

"Is that true?" he asked.

"Maybe," she replied in a seductive voice.

"Stop teasing me."

"Why? You know you like it."

"You're right. Tell me what *you* like."

"I like to fantasize," she said.

He laughed. "About who?"

"Wrong question. It's about what. For instance, I like it when someone overpowers me. When it's dangerous but I'm still in control. I like to talk dirty. Maybe I have a 'safe word.'"

"Are you joking? Are we talking S and M?" he asked.

She gave a short laugh. "It's all about foreplay. I enjoy being told what to do. Sexually, I mean. I like it when someone bends me over their knee and spanks me. The endorphins give me a rush, like a shot of heroin."

"What else?" he pressed in a husky voice.

"I like when someone handcuffs me to the bed, spreads my legs and slowly starts to touch me." The words sounded funny to her as she said them.

"And then?"

"And then I tell him I want him. I want him so bad. I know he's getting hard. He puts his hands all over me. Inside me. I beg him to fuck me, but he keeps saying, 'Not yet.'"

"Shit, Josie. You're making me crazy. Can I come over?"

"Hold on a minute." She placed her cell on the bedside table, swung her legs out of bed and padded to the window. She struggled to slide it open a bit and the night air felt cool and fresh on her skin.

"Josie, are you there?"

She snuffed out her cigarette on the windowsill, wiped off the ashes, grabbed the cell and slipped back under the covers.

"I had to put out my cigarette."

"So, can I come over?" Rob persisted.

"You know what? I'm going to have a serious hangover tomorrow morning so I need to go to sleep."

"Are you fucking kidding me?" he said, incredulous.

"Nighty night," she replied sweetly.

Chapter 25

The next morning, Josie took two Excedrin with a large bottle of water and then made herself a strong cup of coffee. Her head still ached and her mouth was dry as an ashtray. She stared at the check for four hundred grand and slipped it in her purse. The evening had not played out the way she imagined. Not at all. She was still high when she got home from the casino. In another town, with another man, she might feel guilty about last night. Fucking around with Rob and making off with so much money. But this was Vegas, where women are fungible. Might as well use every advantage she had.

She could remember sitting at the Jackpot having dinner with her father when she was little. A man had approached the table and said, "Hey Roy, can you get me some girls tonight?" As if women were a perk, a part of the hotel loyalty program. She grew up with that.

Frankly, Josie thought, it felt good to have the power over Rob. Getting what she wanted. And what she wanted was to be in control. The card counting was just the beginning. Normally, the head of security would tell the card counter to take their winnings and leave the state. Then they'd alert all the other casinos. She knew Rob wouldn't do that.

By the time she got to the office it was nearly noon. Josie walked past the velvet roped-off area reserved for the whales. She felt her head throb as she tried to ignore the barrage of blinking lights and clanging bells just outside the ropes.

She strode into Frank's office, ignoring Lionel, who was settled on the couch as though he were Frank's probation officer. Josie turned her back on him and faced her brother.

"I had a meeting with Rob McCarthy yesterday about the union negotiations. And as you know, he's been—"

"Fucking us over with his sandwiches and cookies," Frank interrupted.

"Anyhow," Josie continued, unfazed, "he's giving us the name of these DC labor lawyers who helped him turn things around. I'm going to call them."

"Those East Coast suits always charge a fortune," Frank scoffed. "Our local guys are just as good."

"We're getting nowhere as it is. I'm going to have an initial meeting with a different firm and then we'll talk," Josie said.

Frank thought about it for a minute. "Okay. What the hell. *You* do it. But I don't want a herd of them flying here first-class and charging us a couple hundred grand. That's their little trick, you know. Why bring in one lawyer when you can bill five, including all their fucking associates."

"If they resolve this, it'll be worth every penny," she said, walking toward the door.

Then she stopped, hesitated and turned back around. Should she ask him about the finances now? Lionel was staring at the wall with flat eyes.

"I need to look at the books," Josie said. She noticed Lionel's eyes track slightly her way.

"Talk to Trotter," Frank hedged, then looked down as if engrossed in a document, signaling that the meeting was over.

After Josie left, Frank walked over to the door and shut it with a slam. God, she was so fucking persistent, he thought to himself. Even when they were kids, she got on his nerves. Lionel shook his head and closed his eyes.

"I told you she'd be trouble," he reminded Frank.

"Josie's not going to find anything. Believe me, if the IRS came up empty, she will too. We've got it under control. We're airtight."

"I don't like it."

"Look, if she *does* see something, which she won't, she'll come running straight to me."

"Sure she will. But her office is wired, just in case." Lionel's voice was tight.

"Unnecessary."

"Let's call it insurance, Frank."

Chapter 26

A few hours later, Josie closed the door to her office and called Rob. He picked up right away and laughed lightly when she asked if she had dented his profit margin.

"Not to be dramatic, but I'm just getting over what you did to me last night," Rob conceded.

"You mean at the casino or later on?"

"Both," he said.

"Sex is a game." Josie laughed. "You know that. Just like blackjack."

"You're giving me whiplash."

"Why, thank you. It was fun."

"I'm glad you think so. But try not to have 'fun' in my casino again. No one likes to lose four hundred grand," he admitted, "but the performance was impressive."

"You ought to see me when I'm sober."

"I can only imagine."

"I'll return the check as a thank-you if you'll introduce me to your attorneys."

"Better yet," he said, "I'm flying to DC next week to meet these guys. Why don't you come along?"

Josie thought for a minute. Made more sense than flying them here and charging her brother an arm and a leg. She'd do the initial consult there, and then figure out if she wanted to hire them.

"That's very generous of you." It was nice to have one thing be easy.

"Not a problem. I'm a big client. I'll have my office set up the appointment. Meet me at Atlantic Aviation next Monday. We're wheels up at nine."

"You're sure it's okay?"

"The plane seats thirteen and so far it's just me. Plenty of room."

Josie hung up and leaned back in her chair. She wanted to meet the lawyers and this just fell into her lap. A private jet with thirteen seats—no lines, no crowded terminal, cashmere blankets on your lap and an attendant offering you a Bloody Mary before takeoff. Her ex might hate the rich, but even he'd have to admit there were some advantages.

It wasn't until Josie started reviewing the casino's most recent financial statements—balance sheets, cash flow, income, assets and liabilities—that she realized what a time-consuming project she'd created for herself. Finding out if Frank was skimming would not be easy. Normally a team of accountants would be assigned this job and given a few months to do it. She scanned the narrative for the disqualifier—anything that stood out—then moved down to the tax summaries. Forensic accounting was one of her areas of expertise when she worked at the firm in LA, so she knew how difficult it was to discover irregularities if someone sophisticated was trying to hide them.

Sam had set up a meeting with his friend Scotty to see if he could investigate on-site—look for any red flags. They planned to meet at the ranch after work. Before she left downtown, Josie stopped at the bank and withdrew ten grand in cash.

When she arrived at the ranch, she felt a rush of emotions. She still couldn't envision this place without her father. The loss was palpable.

Crystal, Sam's new squeeze, answered the door in a half-tied silk robe and fuzzy pink slippers. It felt like a rebuke. Her father would have been appalled. She was a twenty-something "entertainer" he had met at a topless bar. Sam came barreling down the stairs in his boxers, kissed Crystal on top of her head and whispered something in her ear. She giggled and backed out of the room.

Sam, as usual, seemed hungover. He rubbed his eyes and ran his fingers through his messy hair. Then he shook his head like a wet dog.

Scotty arrived a few minutes later in a banged-up piece-of-shit Toyota Tacoma. He gave Sam a big, loopy grin. Scotty had bleach-tipped hair and puka beads around his neck and was wearing a faded Mick Jagger Hot Lips T-shirt. His black-and-white-checkered Vans were old and dirty with worn-down soles. This was the man who was going to untangle Frank's secrets?

"Hey, thanks for coming on such short notice," Sam said, introducing Josie. "Want a beer?"

"Well . . . why the hell not? Nice to meet you," he said, taking Josie's hand. Then he turned back to Sam. "Hey, you never told me she was a ten."

"She's my sister, for Christ's sake. Let's get to it."

The three of them sat down and Rex trotted in, flopping at Sam's feet. For once, Josie thought, the dog seemed quiet and obedient.

"This has to be totally confidential," Josie began. "I was given some information that could be completely bogus, but this person alluded to the fact that there might be stuff going on at the Jackpot that is not exactly legal."

Scotty nodded. "I spent ten years of my life investigating douchebags who were trying to get away with this shit."

"Did you catch many?" Josie asked, slightly amused.

"Some. You know, it used to be no problem. Guys would just slip into the counting room and grab stacks of cash, go to a table, sign a marker and play the cash out," Scotty explained, "then, of course, the marker would disappear. When the laws changed, everyone had to get more creative. They rigged the scales in the counting room to weigh the money so it registered ten percent less. They'd pocket the ten percent. In the old days, the Stardust was able to steal three hundred K a week using that method—the mob took down almost a hundred mill before anyone caught on. But of course, that's old news."

"So if they *were* into something at the Jackpot, could you spot it?" Josie asked.

"Depends on whether they're skimming or laundering or a combination of both. I'll have to get in there, talk to some of my contacts and see what I see. Sometimes it's all over the map. Shell companies, over-invoicing, crooked suppliers."

"So if I gave you ten K, would that be enough for you to get a sense of what's going on?" Josie asked.

"In cash?" He sounded thrilled.

"Well, yes. Keep a grand for yourself and use the rest to get information."

"This should be plenty. I had this source once, a totally respected gambler, a pro. He knew the business inside and out. King of the con. His luck was good and bad. But then the hotel owner spots the pit boss slipping him a marker for ten large, which he took over to the cashier and cashed out. Got caught red-handed. This is the bad luck part of it. So he gets in his Lincoln and drives off, but the hotel owner, he's pissed as hell, so he gets one of his guys to follow him, and when he stops at a light, this guy opens his window, points a shotgun and pops him. Bam, bam, bam—just like that. It was a mess. The windshield shattered and blood all over the place. So the police, they come to the hotel looking for the shooter, and they find him. They take him in, but they shoot him in the car on the way to the station. Said he was resisting arrest. Me? I never said a word, even though I know the hotel owner took care of the cheater *and* the shooter." He took the last swig of his beer, then leaned in and looked Josie dead in the eye. "My point is, you can't trust anyone. They snitch on you when they're supposed to be your friend. You know what I'm saying?" He set his beer bottle on the table and rose to leave. "Anyway, I'll ask around."

Josie and Sam looked at each other in silence as Scotty took the envelope of cash and stuffed it in his back pocket. Josie wondered what the "good luck" part of the story was.

Chapter 27

After meeting with Scotty, Josie had a few hours to kill before her daughter was due to arrive for the weekend. She raced to the market to stock up on soda, cookies, ice cream and chips, stuff she would never eat if Billie wasn't around.

It was late, after ten, when Billie appeared in baggage claim dressed in a hoodie, flannel pajama bottoms and sheepskin-lined moccasins. Her oversize backpack was jammed with clothes and textbooks and she smiled groggily at her mother, her mouth full of braces and rubber bands. Her daughter was twelve, tall for her age. Josie noticed she slumped her shoulders to hide her height. But she couldn't hide her excitement. She loved coming to Vegas and staying at the ranch. Her grandfather, Sunny and Sam always fussed over Billie, taking her riding and hiking and letting her run wild in the casino, making a nuisance of herself until the pit boss told her to "settle down." But Billie's favorite game was pushing all the buttons in the elevator and then jumping out. Billie could do whatever she pleased. No one bothered the King granddaughter.

Josie had made plans to spend the weekend with Billie. She would take Friday off and the business would have to live without her.

"So how's LA?" Josie asked Billie.

"Dad was in a bad mood when he drove me to the airport," Billie said as she tumbled into the car. "When I said I couldn't wait to get to Vegas, he said, 'You *do* realize your grandpa was a gangster.'"

"What?" Josie asked. She wasn't expecting this. She had avoided discussing the controversy surrounding her father and wasn't ready to talk about it now.

"Well, was he?" Billie repeated, baiting her mother.

"No, he wasn't."

"Then why would Dad say that?" she asked.

"Some people think that everyone who lives in Las Vegas is somehow tainted. Your grandfather was a complicated person and it was a different time . . ." Josie said, trying to keep her voice light. What a low blow for Stuart to keep bringing this up. She felt a hot wave of anger.

"Dad says the FBI tried to arrest Grandpa but couldn't," Billie pressed. She didn't seem shocked or even upset. Just curious.

"That's because there was no evidence. They were harassing him. Your grandfather ran a legitimate business. He was a respected citizen. Ask anyone."

Josie felt a twinge of guilt about lying to her daughter, but not enough to cop to anything. She remembered when she first moved to LA, she stopped telling people she grew up in Vegas because they all imagined it as a mobster metropolis. "I didn't know anyone actually *lived* in Las Vegas," they'd say. So she hid her hometown, like porn under the bed, and went to work for an accounting firm in the Valley. She wanted boring—she got it. But at least her daughter had a normal suburban life. Josie had seen to that. Billie glanced up at her with a half grin.

"Can I have a gun?" she asked. She already knew the answer.

"Absolutely not."

"Uncle Sammy says *you* used to shoot when you were my age." Billie rolled the window down. "Younger even."

"That was different. Close the window, it's freezing."

"How was it different?"

"We lived on a ranch."

"So did you kill coyotes or what?" She sounded genuinely intrigued by the idea.

"No. I would never hurt an animal. We went to a shooting range."

"Where?"

"Up in the mountains."

"So why can't I go?"

"Because I said so. Anyway," Josie said, changing the subject, "I hope you like the new house. You have the biggest bedroom."

"At Dad's house, I didn't even get to pick my room. His new family hates me," Billie said, taking a breath. For the first time since she got off the plane, she looked sad. "Her girls got first choice and I got the shitty room over the garage."

"I'll speak to your father," Josie said, struggling to keep a neutral voice. Stuart always followed the path of least resistance, which included not standing up to his new wife.

Stuart still worked at the same accounting firm where they met thirteen years ago. Back then Josie was a first-year associate, under the supervision of senior staff. Mid-year, she was assigned to Stuart, whose top client was being audited. He was a senior partner, thirty-five, athletic, charming—the kind of man to whom people always said, "I can't believe you're an accountant."

They spent long days together and, eventually, long nights. Her former boyfriends had been students in jeans and backpacks with vague plans about touring Europe or joining the Peace Corps. They seemed like boys and Stuart was a sophisticated man with a promising future. He took her to the symphony, the opera, expensive restaurants downtown. And when he proposed after six months, she was over the moon. A year later, her daughter, Billie, was born. Josie was twenty-two years old.

But she should have listened to Sunny at the time. Her sister had arrived in a huff right after she heard about the engagement, summoning her to the Polo Lounge at the Beverly Hills Hotel. The maître d' had given them the best booth—and Sunny the best suite, professional courtesy between hotel owners. Sunny shrugged off her Chanel jacket, ordered two vodka rocks, and got down to business.

"He seems too slick to me. Guys like him are all over Vegas. They have rings on their fingers and escorts by their sides. I bet you two to one he's a player. You should know better. You didn't grow up on a farm, for God's sake."

"He's sexy, intelligent, with a respectable career," Josie retorted. "I mean, he's on the mayor's economic council! And by the way, everyone hated Trent and you married him anyway."

"Everyone did *not* hate him!"

"You're right," said Josie, swirling the ice cubes in her drink. "Only Dad."

"Is this your little rebellion?" Sunny shot back. "Trust me. This is a colossal mistake. At least get a fucking prenup. Don't be naive. You're beautiful but you're also a meal ticket."

"Jesus, Sunny. I'm not that stupid. Of course I'll get a prenup. With an arbitration clause. But stay the fuck out of it," Josie retorted hotly. "It's my life."

"Face it. Guys like that always have a secret. They're broke. Or they're in the closet, blowing guys in gas stations. Or they like to fuck teenage girls they meet online."

"Stop! It's done."

"I give it two years," Sunny said. And she was right.

Chapter 28

Josie thought back to the last meeting with Stuart, which took place shortly after she heard the terms of the will and she had decided to move back to Vegas. They met in LA at a local bar near his Century City office. He had offered no words of condolence when her father died. She was not surprised. He'd always hated Roy King, and Roy's high-powered lawyers had enforced the prenup and extracted Josie from a bad marriage. Under the terms of the deal, since they'd been married only two years, there was no big balloon payment and Billie's expenses were divided equally.

During the course of the negotiations, Josie discovered Stuart was in debt big-time. The fancy cars, the expensive restaurants and the Beverly Hills–adjacent apartment he had rented were all for show. But that wasn't the reason for the divorce. It was the old girlfriend he was still fucking and refused to give up, paying her rent with Josie's money he siphoned from their joint bank account. After the divorce, he married the woman and moved in with her and her two girls.

As for Billie, after Josie's lawyers had thrown some additional money at Stuart, he finally agreed to visitation every other weekend rather than joint custody. Josie knew that whatever Stuart might say about loving his daughter, money talked.

At this point, Josie had only one crucial item on her agenda. She tried to sound calm and businesslike. "Look. There's a situation. I have to move to Vegas and I want to take Billie with me."

"And I want to fuck Angelina Jolie, but it's not gonna happen."

"Can we keep this civil?" Josie gritted her teeth and tried to disguise it as a smile.

"If you wanted to keep things civil, then Roy fucking King should have been more 'civil' to me and my wife when we were in Vegas last year. He didn't even comp the showroom, much less our suite." Stuart mopped his forehead with a napkin and ordered a bourbon rocks.

"Make it two," Josie said to the waitress.

"And I'm exhausted," he went on. "Not in the mood for this shit."

Josie threw up her hands. "Okay. I'll make it short. I'm taking Billie. We're moving to Vegas. We can work out the details later."

"Fuck you. *I'll* make it short. The answer is no." He looked at her with righteous indignation. "So tell me. Did the whole town turn out for Crooked Roy?" Stuart mocked.

"Actually, yes," Josie replied coolly. "And it wasn't the whole town. It was the whole state."

"Gee. Hated to miss the mafia hoedown. Lemme tell you something." Stuart leaned forward and she could smell the alcohol on his breath. "You're never getting full custody. I look at you and I see dead bodies in the desert."

Josie calmly took a sip of her drink. "Stuart, I look at you and I see someone who will agree to my terms."

He sat back heavily.

"Jesus, strong-arming just like your father." There was a pause as Josie watched him finish his drink. She wished she had a gun.

"Make me an offer," he said.

"Okay," she said. "Let's get down to it."

"You know, you don't always get to decide how things play out."

"We'll see." She kept her voice neutral.

In the end, for a substantial payout, Josie got him to agree to everything she wanted. Billie would move to Vegas full-time after Christmas in exchange for July and August in LA. In order to land the deal, in addition to the balloon payment, Josie took on all of Billie's expenses.

As he accepted the wildly generous offer, Stuart added, "I know I'm not perfect, but I try. And I don't want my daughter disappearing from my life."

"Right," Josie said, humoring him. The fact was, she had been willing to pay even more.

Josie brushed off the memory of dealing with Stuart and looked at her beautiful daughter sitting next to her in the car. When they finally got home, she grabbed Billie's duffel and watched as her daughter walked tentatively through the front door, looked around at the strange new environment and then climbed the stairs to her new bedroom.

Josie had made a point of turning the bedroom into a preteen paradise. The walls were painted Billie's favorite colors, turquoise and pink, and there were framed corkboards with pictures of Billie's friends and her latest boy band crush. On the bed were some new pajamas, pink fuzzy slippers and a duvet with pillows to match. Sunny, the compulsive shopper, had ordered everything for her niece, including slipping in a small Louis Vuitton shoulder bag that was far too expensive for a twelve-year-old.

It was past eleven and Josie could hear sounds of the neighborhood shutting down for the night. The suburbs were not at all like the silence of the desert near the ranch. A few dogs were barking in the distance. The occasional car drove by; people were shutting off their kitchen lights, closing their gates, dragging trash cans across the gravel to the curbside.

Out at the ranch the sounds and smells were so different from the city. Life came alive at night, and you could sense nocturnal creatures in the dark—nighthawks catching moths, screeching owls searching for a mate, and the intoxicating, sweet fragrance of wildflowers. If you listened closely, you could hear a multitude of birds calling to one another, a rising and falling of wild sounds that were often high-pitched and insistent. Then there would be a silence, as the birds flew higher and disappeared from view like angels.

She glanced up as she heard Billie coming down the stairs.

"I love it! Why can't I live here with you?" Billie asked.

"You will. I promise. I worked it out with your father . . . after Christmas."

"After Christmas," Billie whispered, her voice catching.

Chapter 29

When Josie was young, she and Sam would shove pistols in their jeans, load up their backpacks with tin cans and empty bottles, and hike up near the base of Gold Strike Canyon. They'd find a flat spot, and then they'd spend the next few hours blasting targets to smithereens. Josie remembered watching shards of glass fly into the sky, and the enormous rush of adrenaline as the bullets hit the mark. Sam would tell her not to "dead fish" her grip, and helped her feed ammo into the empty chambers. They were two bored rich kids blowing shit up. A great outing on a lazy afternoon.

As the town got more crowded, hikers were always ducking bullets. Some were lucky and others weren't. Half the people in Clark County owned guns, so the desert shooting had to stop. That's when gun ranges sprang up all over the valley. They offered beginners and experts targets and burgers, although they'd have to wash their burgers down with soft drinks. The gun range Sam and Josie preferred was out on Decatur Boulevard near Paradise Valley.

In the morning, she called Sam and asked which was the closest shooting range, and if there was an age minimum. She wouldn't buy her daughter a gun but she had changed her mind about target practice as long as there were no human-shaped targets. Since Billie was going to be a Vegas kid, Josie might as well give her a taste of her own Vegas childhood.

"I've seen five-year-olds there. Are you taking Billie? She'll love it," Sam said. "They also have archery, but that's for Girl Scouts and pussies."

When Billie woke up, Josie told her that she had changed her mind and they were going shooting.

"Really? With an *actual* gun?" Billie asked, thrilled.

"Yes. An actual gun. This is Nevada, kiddo." Josie could see by Billie's reaction that she had made the right decision.

Early that morning, she had opened her gun safe and pulled out the Smith & Wesson .357 Magnum that Sam had given her as a housewarming present. On the drive over, she gave Billie the requisite lecture—treat every gun as if it were loaded, never point it at anyone, always unload after using. Billie had listened with wide eyes, feeling grown up and important.

As per the rules, when they arrived at the shooting range, they were informed that the gun must be unloaded and cased. No holstered weapons were allowed. The staff explained the procedures and suggested they watch a safety video before starting.

When they got to their station, Josie handed Billie the pistol and showed her how to load it with the muzzle pointing down. They were both wearing yellow plastic shooting glasses and earmuffs. Josie couldn't remember the last time she had held a pistol, and she had forgotten the sheer pleasure of it all. She felt the curve in the lower part of the grip, and centered the web of her hand into the tail. It was like trying on a shoe that fit perfectly. It was almost sensual.

"Now keep your finger *off* the trigger until you're actually going to take the shot."

"It's really heavy," Billie said with a big grin. She looked up at her mother.

"You'll get used to it." Josie smiled. "Hold it with your right hand high up on the slide and then put your left hand over your right. That helps control the recoil."

Billie held it so tight that her hands were shaking.

"Okay, sweetie. No death grip, relax. Hold tight, but not that tight."

Billie loosened her fingers.

"How's this?" she asked.

"Perfect. Now square your body toward the target, with a slight bend to your elbow. Bring the pistol to eye level—don't drop your head."

Billie was trying hard to concentrate as she aimed at the target.

"And don't close one eye," Josie instructed. "Big mistake. Keep both eyes open."

Billie's palms were sweating as she squeezed the trigger with the pad of her finger. She missed the target altogether, but she didn't seem to care. Nothing could prepare Billie for the thrill that coursed through her body.

Later on in the car, she turned to her mother and laughed.

"Dad would kill you if he knew you taught me to shoot."

"Don't tell him, then."

"Did you ever want to shoot anyone?"

"No," Josie lied.

"Never?" Billie looked skeptical.

"Never." Only your father, Josie thought. And sometimes Frank. And then there's Lionel . . .

After they left the range, Josie decided to drive Billie out to the ranch to see the horses. That always lifted her mood. Sam was living there now, so she called ahead. He suggested they come by in the late afternoon, obviously giving him time to get rid of whoever had spent the night.

They arrived at dusk. Sam took Billie's hand and they set out for the stables. Billie loved being with Sam, the crazy, favorite uncle. Josie hung back, wandering around the property until she reached the edge of the desert. She had always liked to hike this time of day, when the sky was filled with scattered light of all colors, diluting the blue.

As a kid, she would start out on a trail with cactus, scrub brush and acacias. She knew the desert like the back of her hand, never needing a map or a compass. Along the way, she would see bobcat tracks, traces of deer bones, dismembered ring-tailed cats lying near coyote scat. Occasionally, she would pick chokecherries, which grew on the rocky slopes. They were edible, but she had to be careful because the pits contain cyanide.

When she finally climbed to her favorite spot, Cathedral Rock, she could see across the vast valley, to Mount Charleston, Lee Peak, Fletcher Peak and views down into Kyle Canyon. She looked out toward the west as the sun was descending behind the mountains, the sky glowing a beautiful shade of red. Here, she was king of the universe. Josie would stretch out her arms and shout across the void, her voice echoing all around her. Her problems disappeared and the world gleamed with promise.

Chapter 30

Josie had hoped that Billie would find a friend and that weekend she did.

"Mom, this is Cassie," Billie announced with enthusiasm. A skinny blonde about the same age as Billie waved her hand hello and then gave a shy smile. Her T-shirt barely covered her midriff and she had chipped red nail polish.

"She's staying for dinner because her parents are at work. She lives next door."

The girls had met that afternoon and Cassie had showed Billie around the neighborhood. Josie learned that Cassie was a pure Vegas latchkey kid, the kind she had gone to school with years ago. She knew the drill by heart. Cassie's mother worked swing shift at Caesars, leaving the house a little before 4 p.m. and getting home after midnight.

"My dad's a pit boss now and so was my grandpa," Cassie said, gobbling down a pizza Josie had ordered for the girls. "That's why we moved back. He used to be a floorman at the Sahara, and then we moved to Reno, but now he's at the Bellagio and the pay is better. I get a lot of new stuff because they're getting a divorce so it's cool."

"And your mom?" Josie asked.

"She's in housekeeping at Caesars. She says she knows everything about everybody. And I'm not kidding. She doesn't tell me that much, but I listen in. You can't believe what goes on . . . like I mean—"

Josie cut her off. "Okay. We got it."

Josie could only imagine what this kid knew. And she was pretty much left alone until midnight. Not ideal, Josie thought. But Billie needed a friend to get her life in Vegas started, and this one appeared like magic.

What *wasn't* magic were the bags of shoplifted makeup that Josie discovered Sunday night after taking her daughter back to the airport. The stolen merchandise was shoved under Billie's bed. Everything was brand-new with the price tags still attached. She felt sick. She'd have to pay Cassie's mother a visit before she headed to DC with Rob. The trip was still on for the next day, although she had second thoughts about going.

She walked next door and rang the bell. A woman answered in a robe and bare feet. She was holding a basket of laundry and she had a few curlers in her hair. There were dark smudges around her eyelashes and down her cheeks, as though she hadn't bothered to remove her makeup before going to bed the night before.

"Hi. So sorry to bother you," Josie said. "I'm Billie's mother, from next door."

"Oh. Glad to finally meet you. I'm Flora." She smiled, setting down the laundry and pulling the curlers from her hair. "Cassie's so happy you moved here. Please come in. Have a cup of coffee."

"Thank you. Some other time. I really can't stay," Josie said, feeling slightly guilty. This was not a social call. She hesitated a minute, wondering if she should bring it up at all. But hell, there's no good time to call someone's daughter a thief. After a few niceties, she gently broached the subject.

"I found these shopping bags in Billie's room. I was wondering if you bought these things for the girls?" Josie asked, knowing that she hadn't.

"Oh no," Flora groaned, shaking her head in frustration. "I've been over this so many times with Cassie. I even had our LDS bishop talk to her. Honestly, I don't know why she does it."

"Where did they get this stuff?"

"They walk on over to the mall or the drugstore," Flora explained. "Cassie was probably showing off to Billie. She knows better than to bring it here. With my schedule, it's hard to stay on top of all the mischief she gets into."

"You're swing shift, right? Four to midnight?"

"Yes, been trying to change for months, but I don't have seniority."

"Maybe I could do something about it. Talk to someone in HR at the Jackpot."

"My God, that would be incredible."

"I can't promise anything, and with the strike going on it's complicated, but I'll try," Josie said, thinking that if Flora was home in the evenings, it would be better for Cassie. Better for Billie. And not bad for Josie either.

Chapter 31

Josie arrived at the private jet terminal, per Rob's directions, at exactly 8:30 a.m. She wondered how Scotty was doing and if he was finding anything useful about Frank. She still couldn't believe her brother was involved in these reckless schemes. But she'd been gone a long time. In many ways, Frank was a stranger to her. She felt uneasy about sneaking around behind his back, but if he was skimming, she needed to know.

Josie had flown private before but nothing as lavish as Rob's navy-and-white Gulfstream with its Rolls-Royce engines. It took off like a rocket and reached forty thousand feet in about eighteen minutes flat. The cabin had satin cherrywood cabinets with polished chrome plating. LCD monitors were placed in the main cabin, along with a printed list of first-run films.

There was a small galley up front with a very impressive Italian espresso machine. In the back, behind a lacquered wood partition, there was a bedroom with a fluffy down comforter rolled at the end of the bed (an amenity for the mile-high club) and a bathroom with a black marble shower and hammered silver sink.

Josie settled into her seat and Rob, always the gentleman, sat across from her, facing the back of the plane—their knees almost touching.

After they leveled off, a male attendant, who introduced himself as Oscar, served mimosas, truffled omelets with berries and fresh croissants.

Who lived like this? Rob McCarthy lived like this. Even though

Roy King could have afforded this setup, he never had a private jet. Not in line with his frontier mentality.

Josie decided not to mention her win at the casino and especially not that phone call afterward.

"So, how long have you owned this plane?" she asked innocuously, looking over the crisp white linens covering the table.

"Once the hotel was up and running and I was doing a lot of business travel, the company bought it. We use it for whales, VIPs, celebrities. We bring them to the hotel in style and they gamble ten times the cost of the flight, plus they become loyal customers. It's just good business. In fact, in January, we take delivery of a second jet with international range. Vegas to Singapore, nonstop."

"A solid business decision," Josie said with a smile, acknowledging this was no sacrifice for him.

"Okay. I admit, I'm spoiled. I'm never flying commercial again."

"Did you grow up this way?"

"Not even close." He laughed.

He told her that his father started out "in trucking," which usually meant the mob, and graduated to low-rent bookmaking joints, initially in New York and then in Vegas. He earned enough to send his son to private schools and on to Cornell, where Rob majored in business and pretty coeds. When his father died unexpectedly, Rob left college, moved back to Vegas, sold his father's business and began working his way up in the casino world. His first job was at the Riviera Hotel, where the owner was an old friend of his father's. It seemed he had a knack for attracting whales, he told her, without sounding arrogant. Or maybe he was just lucky, he added.

"I was promoted to management and then able to earn enough to buy a majority interest in an off-Strip casino, Buffalo Bill's, which, as I recall, you visited."

"And as I recall, you neglected to *properly* introduce yourself. Bobby."

"At the time, it didn't seem you were that worried about being proper. In fact, I've noticed that being proper is not high on your list . . ."

"You'd be surprised by what's high on my list. Let's just go back to your illustrious history."

"With pleasure. Finally, I had enough backing to start Desperados." He mentioned a brief marriage to an actress she'd never heard of.

"What was it like to be a casino kid in Vegas?" he asked, turning the conversation back to Josie.

"My brother and I used to sit out at night in the dark, play cards and shoot snakes," she told him.

"Me too. But it was in Brooklyn. And the snakes would shoot back."

Josie laughed despite herself.

"Seriously," he said. "What was it like?"

"You really want to know?"

"Yeah. I want to know," he answered sincerely.

"Okay. So picture this. I was twelve years old, a geeky kid who loved math, science and climbing rocks. My best friend was a turtle. That tells you everything you need to know.

"So one day, I was waiting for my dad's driver to pick me up from school and this really cool older kid walked over and started flirting. I couldn't believe he was interested in me. He picked up my backpack and started twirling it around, asking me why it was so heavy. I found out later that a fed bribed him to plant a few grams of coke in my backpack so my dad would be more 'cooperative.' Luckily, my dad's attorney got wind I was being set up; he raced over and dumped the stuff before anyone could arrest me."

"Jesus," Rob said, switching out his mimosa for a scotch. "That's some story."

"Wait. Don't you want the happy ending?"

"I thought that was it."

"Nope. Even happier. My dad's friend, the sheriff, arrested the little shit and scared him with serious jail time. He spilled the beans about the fed's setup. The judge went fucking nuts, threatened to expose the whole investigation and charge them all with child endangerment . . . which forced the feds to drop all the charges against my dad."

"Sounds like an idyllic childhood," Rob joked.

"American as apple pie," Josie said.

"Right. Apple pie with a Beretta in it." He laughed.

All joking aside, it was difficult for Josie to think about that time, and the long, miserable days and nights that followed. Glancing over her shoulder wherever she went. Wondering if her father would get sent to prison and who would take care of her. She would never have an ordinary day in an ordinary place again. Leaving Vegas seemed like the only way to have any kind of normal life.

"No more questions," she said, cutting off the conversation. She pulled a brand-new deck of cards from her purse. "Let's play a few hands."

"Not on your life! You cheat."

"It's not cheating. It's just math."

"Bullshit. You count cards. How'd you learn, anyway?"

"I taught myself." Josie began dealing onto the burled wood table between them.

"C'mon. Really?"

"I watched my brother and his friends play. And then I practiced on my own. There wasn't much else to do on the ranch."

"How old were you?"

"Ten, I guess?"

"You're kidding." He picked up his cards.

"I'm good with numbers." Josie set the deck between them.

"That's an understatement." He fanned the cards in his hands and looked at her. "What did your father think about all this?"

"Good question," Josie said, thinking back to the first time her father saw her counting cards. "It's complicated."

Chapter 32

Josie was twelve when she had her big debut at the casino. She had spent every weekend watching Sam's backyard game, standing quietly by his side, memorizing each card, each hand, predicting when the high cards were enough to give him an advantage.

"You should have bet on those last hands. The count was plus eight," Josie told him after one game. He had managed to lose a hundred bucks and was lighting up a joint.

"You know, sometimes it's just about getting lousy cards. That's a fact," he said, sweeping up the decks.

"It's really not. I could have told you when to bet. I *knew* you were screwing up."

"I've created a monster," Sam joked, but he shook his head in admiration.

Josie could feel the glow and basked in it, then she was emboldened.

"Try me. I can tell you when to bet and when to pass."

"So I should risk money on my little know-it-all sister?"

"I'm a sure thing, Sam," she boasted.

"Okay. Next week. We'll see how you do. When you think I should bet, tap me on the shoulder."

"Geez. That's so obvious. I'll just walk over to the grass . . . then you'll know. And don't smoke a joint. It makes me sick."

"Yes, ma'am."

After Sam won $500, his "best night ever," he decided Josie was ready for the big leagues. His plan was to stage a little presentation and invite their father. While some of her schoolmates were performing in Miss Ginger's ballet recital, Josie was strolling through the casino, getting ready to show a group of card pros the fruits of her extracurricular activity.

She watched as tourists walked by with buckets of coins, bills and purses filled with twenty-five-dollar chips. Sam had roped off one of the high-stakes tables. Josie was underage and casino owners were not allowed to play in their own establishment, so this private little exhibition was for show only. Sam had gathered a few good gamblers to play against Josie. The dealer was one of the best. Their father sauntered in with his head of security and Frank. Sam had invited his father and brother without giving them the whole story. Roy King looked at his daughter, confused, his eyes narrowed.

"Sam, what's going on? What's Josie doing here?"

"Just watch," Sam said, giving his father a mischievous grin.

Each player was given $500 in chips. Josie knew they were all watching her. Stay calm, she thought to herself. Act normal. Be patient. Sam caught her gaze and winked at her. He sat her at third base and said, "Let the play begin!"

Josie had never sat at a real blackjack table with smooth green felt and actual chips. She felt the cool leather of the seats and looked around at the other tables with the high rollers. She knew she was in the velvet-roped high-stakes area, which was usually reserved for the whales—the really big gamblers, guys who think nothing of dropping fifty grand a hand and then upping it to a hundred. The dealer was a balding older man, who gave her a patronizing look when she sat down. He began with two decks in the shoe.

At first Josie felt out of her league. Sam had put her on the spot but hadn't prepared her for the pressure. Despite the casino's icy air-conditioning, she felt a trickle of sweat run under her arms. She didn't dare look at her father, and tried to ignore the adrenaline-charged crowd and the barrage of blinking lights and clanging bells just outside the ropes.

"Are you ready, little lady?" the dealer asked. That smile again. He was one of those guys who used to have an athletic build, but his broad shoulders slouched down to a visible gut. "I guess you know how to count to twenty-one. Right?"

"Right," Josie answered politely. What a jerk, she thought. Then she wondered how much Sam had paid them for the demonstration. They acted as though Josie didn't even know how to count. They didn't realize why she was there.

"And if you go over—" the dealer started to explain.

"Yes, I know," Josie interrupted. But then she reminded herself to sound more naive, to play along. "Thank you. I think I know the rules."

As the game began, she pretended to be hesitant and not quite sure of herself. She placed only modest bets on the table. She was initially dealt a pair of nines but didn't split them, which would have made it easier to win. Likewise, she split two face cards, a major no-no. This was the big bluff. Making people think she didn't know what she was doing. Everyone was humoring the boss's kid, and she'd happily make the most of it until the high-numbered cards started coming through.

When they did, Josie was rolling. She looked the dealer in the eye with a blank stare, pushed a stack of chips onto the table and started betting and winning big. Sam stood next to his father, elbowing him every time Josie won. Roy watched, his eyes widening with Josie's every play. He took off his glasses, wiped his brow, then turned to Sam at one point and said, "What the hell. Did you coach her or what?"

"Don't you know how good she is at math?"

"Of course! I read her report cards. Being good at math doesn't naturally translate to killing at blackjack."

"It does for Josie. She has a gift. She remembers everything."

"Let's try four decks," Frank interrupted, apparently not as impressed as his father or Sam. "Two is pretty easy."

"Oh yeah? Let's see *you* do it," Sam scoffed.

"Why don't we try six?" Josie suggested innocently.

The dealer opened six fresh decks of cards, fanned them out on the felt table and then shuffled and cut. Josie's expression never changed, play after play, until the shoe was empty and the dealer raised his hands signaling that it was time to shuffle up again. At this point, she was up thirty grand.

"Okay, I've seen enough." Roy looked a little shell-shocked.

Josie peered up at her father's face. He didn't seem proud. He wasn't beaming like Sam. She detected something else in his expression.

"My daughter seems to have a knack," he declared to everyone around the table.

"A knack—my God, Roy, she's one of the best!" the dealer blurted. He couldn't hide how impressed he was. Josie tried not to smirk.

"Okay, thanks, guys, you can go back on the floor," Roy said, dismissing them.

"Jesus." Roy turned to Sam. "How did this happen?"

"She was watching my games at home with my friends, and I gave her a few pointers."

"She's only twelve years old, for Christ's sake," Frank said.

"Shut up, Frank, we all learned to play cards when we were kids," Sam snapped.

"Plus, I practiced," Josie added, climbing off the stool.

"Where?" Roy asked, affectionately pushing her auburn hair back behind her ears. She looked up at him. Green eyes, a sprinkle of freckles across her nose that reminded him of his wife.

"In my room."

"With who?"

"I play against myself," she told him.

"I'll be damned."

There were enough crazy King stories without adding this one, but Josie enjoyed the look on Rob's face as she told it. It was getting dark outside as they flew east. They played a few hands, and as the plane approached Washington National Airport, Rob laid down his cards.

"So if we played right now in my casino, would I have half a chance?" he asked.

"No. I'd kill you," she answered lightly.

"You already have." His gaze moved over her.

Rob McCarthy had been around many beautiful women. In his world they were a dime a dozen. But there was something about Josie that drew him in. Maybe it was the whole Vegas royalty thing. Roy's daughter, for Christ's sake. She was complicated, out of control and a fucking genius with numbers. He'd never met anyone like her. It had been a long time since he was this attracted to someone. On the other hand, she was his competitor, so he would have to tread carefully. There was a lot at stake.

Josie packed up her briefcase. She couldn't make up her mind. Should she trust him or not? And did it even matter? She was overwhelmed with what was going on in her casino. Rob's snide remark the other night basically telling her she wasn't up to the job still grated on her. Her father had always told her to never trust anyone outside the family. But "the family," specifically Frank, *was* the problem here. She could ask Rob for advice. But she couldn't ignore the fact that he was her competitor and might use it against her. In Vegas, alliances fell by the wayside when money was at stake.

She turned to Rob as the wheels hit the tarmac. "Thank you. You've made it so easy for me. I can get a cab to the Four Seasons. You don't have to do anything more."

Rob tried to hide his disappointment. No dinner? No drinks? No sex, that was for sure. He could tell from the detached look on her face. She was all business. He'd talk to her in the morning.

Chapter 33

The law offices of Hogan and Connolly were across town in a classically inspired marble building with fluted columns and ornate cornices. Josie was escorted to a reception area filled with gilt-framed portraits of famous racehorses like Secretariat and Seabiscuit. The meeting went well—even though, as Frank had predicted, there were four lawyers and three associates, all charging by the hour. Ka-ching. Regardless, Josie unilaterally decided to hire them. She'd tell Frank when she got home. If they could negotiate the Jackpot out of a full-on union shutdown, they'd be worth the money.

Rob met her after his meetings and offered to give her a ride back to Vegas later that evening. As they were taxiing toward the runway, Josie's cell rang. It was Scotty.

"Hey, Josie, where are you?"

"On a plane, about to take off. What's up?"

"I think I've got something."

"I'm listening." She turned her head toward the window and lowered her voice.

"It definitely doesn't look kosher. When are you back?"

"Late tonight. We can meet in the morning," she said in a barely audible voice.

"Okay, I'm still here at the casino. I'm pretty sure Lionel's dirty. Sounds like he's fucking over everyone. I have a source . . ."

"Wait! Scotty. What does that mean?"

"Shit." She could hear the engines revving up for takeoff. "Gotta go. Talk tomorrow."

She knew it! She knew something was up! And she knew it had to do with Lionel; she could smell it. She'd find out the full story in the morning. She was exhausted and the call from Scotty left her with many unanswered questions.

Josie twisted her hair into a low ponytail, then fastened her seat belt. Rob stared at her tense face and waited for her to say something but she didn't.

"I'm going to freshen up," she said after the plane leveled off. She walked back to the bathroom, looked in the mirror and tried to compose herself. The worry line between her eyes seemed even deeper than usual. When she returned to her seat, she gave Rob a slight smile and tried to act as though nothing was wrong. She began to describe the meetings when he interrupted.

"Now, as much as I enjoy business talk," he said, grinning encouragingly, "tell me something personal instead."

"Jesus. Umm. Let's see. I don't like blue cheese or olives or cats . . . and when I was thirteen, I snuck into the counting room at the casino, stole a hundred and twenty thousand dollars in C-notes, put it in my backpack and buried it in the backyard."

Rob started laughing. Josie rolled on.

"A few weeks ago, I went back to the ranch, dug four holes and finally found it. Everything was a little moldy, so I put it in a plastic bag and stuck it in my safety-deposit box. Cash is cash."

"Keep going," Rob said, leaning back and enjoying himself immensely.

"Okay. I like romance novels, especially regencies. It's the sudden twists of fate that I like and the unexpected love affairs—you know, the village girl who fucks the duke. Are we done here?"

"One more. Sing for your supper."

"Why not. Last one. You're going to like this. When I was fifteen, I had a crush on one of Sam's friends. He was shit at blackjack so he asked me to help him. He needed to pay off his car so we went to the

Jackpot. I sat behind him and coached him. We ripped off Dad's casino for twenty grand. The only problem was the fucking Eye in the Sky caught me. My dad came roaring over, banned the kid from our house and grounded me for a month. Also, I smoke cigarettes after sex." She looked at him. "Sometimes before. Your turn."

"I can't compete." He held up his hands in mock surrender.

"Remember that," Josie responded with a smile.

Rob had a limo waiting at the private terminal. It was past ten as they slid in the back seat and he poured each of them a glass of champagne from the minibar.

"I have dinner waiting at my place."

Decision time was right there in front of her. Should she or shouldn't she? Oh, what the hell, Josie told herself.

Rob's four-thousand-square-foot penthouse spanned two stories, with floor-to-ceiling windows and white marble floors that Rob told her came from a rare quarry in India. The apartment was filled with modern art, plus a fabulous Harry Jackson bronze sculpture of a cowboy on horseback.

Rob gave her an informal tour when they first arrived, showing off his five-thousand-gallon aquarium stocked with tropical fish. To service this tank, a scuba diver entered through a hatch in the front coat closet. So much for the goldfish in a bowl she'd had as a kid. The kitchen had been stocked with Beluga caviar, sushi and smoked salmon, and on the bar, chocolate strawberries and a bottle of Dom.

Rob poured her another glass of champagne as they stepped onto the wraparound terrace next to his private infinity pool. Josie gazed out at the Las Vegas Strip, glittering with flashing neon lights. Looking out at the hotels was like taking an acid-soaked tour of the world—the canal at the Venetian, the Eiffel Tower at Paris, ancient Rome at Caesars Palace, the Statue of Liberty at New York-New York and the Egyptian pyramid at the Luxor. The sky beyond the hotels, past the suburban sprawl, was total darkness. Black and desolate.

Josie shivered. It was cold in the desert at night. Rob put his hands on her shoulders, leaned in and kissed her. As much as she wanted to respond at that moment . . . she pulled away and walked back inside. He followed her and closed the glass doors behind them. If he wanted her, she thought, he was going to have to work for it. But then again, she looked up and saw him as others saw him. Hot, rich, and self-assured. She brushed her fingers across a vintage inlaid card table that didn't quite fit into the ultra-modern setting. Rob told her he bought it at auction in New York, and it was made in the forties for Bugsy Siegel.

"Interesting choice."

"I thought so. Here's the best part. There was a secret drawer."

"What was in it? I heard he kept a list of all the people he killed."

"Sadly, no list. Although he personally copped to murdering ten men."

"Twelve," she corrected. Everyone who grew up here knew about Bugsy's dozen. "Tell me again why you wanted his table?"

"It's history. He ran the first luxury casino, the Flamingo. Anyhow, after they 'retired' him, I happened to see an old video of the Kefauver mob hearings from the fifties."

"I know where you're going. The infamous quote. When the senator asked Virginia Hill, Bugsy's mistress, why she was such a favorite with the boys."

"Yeah. Remind me what she said?" he asked, teasing her.

"You just want me to say it, don't you?"

"I do." He nodded with a grin.

"The lovely Miss Hill said under oath and on *live tv*: 'Senator, I'm the best goddamn cocksucker in the world.'"

"Well done," he said, taking her hand and leading her to the bedroom.

On the way, he grabbed the bottle of Dom, uncorked it and took a swig.

He sat at the end of the bed and watched her slowly undress. Then she sat next to him, wrapped her arms around him and pulled him toward her. He ran his hand along the inside of her thigh and then leaned into her and kissed her on the mouth.

"I really want you," he whispered.

"That's my line," she said.

"I remember. Along with the handcuffs?"

"Next time," she answered in a low sultry tone as she began unbuttoning his shirt.

He gently touched the side of her body, caressing the curve of her breast. Her fingers weaved through his hair. His lips were soft and warm as he kissed her again. He took off his clothes and moved his hand between her legs. She closed her eyes and let him touch her, murmuring, "Yes. Yes . . ."

Their bodies were pressed tight together as he put his hands on her hips and pushed deep inside her.

"My God," she murmured, "don't move."

Afterward, he gazed at her naked body. "Was that good?" he asked.

Her cheeks were flush and her body warm. She nestled against his chest and sighed.

"Did I make you happy?"

"Extravagantly," she said. She closed her eyes and listened to the sounds of the city. The doors to the bedroom terrace were slightly ajar and she could feel the night wind on her face. They both fell asleep, her legs wrapped around his body. This time they slept together like lovers.

Josie woke up at 5 a.m., anxiety sweeping over her. She began to wonder what Scotty had to tell her. She turned over and tried to go back to sleep but couldn't. She considered every conceivable scenario—the what-ifs that always plagued her at dawn.

She got dressed and brushed Rob's cheek with a kiss. He sat up and looked at her in disbelief. "You're leaving? Again?"

"Sorry," she said, trying to be tactful.

"You know, you're starting to hurt my feelings," he said, smiling. "What can I do to make you stay? Name it. Pancakes?"

He raised his eyebrows and pushed away the covers as he waited for an answer, which she didn't give him.

"Okay, I get it. Say something nice on your way out, at least." He laughed.

Josie paused and pretended to think. "Thanks for the ride to DC."

"Try again."

"Thanks for helping with the lawyers. My family is a shit show, as if you didn't know, and I'm under a lot of pressure." She paused and looked at him seriously. "I like you, Rob. I do, but I just don't have time for a normal relationship right now."

"Did I say I wanted normal?"

"No," she admitted, "you didn't."

Chapter 34

Josie took a cab home from Rob's place and crawled into her own bed. In the distance she heard the eerie howls of a pack of coyotes on a kill. Sometimes she forgot that they prowled just outside the neighborhood, along with bobcats, rattlesnakes, lizards, hawks and other nocturnal desert predators. It was no coincidence that someone tacked a sign on a tree with a photo of their white chihuahua. "Missing," it read. Fat chance it was still alive, Josie thought. She had seen coyotes flatten themselves out like rats, slide under a fence and, in an instant, grab a cat or a small dog from the yard. It happens all the time. All they leave is the collar.

Josie slept a few more hours, then padded downstairs in sweats and a T-shirt and checked her cell. It had been turned off since the plane. There were four messages from Sam and a couple of missed calls. She dialed his number.

"Where are you?" Sam asked.

"Home. What's up?"

"You better step outside."

She put on a jacket and walked out to the back patio.

"You're making me nervous. Did Scotty do something?" Josie whispered.

"Yeah." Sam's voice was flat. "He died."

"What?" Josie instinctively pulled her jacket tighter around herself.

"Car bomb. In the parking structure on Fourth and Fremont, a few blocks away from the Jackpot. People heard the blast for miles. Scotty's body was burnt to a fucking crisp. They only identified him by his dental records."

Josie couldn't speak for a moment. Her heart was pounding in her chest. She sank down into one of the lounge chairs.

"Are you there?" Sam asked.

"Oh my God." Josie's voice shook. "Is this our fault?"

Sam tried to calm her down, but it wasn't working. She could detect a waver in his voice as well.

"It might have nothing to do with us. Scotty made a lot of enemies, inside and out," Sam said.

Car bombings were rare but not unprecedented, Josie knew. When someone wanted to send a message, there it was. Loud and clear. Last year there had been a bungled car bombing, and the intended victim—a bookie who might have been scamming the wrong client—had cut and run.

"I think it's on us," Josie said. "He found something. He called me, dammit. I couldn't take the call because I was with Rob. I was supposed to talk to him this morning, but I should have called him the minute I landed," she said in a low voice.

"Jesus! Who else knows we hired him?" Sam asked.

"No one. I didn't tell a soul. Did you?"

"I didn't tell Crystal, if that's what you're asking. My guys tell me that Scotty was walking around the Jackpot earlier in the day. Christ! Someone wanted him gone."

"We need to know what he found out and who he was talking to." Josie rubbed her eyes.

"I can nose around. The police aren't gonna find shit. No fingerprints, no witnesses, everything blown to smithereens." She could hear the pop and hiss of Sam opening a beer.

"I wonder if he kept any records?"

"Did he look like the kind of guy who kept records? I guess we could stop by his mother's house and poke around," Sam said.

Josie felt sick. And scared. What the fuck had Frank gotten himself into? Then it dawned on her that she and Sam might be in danger as well. She agreed to meet Sam in front of Fremont Junior High, their old school. That's where Sam and Scotty first became friends. Scotty's mother still lived nearby.

The neighborhood had not aged well. Low, flat-roofed, mid-century houses were painted different pastel colors, with gravel and cactus gardens bordering the cement carports. Scotty's home was on Sombrero Lane, a faded yellow ranch with peeling paint. Some of the houses had rusted bikes on the lawn, old tires and broken-down cars in various stages of dismemberment resting on cinder blocks.

When they arrived, Scotty's aunt, a small, elderly woman wearing a drab, flowered housedress, told them that her sister was sedated in her bedroom. She wasn't receiving visitors.

"I don't know how she's going to manage," she sighed. "Scotty did everything for her. The police are coming over this afternoon to interview her. She wasn't up to it this morning."

Sam took the aunt's hand and sat down on the couch with her while Josie stood by the door. There was an awkward silence. At one point, she excused herself and asked the aunt if she could use the bathroom. There were a few flower arrangements sitting on the floor, so she maneuvered around them and walked down the hall.

Scotty's room connected to the bathroom. It looked like Godzilla had stomped all over everything. There were squashed beer cans, crumpled-up balls of paper, a large glass bong and an unmade bed littered with empty take-out cartons. In the corner, by the window, was an old pine desk that had probably been there since high school. She wandered over and spotted a bunch of blue Post-its stuck to the wall. A few had fallen on the floor. Most of them were illegible, but one scribbled name, "Bill Woods, Jackpot 4 p.m.," sounded familiar, and another one said, "RM, Tues." Josie scooped them up and crammed them in her purse.

When they left the house, Josie took Sam's arm and they walked to the end of the driveway. She opened her purse and handed him the Post-its.

"This name mean anything to you? I took it from Scotty's room."

Sam squinted at the paper. "Bill Woods is a casino flea who hangs out downtown. Hits all the casinos until he runs out of money and then comes back when he has more cash. I always thought he was hooked into the mob somehow."

"Scotty was meeting with him, obviously. But we don't know if it was nine months ago or yesterday," Josie said.

"I can find out," said Sam. He folded the note into his pants pocket, which was bulging with a flask. He took it out and offered it to Josie. She frowned and shook her head.

"I'm going back to the casino," Josie said, thinking that this was a hell of a cautionary tale.

She climbed into her car and paused for a minute before turning the key in the ignition. When the car started up, she exhaled, then put it in gear and drove away.

On the way to the office, Josie tried to keep it together. She shivered with a cold rush of fear topped with guilt. She pulled over on Flamingo, into the Terrible Herbst gas station, and was filling her empty tank when a dark green sedan pulled in behind her. FBI agent Max Gavin got out of his car and approached her casually, like an old friend.

"I assume, Ms. King, since you were just at Scotty's mother's house, you know something about his demise."

Josie gave him a sharp glance. "You were following me?"

"You're lucky it was only me. There are other players and they won't be so nice. We know what's going on."

"If you really knew what was going on, you'd have a warrant."

"We still need a little thing called probable cause." He drummed his fingers on her car hood. "That's where you come in. We want you to wear a wire and help us out before more people get killed."

"I'm not going to wear a wire to spy on my brother."

"Who mentioned anything about your brother? I don't think you appreciate the danger you're in. These people have no problem coming after you or your family."

"What are you offering? I testify and you give me witness protection? We know how well that turns out. The desert is filled with dead witnesses. And as far as I can tell, you have nothing that would hold up in a court of law."

"We're getting close."

"I won't be a part of some fishing expedition." She turned away from him. "When you have more, let me know."

Josie removed the gas pump and got back in her car. Everything was telling her to get out while she could. But it was too late for that. She was Roy King's daughter and she wasn't about to let some washed-up fed push her around, or some thugs steal a business that had taken her family generations to build.

Chapter 35

Josie knew all too well the history of FBI informants in Las Vegas. When she was a teenager, a group of mobsters and casino bosses, accompanied by several showgirls, took a beautiful mahogany Chris-Craft cabin cruiser out on Lake Mead. It was one of those perfect summer days. No wind. Calm waters. A few of the guys were lounging on the deck with cocktails when one of the showgirls decided to take a dip to cool off. Tragically, the captain switched on the engine and the cruiser backed up full speed, cutting her glorious body in half. The *Las Vegas Sun* later reported that the woman had recently turned state's evidence in an upcoming trial. All possible witnesses to the incident said that they were napping below deck and had seen nothing. No, Josie wasn't about to wear a wire.

When she pulled up to the casino executive parking lot, she noticed even more strikers today. They were bundled up, standing outside the security booth and carrying signs that read "On Strike, Merry Christmas." Some were even with their kids, laughing and socializing like they were all on a fun field trip. It looked like Rob was at it again. She spotted urns of Desperados' famous hot chocolate and platters of Christmas cookies. What a guy.

Josie silently cursed herself for ever involving Scotty. She wrapped her coat around her as defense against the icy wind that whipped through the parking structure. The grim connection between Scotty's murder and her clandestine investigation was not lost on her. The question was what to do next.

A headache throbbed behind her left eye as she entered her office. She took a file out of her briefcase and set it on her desk. There was a knock at the door.

"I hope I'm not interrupting anything. You heard about the explosion last night," Cindy said with a frown, handing the newspaper to Josie. "Terrible, just terrible."

Josie glanced at the headline, "Deadly Blast on Fremont Street, One Fatality."

"Oh, I forgot," Cindy added, taking a message from her pocket. "Mr. McCarthy called while you were out."

Josie didn't feel like talking to Rob; she had a murder on her conscience and she didn't know who was next. She called him back anyway and told him she just had a minute, "with the strikers outside and all."

"Yes. They're really cold out there," he said.

"But not hungry or thirsty. You're a saint." She pressed her fingertips to her throbbing head.

"I try."

"Listen, I can't really talk right now. I have to take off . . ."

"Like last night?" he teased, in his usual self-confident tone.

"I know. I'm sorry."

"When can I see you again?" he asked, undeterred.

Josie couldn't even attempt to figure out the next time she'd be free.

"It's kind of complicated . . ." she said, trying to be honest.

"Everything's complicated. Are you playing hard to get?"

"Yes," she said, thinking this man had some ego. "That's what I'm doing. Playing hard to get. Doesn't that *always* work?"

"Not really. Why don't we do this? Next time you're free, call me."

She knew he was annoyed, but she couldn't deal with that now.

After she hung up, Josie opened the newspaper and read the story. She remembered Sam saying that Scotty had enemies. But this was too much of a coincidence. Scotty had found something. She knew it. She had to talk to Frank. The best thing for her to do would be to fess up—about the FBI and everything else. She walked down to Frank's office and entered, once again without knocking.

Frank was sitting behind his desk. He had a raft of what looked like financial statements piled in front of him, and the morning newspaper tossed to the side. Lionel was there, of course, settled in his usual spot on the couch. Frank casually turned the documents face down as she approached.

"So, how was the trip?"

"Good. I hired the labor lawyers from Hogan and Connolly. I'll be sending them more information over the next few days."

"You might have discussed it with me first."

"I'm discussing it now," Josie said. She paused, took another look at Lionel and changed her mind about saying anything else. She needed to talk to her brother alone.

"We can go over it later when I have their retainer agreement," Josie said, hesitating a moment. Then she nodded her head as if she just thought of something else.

"I guess you read about that car bomb," she said, picking up the newspaper from his desk.

"Read about it? The whole fucking building shook. Who knew this shit still went on," Frank said.

"Yeah. Who knew?" Lionel echoed, staring at the floor.

Josie was seething when she left Frank's office. She crushed the newspaper in a ball and threw it in the trash.

Lionel stood up and closed the door behind her.

"Well, you said she'd come running if the feds approached her. Our sources say they talked to her and nada," Lionel said.

"That doesn't mean she's cooperating. They're always sniffing around. And besides, she doesn't know anything," Frank insisted.

"So why not come clean?" He cracked his knuckles, making Frank wince.

"I know my sister. Maybe you make her nervous. I'll find out."

"Okay. You do that," Lionel said. But he didn't trust the whole bunch of them.

Chapter 36

Josie's next visit was to Cindy—unobtrusive, cheerful Cindy. Cindy doled out coffee, the mail and messages. Her desk was right outside Frank's office and she probably heard every fucking thing that went down.

"Hey Cindy, talk to me." Josie tried to sound light but her tone was strained. Cindy looked at her, then glanced up at the cameras. The signal wasn't lost on Josie.

"I know it looks different downstairs," Cindy said pleasantly, avoiding Josie's gaze. "I'd love to show you the new construction. Follow me." They walked out of the office into the casino and stood by a row of slot machines. The clanging bells and loud whistles, even at this early hour, would drown out most conversations.

"What can I tell you? Everything's gone to hell since Moe left," Cindy said softly.

"Why did he leave? He was Dad's head of security for years."

"Lionel moved in and got rid of everyone. I'm lucky *I'm* still here."

"I don't get it. And Frank just stonewalls me when I ask."

"Well, be careful. Look over there." Cindy glanced at a beefy guy in a blue sports jacket standing near the roulette table.

"I've seen him a couple times before."

"One of Lionel's guys. And the other one by the craps table in a Rebels jersey. Have you noticed him too?"

"Shit. Yes."

"Stay away from both of them. They're bad news. And remember, cameras and bugs are *everywhere*."

"Cindy, what *is* all of this?" Josie asked, beads of perspiration shining on her upper lip.

"Why don't you talk to Moe? He lives in a cabin on Mount Charleston now."

Josie noticed that Cindy's usually relaxed and affable nature had disappeared. She was trying to look casual but her eyes kept darting around the room. She pulled out a little red address book from her purse, jotted down a phone number, then tore the page from the book and handed it to Josie. Both women looked around, pretending to inspect the new construction, then Cindy composed her face into a pleasant mask and walked back upstairs.

Chapter 37

When Josie was a child, her father would pile all the kids into his sky-blue Cadillac Seville and drive sixty minutes up to Mount Charleston to escape the dry desert climate. Hidden at an elevation of seven thousand feet, among the junipers and sweet ponderosa pines, the beauty of Humboldt-Toiyabe National Forest surrounded an old snow-covered A-frame lodge, where they would sit at long, wooden tables and spoon out hot chili with cheese melted on top. Afterward, he would tell them to go play outside, and try not to kill each other. When their mother was healthy, she would join in the snowball fights and then teach them how to make snow angels.

Everyone was happy then and Josie thought they would be happy forever. But the next winter, their mother was too frail to make the trip and they went up to the cabin without her. Sam's birthday was the next week. The children brought the cake up to her bedroom and Sam blew out the candles in front of her. That was the last birthday he would ever have with her. He was her "little prince," the one she indulged above all the others. Sometimes she called him a scamp, but he charmed her just the same. The two of them had a bond, and years later when memories of his mother came up in conversation, Sam was always elusive and distant, withholding his thoughts.

Life was different after her death. Roy would sit in the lodge hunched over a coffee spiked with whiskey, while the kids ran around outside like little banshees. Every once in a while, Josie would venture in and ask her father if he was okay. He would tousle her hair, smile and tell her he was fine. She seemed to be the only one who noticed his depression.

Sam picked Josie up at around 7 a.m. and shoved Rex in the back seat. Josie climbed in the front with a mug of hot coffee. They headed northwest on Route 157. It was that time of morning when the moody light filtered through the trees, and drifts of vapor hung in the air. During the night, the temperature had plunged to the thirties. Outside on the highway, Josie gazed at monotonous views of scrub oak, yucca plants, tumbleweeds and stiff brown grass.

Sam wore Ray-Bans, and shoved down the visor. Josie could tell he was hungover, and the smell of alcohol and weed permeated his shirt. She opened the window without comment.

Growing up, Josie used to think Sam was so sophisticated, self-assured. When had all this changed? Maybe the years she was in LA? She suspected the reason for Sam's addiction was not only his mother's death but also that he'd been so young and impressionable when he was following their father around the casino. Too young to handle the tension, the menace, the outright violence, and Roy King's endless justifications and evasions. Sam—delightful, difficult and hopelessly addicted.

Just before they headed up the mountain, they pulled off the highway for a minute and looked back toward town. The road was straight and empty for at least ten miles. If they had been followed, they would be able to see the car.

Josie thought about what Cindy had told her. Moe would know what was up, but would he help them? She had known Moe practically her whole life. When she was a teenager, he had been the one person at the casino who she could talk to and who would listen. He had grown up in Vegas, carried his high school to the state championships and was considered one of the two best football players ever to play in the city. He was the first Black quarterback at UNLV, a local hero when her father hired him right out of college. Over the years, Moe worked his way up from floorman to pit boss to head of security. Now he was exiled to the mountains, and even though he had agreed to the visit, Josie wasn't confident he would be forthcoming. But one thing she knew for sure, her father had trusted him. She would too.

After they drove past the lodge, the road to the cabin was steep and rocky and got steeper, narrowing down to a slim path. The area was impassable in the winter, especially when it snowed, and it looked like they might need chains to get through. After Sam parked the car, they put on their jackets and boots and began trudging up the path. After twenty minutes there was still no cabin in sight.

"Jesus, how far is this? I feel like the fucking Donner Party," Sam muttered.

"Didn't they all die?"

"Well, no. Some survived. They ate each other."

"Shut up and keep walking," Josie said with a half-smile.

Rex bounded ahead of them, darting in and out of the thick brush. At one point, the dog treed a squirrel and whined, then gave up and followed behind them.

The smell of pine needles and fir filled the air as they neared Moe's place. The air was heavy and damp. A tumble of twisted branches and deep, rotted trees were filled with silent decay—a primeval feeling. Josie thought this seemed like a place where lost things go. Everything was quiet, except for the occasional grinding of snowmobiles in the distance.

Moe was standing on the wraparound porch of his stone cabin, waiting for them. There were a couple of plastic chairs leaning against the wall, a hammock, a set of barbells and a worn-out football. He looked older than Josie remembered, with gray stubble on his chin. He was wearing multiple layers—an open parka and a plaid flannel shirt unraveling at the edges. It was a far cry from his uniform in the old days: black silk suits and custom white shirts with his initials embroidered on the cuff.

"Sorry about the mess." Moe pointed to a puddle of water. "The coyotes chewed through my irrigation pipe again to get a drink. Come on in. I don't get many visitors."

Rex rushed by them with a big stick in his mouth, which he immediately started gnawing on the woven throw rug. Splinters of bark flew everywhere.

"Rex! Leave it!" Sam shouted.

"It's okay. My dog Tag died a few months ago. There are still a few toys here and there for Rex if he wants them."

Josie looked around the cabin. Husky oak pillars supported a beamed ceiling, and the hardwood floor was dark and warped. A big stone fireplace in the center of the room was decorated with spruce and pine cones. Mistletoe hung wistfully to one side. The place was small but filled with heavy, oversize furniture, as though a much larger house had been downsized in a hurry. Half-burned candles with globs of splattered wax hardened on the table and floor. A banged-up guitar leaned against one wall.

Josie noticed the smell of Pine-Sol and cigarettes, and indeed, a pack of Marlboro Lights was sticking out of Moe's pocket. He had been a heavy smoker in the old days and Josie could hear it in his deep, throaty voice.

At first Moe sat quietly and listened. At one point he absently leaned down and patted Rex's head. Sam and Josie laid it all out—the FBI warning, the accusations of skimming, the cameras, the bugging, the secret, locked room. There was also Bowden's car accident and Scotty's murder.

"So do you know what's going on? Is it skimming? Is Frank calling the shots, or is it that fucker Lionel?" asked Sam.

"And what do we do about the feds?" Josie added.

Moe leaned back and took a breath.

"Listen, in the old days, sure, there was skimming going on—there were a few made men at most of the hotels. The Chicago, New York and Kansas City mobs had their noses in the trough. But it wasn't pervasive. The cops mostly looked the other way. I'm not saying everyone was complicit, but gambling was legal and we provided over a third of the state's jobs.

"But then an FBI guy named Yablonsky rolled in like a man on a mission—they called him the King of Sting," Moe went on, "cracked down on us with fire and brimstone. Wiretaps, undercover operations, unmarked cars on every corner, harassing witnesses, subpoenas flying. Stomping on people's rights. It was war. The FBI brought a slew of cases, and only your father and Mel Davis were never convicted of anything."

Of course Mel Davis would have gotten away with it, Josie thought. In the old days, he was as connected as it gets, but now he was Mr. Las Vegas.

Moe went on. "The Chicago gang was out. The FBI had New York, Detroit and Kansas City on the run. That's when your father cleaned house. It stayed clean until Frank took over."

"What changed?" Josie asked.

"Your brother has a gambling problem. I happen to know from my sources that he lost five mill in a gambling spree at a tribal casino in Connecticut. He stayed away from the Strip and mostly hit East Coast tribal operations. They would send helicopters to pick him up when he went to New York on business. He was their biggest whale."

"Shit," said Sam. "Mr. Model Fucking Citizen."

Moe continued. "About a week before the last spree, he apparently signed markers totaling six mill to pump up his line of credit. The markers were checks drawn on his personal account. When the casino went to cash the checks, guess what, they all bounced. After that Frank went to a loan shark to cover his debt and pay off his markers."

Josie put her head in her hands and sighed. "Jesus Christ," she said. "Go on."

"I heard he told the casino that the money came from a 'third party,' but it actually came from guys in the waste management business, if you know what I mean. Your father and I found out about it last year.

We were trying to negotiate a settlement when Roy died. The mob saw the opening and moved in to protect their investment. They fired me and that's when the skimming started up again."

"Is that when Frank brought in Lionel?" Josie asked.

"I wouldn't say Frank brought him in. He was dispatched. I know the guy," Moe went on. "He's bad news. Started out okay. Army helicopter pilot in Afghanistan, ex–New York cop. He found that doing a different kind of enforcement was more lucrative. I was actually happy to get out while I still could. Look, I know too much. If the feds started sniffing around, which they obviously are, I'd be the first witness to get whacked."

"Moe, what can I do? The FBI wants me to wear a wire," Josie said.

"That's a good way to get yourself killed." He paused for a long moment, then continued, "Let me think about it. We need to find out how they're skimming and where the cash is. And we need to do it before the feds arrest Frank and shut down your casino."

"By the way, there's a locked room by Frank's office with serious security," Josie offered.

"If that's where they're holding the cash, at some point they'll move it to offshore accounts—the Caymans, Bermuda, Panama. When they do the transfer, they'll shut the cameras down."

"So that means I need to get in before they move the skim, right? Who works graveyard security these days?" asked Josie.

"Let me check. If it's part of my old crew, they'll look the other way if I ask them."

Moe stood up and stretched. "You want a cup of coffee or anything? Or some bacon for the dog?"

Sam looked around and realized Rex was gone. The back door to the cabin had been slightly ajar, and the dog had apparently slipped out while they were in deep conversation.

"Shit, I hope he hasn't run off. I'll never find him out here," Sam said, his face turning ashen. God, Josie thought, Sam was so attached to that dog.

Moe smiled at him. "Follow me," he said, and opened the door to what looked like a large closet. He switched on the light, revealing a row of monitors covering the back wall. Each one of them contained a camera with different views and angles of the entire property—from the road to the path to the perimeter of the house. A few of the cameras were aimed at the trees. A five-foot-high gun rack stood in one corner.

"Jesus, Moe," Sam blurted.

"I like to be ten steps ahead, if you know what I mean. If I had to, I could hold off a fucking army up here."

"Well, let's hope you don't have to," Josie said.

"There he is!" Sam shouted in relief, looking at Rex on one of the monitors. "By the truck."

On the drive back into town, Josie thought about danger and how it loomed over her every move since she was forced back to Vegas. This was not how she wanted to live her life. Seeing how Moe dealt with it was a wake-up call. Even being sixty years old, retired and living way the hell up in the mountains, safety was not guaranteed. You still loaded up with cameras and guns, waiting for the day someone came for you.

Chapter 38

Sam hadn't even hit the 157 when Josie got the call from Moe. His contact at the Jackpot was still working graveyard and he owed Moe big-time. He knew the room. The door was set up with solid steel bolts and heavy-duty strike plates and the lock was equipped with military encryption. It was virtually tamperproof. The code changed every forty-eight hours and the door relocked itself after fifteen minutes. She had to be out of there by then, not a minute longer, Moe warned, "or she would be locked in and fucked." The guard would, for ten grand, give her the code, turn off the cameras and look the other way. And "don't touch any-fucking-thing."

"Can he cover us tonight?" Josie asked.

"Tonight? I'll try," Moe said. "You sure?"

"Yes," Josie told him firmly. "We have to do it tonight. Where do I leave the cash?"

"In an envelope on your desk. He'll take care of the second guard out front. Park down the block, and Josie . . ." he said, his voice going suddenly soft.

"I know. I'll be careful."

Josie was playing a hunch. There were other avenues to explore, but they'd take more time. In all the years she visited her father, she never remembered a locked door with security right outside his office.

At a little after midnight, Josie dressed in a long-sleeved black sweater, black wool slacks, black boots and a UNLV baseball hat. She pulled her hair back in a bun and wiped off any remnants of eye makeup so her face looked pale and unremarkable. Except for the old biddies at the slots, most of the women who frequented the casinos were dressed in a way to call attention to themselves. When you wanted to do the opposite, it took just as much time and effort.

Before leaving the house, she slipped a small, powerful flashlight in her purse, along with ten grand in an envelope. She had stopped off at the bank on the way home. She opened her locked gun cabinet, grabbed her pistol and the ammo, sliding the bullets into the chamber one by one until it was fully loaded. You never know. Her hands were sweaty and she kept checking her face in the mirror. She looked ordinary. Just what she wanted.

She drove through heavy, stop-and-go traffic, turned off the radio and parked her car at the city lot on Fourth near Fremont. It was a busy night in downtown Vegas. There were crowds of tourists strolling down Fremont Street, dressed in puffy parkas and cocktail dresses, as she passed under the glittering facades of the casinos. Christmas lights had been strung from one side of the street to the other. She moved along with the throng, pressing her purse to her chest and weaving her way to the Jackpot.

This was an impulsive, crazy idea. Maybe she should turn around and forget it. Let's say she *did* find something. What then? She had no plan. Shit. But the one thing she definitely had going for her was access. Play it out, she thought. Be tough and see where it goes.

The casino was packed. She made her way past the blinking, chiming slot machines lined up like soldiers, the green, felt-covered blackjack tables with dealers mechanically determining each player's fate, and spectators holding their breath in anticipation as roulette wheels spit out random numbers, black or red. She knew that security up in the catwalk would pick up her image, but with her dark clothes and cap, and the angle of their cameras, she was almost unrecognizable. Across the floor, she heard shouts of victory from a craps table as a man wearing hand-tooled leather cowboy boots threw his Stetson into the air.

As she passed the shops and approached the executive offices, her anxiety level increased. She felt a slight chill, and her hat pinched the hair around her ears. As promised, there was no guard on duty. She opened the large, mirrored entry door and closed it behind her, keeping the lights off in the suite. Neon signs from the Strip reflected off the windows, and gave off just enough light for her to find her way down the hall. But even in this gloom, she could tell the reception area still hadn't been serviced. There were sections of newspapers left on chairs from the day's visitors, trash in the cans and coffee cups with lipstick-smeared rims on side tables. She walked tentatively to her office in the dark and placed the envelope with the cash on her desk. She hesitated a moment, calming herself, and then approached the door of the locked room like an accused walking the walk. She checked her watch. Once she was in, she had fifteen minutes.

Moe had called her back with the code, and she punched it into the keypad of the heavy reinforced door. She knew there were three alert modes (activity, tampering and forced entry), and she didn't want to activate any of them. She held her breath as she entered the windowless room. Total blackout. There wasn't a sliver of light and she couldn't even see her hand in front of her face. She had never been afraid of the dark: Lord knows, she had been alone in the desert at night countless times. But this was far more unnerving. She turned on her flashlight and swept it across the room.

Unlike the rest of the suite, this area was industrial-looking with exposed pipes crisscrossing the ceiling and hanging fluorescent lights. There was a row of metal desks down the center of the room, with large state-of-the-art monitors, headphones, computers and a bank of locked, gray file cabinets against the wall. She tried to pull open one of the file drawers. A light flashed on an overhead panel that said, "ACCESS DENIED." Shit. She didn't think she'd see incriminating papers just lying around on the desks.

Now she was feeling lightheaded. All this effort and so far, nothing. Ten minutes left. She pointed her flashlight at a few blinking ten-line phones, thinking the whole setup looked like something the

CIA would use to carry out covert activities. Glancing down at the trash cans, she noticed a few papers crumpled inside them. She bent down and fished out a pink message slip. Then the thought occurred to her—why not lift one of the plastic bags that lined the trash cans and fill it with all the trash from each desk? Who knew what she would find later?

She slipped the handles of the trash bag around her wrist and moved farther into the darkness. She moved closer and noticed that leaning against the left wall were what looked like framed paintings, covered in brown paper. What was this? She moved her flashlight over the labels written in black Sharpie ink—Pissarro, Manet. My God.

Four minutes left, and she hadn't begun to look at everything. But then, in the far back corner, hidden behind a pillar, were dozens of half-open cardboard boxes piled next to each other. She aimed the beam toward the boxes. Green. Lots of green. Holy fucking hell! There must be millions here. There was so much cash you could fill a giant sinkhole. Money all over the place. Tons of it. Thousands of bills. All hundreds. Everything smelled like money—that greasy, palmed-over, inky odor.

Josie had instinctively known it all along, but she was still rattled. Of course she had heard about these things. It was no secret. In the old days, when the mob ruled, suitcases filled with cash moved in and out of counting rooms in broad daylight. The take was divvied up—one for you, one for me—and ferried across the country to New York, Kansas City, Detroit, Chicago. Everyone had their fingers in the pie. She wondered who was running this show. She'd been wondering that since the first day she started working here.

One minute left. It was time to get the hell out. There was a noise outside in the lobby. She reached for the gun in her purse. Her top was drenched with sweat. Then she heard the sound of a vacuum cleaner. Shit! Housekeeping had arrived. She had to get out before the door relocked and the security cameras went back on.

She turned off her flashlight and peered through the door to figure out which office the housekeeper was cleaning. Josie watched the woman slowly wheel her vacuum into Trotter's office at the end of the hall and turn it on full blast. Now was her chance. Fifteen seconds left. She slipped out the heavy door of the storage room, closed it and heard it lock in place. Then she raced out of the suite, clutching her purse and the plastic bag of trash, which had cost her exactly $10,000.

Chapter 39

Josie drove home in the grip of sheer panic. What she discovered in that room was a land mine. And she had stepped on it.

As soon as she walked out on her patio, she lit a cigarette and inhaled deeply, like one of those people who go to AA meetings and take a break outside to stay sane. Despite herself, she was scared. She could picture herself stopping at a gas station, and a couple guys pulling up behind her, casually walking over to her car window and, bam, one shot to the head.

She needed to come up with a plan, preferably one that didn't get her killed, and find out who was involved and how it all worked. Josie went downstairs to the hall closet, where she had stashed the plastic bag of trash from the security room. She grabbed her rubber gloves from under the kitchen sink, laid down sheets of newspaper on the breakfast table and got to work.

She didn't know what she was looking for but would separate anything that seemed to have significance. Old, balled-up tissues, gum wrappers, banana peels, chip bags, half-eaten sandwiches and empty flip-top cigarette boxes were immediately thrown in the trash. It was the crumpled pieces of paper that interested her. Here was a phone number. Here was a name. Here was a line of numbers that could be financially related to their operation. There were some handwritten notes that were indecipherable, and a few bills from Nassau. Josie didn't imagine the people in this room were traveling to The Bahamas on vacation, so this probably had something to do with offshore accounts. Her eyes were getting bleary, and she figured she wouldn't make much more progress tonight. She needed to examine the names and numbers with a clear head.

Her top was still clinging to her body. She took a long shower, changed into a flannel robe and walked outside, barefoot, in the pitch dark. Her whole system was still on alert, and there was no way she was going to get much sleep tonight.

She heard a rustle in one of the bushes, and then a skittering sound like a tarantula making off into the dry leaves. She imagined the whole garden teeming with sinister, poisonous creatures, hiding just under the surface.

One night, when she was a teenager, she was upset about something and ran outside near the stables at the ranch. She had just approached the barn door when she saw an army of tarantulas crawling across the gravel. Hairy, slow and deliberate, the nocturnal hunters could literally pounce on their prey with brute force, sink their venomous fangs into its flesh and paralyze them. They scared the hell out of Josie every time she saw them. She was comfortable with most living creatures, but tarantulas made her skin crawl. She started screaming bloody murder, whacking at them with her tennis racquet. Her father ran outside to see what was wrong.

"Josie, just because something looks like a monster, doesn't mean they have that kind of power. In fact, these guys are pretty harmless to humans—no more than a bee sting. Next time you see one, just stomp on it."

Sam came over the next morning, and they walked out to the end of the property. Rex trotted after them, and then lay at Sam's feet. The sun was bright in the sky, but a blanket of clouds was moving in.

"Our brother is skimming a shitload of cash," Josie said angrily.

"I'm not surprised. What do you want to do about it?"

"We have to stop him. If we don't, the feds will, and I don't think

Frank will like washing dishes in Leavenworth for the next twenty years. And we'll be implicated."

"Enough is enough, Josie. We need to talk to him."

"What are you going to say?" She made quote marks with her fingers. "'Gee, Frank, we know you're stealing our money to pay back your fucking gambling debts.'"

"That's exactly what we're going to say. In fact, why don't we go over to his house right now."

"Because he's probably in the office."

"So let's meet him at the Pioneer," Sam proposed. "At least we know we won't be bugged there."

Chapter 40

At dawn, the morning after Josie's little adventure, Lionel climbed in his Ford Ranger. Did she think he wouldn't know she'd been in the room? He might just be a field operative, but the scope and the magnitude of his company's operation gave him access to the kind of security she could only dream about. He needed to shut her down. All he had to do was snap a picture of her daughter and she'd toe the line. They always did when you went after their kids.

Lionel headed out on NV-160 to Pahrump, Nevada, a sunbaked town about an hour north of Vegas in the Mojave Desert. It was on the edge of the California border, with Death Valley's scorched landscape looming over a nearby mountain ridge. The town itself was so remote that there had been no telephone service or paved roads until the sixties.

It was originally named Pah-Rimpi by the Paiute Indigenous peoples, meaning Water Rock, because of the artesian wells in the valley. Now it had other names, with some people referring to it as one of the worst small cities to live in America, due to the piss-poor quality of life. Lionel stared at the barren scenery, occasionally passing the sun-beaten faces of ranchers and alfalfa farmers who called this godforsaken place home. He'd heard the area also attracted a growing number of retired vets and meth cookers. Nowheresville, he thought. How long could he keep this up?

When Lionel was first hired by the men in New York who were

part of the Gambassi family, he saw a future for himself, becoming a deputy or maybe a lieutenant. But the years passed, and he was no further up the ladder than when he started. Trust. That's what it was all about. He wasn't one of them and he never would be.

The casino skim was his area of expertise. And each week after he transported the take to a nice little Lear on a private airstrip in North Las Vegas, he was out of the picture. The cash would go on its merry way, freshly laundered, to the partners, the businessmen, the politicians, the judges, all the wheels necessary to keep New York's operation running.

The truth was that Lionel was a bit player in a big operation. He was stuck in a job he couldn't stand, and he wanted out. He was tired of following orders. Tired of the noise and the stupidity. Tired of the bosses back east who treated him like a glorified bagman. He was taking all the risk, and for what? So he decided to take care of himself. That's when he found this piece of property. It had belonged to a paranoid casino owner who had buried his silver coins in a vault in the backyard. All Lionel had to see was the vault, and he bought the place. He didn't even bother walking through the house. He signed the mortgage under his buddy's name, a guy who had been killed in Bagram. Funny how these hicks never asked to see ID.

His van was loaded with boxes, the ones that didn't make it on the Lear that was now headed to Nassau. After he dumped them and made sure everything was locked up in the vault, he drove to the edge of town and headed to the Chicken Ranch, a group of bungalows surrounded by desert scrub—one of the few whorehouses in America actually licensed by the state. There were usually fifteen to twenty girls for him to choose from, and they weren't bad looking either—well worth the two hundred bucks. He drove past the swimming pool, where some of them were sunbathing topless, and parked next to the brothel's private three-thousand-foot landing strip. He walked down the gravel path and rang the buzzer. The madam answered the door and called out, "Ladies, we have company."

Chapter 41

It was mid-morning when Josie, Sam and Frank arrived at the saloon next door to the Jackpot. There were a few old-timers nursing shot glasses at the bar, so they took a booth against the far back wall. Sam was sullen and quiet. There was a tightness to his face, a sealed-off quality, that gave no indication of his smoldering anger. Frank had no idea why they had insisted on a meeting. At least not at first.

"Okay, Frank, I have a question," Josie began. She leaned in so she could see his face clearly in the dim light. "When did you go from being the good son to being the biggest fuckup on the planet?"

"What are you talking about?" Frank looked blindsided. "Is this about the strike? Because if it is, I haven't heard boo from those DC guys you hired."

"No. It's not about the strike. I think you know what we're talking about. What kind of fucked-up mob shit did you get us into?" Josie asked. She waved away a waitress who was handing them menus. The woman hovered until Josie ordered a round of coffee.

"Just admit it, asshole," Sam said hotly. "How in the name of fuck could you fuck us all over, hiding behind your CEO bullshit? At least with my 'little problem,' I only fucked over myself. You're taking us all down with you."

Josie noticed Sam's fingers twitching near his holster and it worried her.

"I don't need this shit from you," Frank spat out. "And I don't need to admit anything."

"This isn't a court of law. You *do* need to admit it." Sam leaned across the table and grabbed Frank's lapels.

"Get off me, you loser," Frank shouted, ignoring looks from a nearby table. "Here I am, working my butt off, and all you two know how to do is cash your checks."

"Don't act like you're taking care of the family!" Sam released his grip so hard that Frank's back slammed against his chair. Sam stalked away from the table and ordered a whiskey from the bar. When he got back, Frank and Josie were staring stone-faced at each other.

"Let me tell you something, Frank." Josie tried to tamp down the anger in her voice. "There's a reason we don't trust you right now. We know you're skimming money to pay your gambling debts. Not to mention getting us involved with some Murder, Inc. crowd that Dad got rid of years ago."

Frank's eyes narrowed down to little slits. He searched his sister's face to see if he could bullshit his way out of this. He couldn't.

"I was forced to do it," he admitted, looking away.

"Someone forced you to gamble and borrow money from some connected punk crook loan shark?" Josie shook her head. "What's the vig? Our casino?"

"Look. I was forced to make a deal with these guys."

"Listen, Frank. I was in your locked safe room with up-the-ass security. I know what's going on. Maybe you didn't think it would go this far, who the hell knows, but the fact is, we're now being dragged through your shit. Don't try denying it. There were millions of dollars in those boxes."

"And Lionel has you sucking up to him like you're his fucking nursemaid," Sam added.

"You two are laughable. Fucking Nancy Drew and the Hardy Boys. You're in way over your head. If you don't leave this alone, we're all screwed. You understand me?" Frank said. His tone was threatening but his face was ashen and his eyes were bloodshot.

"And what's with the art?" Josie asked, ignoring his threat.

"That's all part of it."

"Well, clue us in, why don't you?"

"You have no idea what it takes to run a casino," Frank said. He had lost the tough-guy stare—his expression changing from rock-hard defensiveness to something resembling a form of resignation.

"This has nothing to do with running a casino. This is about your gambling addiction. And I know a little something about addictions," said Sam.

He swirled his glass in front of Frank's face. An ice cube flew out and struck Frank's cheek. Frank took a napkin off the table and dramatically wiped himself off. Sam might as well have spit in his face.

"The art, Frank. Tell us about the art," Josie pushed.

"Okay. You want to know? Here goes," Frank began. "Assume you have a couple mill in dirty money. You buy a Warhol at a gallery, ship it to a climate-controlled storage facility at some free port. After that, the painting can be resold by another gallery or whoever. You think what we do is secret? That's *nothing* compared to the art world. No one knows shit about the buyer or seller. It's all private. The new buyer gets the painting, and voila, whoever sold it now has clean money."

"Fuck me," said Sam in disbelief.

"The art world has always been the perfect place to launder money. Lots of people buy art anonymously—under fake names or shell companies. They pay all cash. This is all tied up with the New York guys. And trust me, I stay away from their operation . . . you get too close and you disappear. I keep my head down and focus on running the casino. I'm not involved in their shit."

"Well, congratulations! We're so happy you haven't killed anyone, you fuckwad," Sam said. "In the meantime, rats chew through our profits and we get scammed while the FBI crawls up our ass."

"What do you want me to do? I'm screwed any way you look at it, aren't I?"

"I don't know, Frank. The FBI is closing in, which means you're going to end up in jail, because if you *do* cooperate, the mob will get you—inside or out. They'll hunt you down and one day when you least expect it: Bang!" Josie said, pulling an imaginary trigger with her index finger. "So it'd be nice to have a plan B, don't you think?"

"Stop ganging up on me. It's always been the two of you against me," Frank sputtered. "What does Sunny know?"

"Nothing, and we're going to keep it that way," Josie said.

Frank turned his head slightly, sneaking a furtive look at the exit. "I'm not a bad person," he protested weakly.

"Well, you're not a good one," Josie snapped back.

"Why couldn't you just leave everything alone?" Frank's face was flushed red. Josie wasn't sure if it was because of rage or humiliation or both. "You *always* fuck up everything, Josie. That's why Dad sent you away."

What a cheap shot, bringing that up, Josie raged to herself. She stared at him coldly. "But then he brought me back, Frank. What does that say about you?"

Chapter 42

As Josie drove away from the Pioneer, she wanted to tear Frank's guts out—not just because of the skimming, but because he'd dare to bring up that awful night of her senior year, the night her father sent her away.

Josie was seventeen. It was three weeks before spring break, Monday night, a traditionally slow time for the casino. She had arrived at the Jackpot directly after school and was scheduled to ride home with her father later that evening. The place was only half-full, and there was a listlessness to the staff—a stale, tangible pall in the air. She ate dinner alone in the Jackpot Grill, and then decided to go up to the catwalk and roam around.

Whenever she was at the Jackpot, she would eventually end up in the catwalks—the maze of narrow walkways in the ceiling, positioned directly over the gaming tables, that allowed the security team to observe the gamblers through one-way glass. Her father called it "Eye in the Sky" and used to take all the kids up there when they were younger. On the catwalks he taught them the ABCs of how to spot grifters, cheaters and scam artists.

She climbed the stairs and noticed that even the usual security guys were just smoking and talking in the corner, nothing much to watch on the floor. Josie looked down the long bridge of the catwalk and decided to follow it to the end. There were a few people playing blackjack, and the craps tables were half-empty. Older women with blank expressions were at the slots, "getting in the zone," mesmerized by the hypnotic effect of the machines, bathed in neon reds and gold.

Josie walked along the catwalk, surveying the crowd below for the entire length of the casino. She was turning back when she spotted a small door behind a pillar. She had never noticed it before. There was a security combination lock on it, but the door was slightly ajar. It was smaller than the usual door so she bent over, like Alice in Wonderland, and walked through. The door led to another long catwalk and a small wooden bridge. For a moment Josie couldn't figure out where she was—maybe over one of the private gaming rooms for the whales? A group of Chinese gamblers had just checked out after spending most of their time in the VIP Baccarat Room. They'd lost close to a million dollars over the weekend.

She continued on the bridge, which led to yet another door. She opened it and stood on a small wooden platform, which had just enough room for one person. It was dark below, but she could hear voices. She heard a lock click and a door open. Then the lights suddenly blazed below and she was looking down into the living room of one of the ground-floor villa suites, reserved for the VIPS.

The suite was divided into two rooms, a living room with a white sectional couch, a round glass dining table with four red leather chairs and double doors that led to a lavish bedroom. Along one wall, a sixty-inch TV screen flashed various scenes from the hotel with canned Sinatra classics. To the right there was a view of a small garden through sliding glass doors.

Josie had no idea these suites could be observed from above and, at first, she was curious. Maybe it used to be a VIP gambling room that was converted to a suite. And someone decided to keep the one-way glass. She was thinking she would ask someone about it when she got back.

The next moment, a couple walked in, followed by a single man. Josie recognized the woman immediately: Gwen, one of the more attractive dealers. She was wearing a tight black dress that zipped up the back with a pair of razor-sharp spike heels. She radiated confidence as she plucked a chocolate from the bar and then licked her fingers. Her face glowed as she nestled herself between a row of fluffy pillows on the sectional couch and tossed her long, wavy blond hair with one hand. Her dress cinched all the way up her thigh as she tilted her head back with a half-smile.

"I think I'll park myself right here, fellas," she said, pulling a pack of cigarettes from her purse and tapping out one. Her date shoved his hand in his pants pocket and gallantly held out a gold lighter. Gwen pressed the cigarette to her lips and leaned into the flame.

"I could get used to this," she said, exhaling the smoke up to the ceiling. It swirled into the air and momentarily clouded Josie's view.

Gwen settled herself deeper in the couch and then bent forward to reveal her ample cleavage. She flung her heels, one by one, onto the rug, wiggling her toes. Her date slid in next to her, lifted her chin and kissed her on the lips. Then he slipped his hand into the V of her dress.

"Come here, baby," Gwen cooed, as the man fell on top of her with a playful laugh.

Josie leaned back, her shoulders touching the wall. She shouldn't be here. But a part of her was weirdly mesmerized by the scene below. It was obvious that she could see them but they couldn't see her.

The other man sat down at the round table, pulled some papers from his briefcase and laid them out in front of him. He glanced at the couple, who were now rolling around on the cushions, oblivious to the world.

"Jesus, Ed. Get a room," he said. He shook his head in annoyance.

"We got one," Ed answered.

"Get another one. Later. We've got work to do."

Ed sat up and straightened his tie and shirt. Gwen still lay on her back, her dress half unzipped and her legs curled under her.

I should get out of here, Josie thought, as she slowly tried to inch herself out of the tiny, cramped space. Then the floor creaked, and her purse slipped off her shoulder and fell on the landing. Thud! The contents spilled all over the place, her lip gloss rolling precariously near the edge.

"What was that?" the man at the table asked, looking up. "Check the door."

Oh shit, thought Josie. Gwen's date, Ed, stood up with a groan and walked toward the door.

"No one there. Calm down, Shik," he said, glancing appreciatively at Gwen.

"How about a drink?" he asked, following her with his eyes.

"I'm giving up my bad habits," she said with a wink.

"I hope not all of them." He smirked. He walked over to the bar and opened a bottle of whiskey. Josie didn't dare move. She watched as the man poured three glasses, doubles over ice. Gwen sat up and took a sip, then provocatively swirled the ice around in her glass with one finger. Shik downed his in a gulp.

Slowly, ever so slowly, Josie leaned over and gathered the contents of her purse. Her fingers trembled as she slipped the lipstick, gum, Kleenex and wallet back in her bag, but then felt a rush of lightheadedness that made her nearly lose her balance. She left the purse by her feet until her head cleared. Just as she decided to make a run for it, there were three short knocks at the door below, and Josie saw a heavyset man lumber into the room, looking tentatively at the other two men.

"Sit down, Coulter," Shik said. "Gwen was just leaving."

"I haven't finished my drink," she protested. "I thought we were going to—"

"Take it with you," Shik barked.

Gwen deliberately slammed her glass down for good measure. She gave Ed a questioning look, but he shrugged his shoulders.

"Sorry, doll. See you later," Ed said, settling himself at the table.

The new guy moved aside to let Gwen pass, and then joined the other two. There were no pleasantries as far as Josie could tell and, in fact, the new guy was visibly sweating and scowling. Now she was curious as to what was going on. She crouched down next to the wall, her eyes on the men.

"We need to talk," the sweating man said.

"What's there to talk about, Coulter? Sign the fucking papers," Shik said, the muscles tightening in his cheek.

"I've reconsidered my decision. I don't want to sell." Coulter's voice quavered.

"'I've reconsidered my decision'?" Shik sneered, mimicking Coulter. "Now I'm a patient man and I do appreciate you coming all the way out here to see us, but it seems that we have a little problem."

"I don't want to sell. It's not a question of money."

"It's *always* a question of money. Cut the shit, Coulter." Ed's face reddened. He glanced at Shik.

"No. Really." Coulter's hands were shaking so much he clasped them together and put them in his lap. "I discussed this with my wife, and she agrees we're better off just keeping the place."

"This has been going on for months! *Now* you want to back out? You trying to hold us up? Because I wouldn't advise it. That would be a very stupid thing to do. You don't look like a stupid man. Does he, Ed?" Shik's voice was low but deadly.

"Nope. Doesn't look stupid to me. But I've been surprised before."

Coulter was quiet for a moment, then he abruptly stood up and pulled a gun out of his jacket. In one quick move he leveled it at Shik's head. A silence descended on the room.

"Now, what the fuck you gonna do with that?" Shik asked, staring down the barrel.

"You two think you can fucking push me around?" Coulter said, his voice rising.

He sounded tough, but there was a shit-scared gleam of fear in his eyes.

"Put the gun down, Coulter," Ed said, his voice calm and controlled.

Don't panic, Josie told herself. If she moved again, they would definitely hear her. She stood stock-still, staring down at the three men. It was like watching a horror movie in a front-row seat. She could feel the sweat trickling down her armpits, and her chest tightened. It felt like there was a vise around her lungs, and it was hard to breathe.

Josie decided to run for it. She scrambled across the bridge to the hidden door connected to the main catwalk, but when she tried to turn the knob, it didn't budge. Oh God. Someone had locked it. She stood there for a moment, rattling the door like a cage, and then it hit her. Her purse was still on the ground, right smack in front of that one-way mirror over the villa. Shit. She had to go back and get it.

As she ran back to the spot, she heard a crash. Sam and Ed had dived on top of Coulter, and Ed was pummeling Coulter's face with his bare fist. There was a wide slash above his right eye and blood poured down his face like a faucet. She recoiled in fear, shut her eyes tight, but opened them again when there was another bloodcurdling scream and she saw Ed give Coulter a direct kick to the head, the sound of bones cracking.

They're killing him, she thought. Her legs were frozen. A frantic refrain kept going in her head: Get out! Get out! Waves of nausea hit her as she lost her balance once again on the platform and fell backward.

Coulter was writhing in pain and jerking wildly back and forth. The gun had slid from his hand to the carpet. He wrenched a turn and made a dive for it, but he was one second too late. Ed grabbed the gun and shot Coulter in the forehead. The force of the bullet knocked him against the table. A spray of blood hit the wall behind him. Josie could see blood seeping from the back of his head and pooling on the floor beneath him. He was lying on his side at an odd angle, his eyes still open.

"What'd you do that for?" Shik asked, breathing heavily and staggering to the bar.

"What do you mean? The guy was going to kill you."

"Now we're fucked," Shik spat. "Call Roy."

Josie felt dizzy and disoriented, and her head was pounding. She turned and fled across the bridge, and this time she banged on the door with both fists. A security guard appeared.

"How'd you get in here, Josie?" he asked. "We keep this door locked."

"Well, it wasn't," she managed to say in a shaky voice as she walked past him. He had no idea what had just happened. To him she was just a kid stuck in a closet.

Dazed, she walked back through the catwalks, and stopped at the viewing platform over the main gaming floor. She needed room to breathe. There were players hitting the tables as usual. Drinking, smoking, the hollow sound of the slots insanely ringing. A hundred different machines. To Josie's shock, the world hadn't come to an end. Nothing had changed. No police sirens. No ambulances. Nothing.

She had no idea how much time passed, as she tried to figure out what to do next. Then she felt her father's hands on her shoulders. He leaned in close to her ear and whispered, "What are you doing?"

"Looking for cheaters," Josie lied, numb, not moving. She was grasping the rail for dear life.

"Find any?"

"No," she answered, staring straight ahead.

"I'm having one of my guys take you home."

"Fine," Josie said, avoiding his eyes.

Josie stood there rigid, her face illuminated by the lights below, as her father moved away from her and began talking in a low voice to a group of security men nearby. She could hear her heart pounding in her chest as she leaned over the railing and saw the place awash in blood reds, yellows, blues, purples and the tantalizing green of money. Sometimes standing there on the catwalk, she'd feel like she was getting high on all the garish flashing neon. She would have a burst of energy and fantasize that everything was bright and full of promise.

That was the secret of this city, the land of twenty-four-hour sunshine, where the glowing lights made you feel optimistic and lucky. But then its darkness could hit you without warning. You had to be vigilant. You had to be smart. You had to keep looking over your shoulder. But then what?

Chapter 43

That long-ago night, when Josie got home, she curled up in her bedsheets, crushing the pillow over her head. There were no words for what she had actually seen. She was still in the fetal position when her father arrived home a few hours later and knocked lightly on her door.

"Josie, I know it's late, but can you come down to my office for a minute? I need to talk to you."

She didn't respond, even though she was wide awake. There was absolutely nothing she wanted to hear from him.

"Do you hear me? Are you awake?" he persisted.

She told him she'd meet him downstairs, then stalled, sitting on the edge of her bed. She instinctively knew what he was about to say, but that didn't change the fact that she was terrified to hear it. She wished she could plug her ears like a toddler.

Her father was sitting behind his desk, where he usually worked late into the night, chain-smoking and reviewing the previous day's casino receipts.

"Are you okay?" he asked, peering into her face. In his hand was the purse she had left on the platform.

"No," Josie murmured, finally meeting his eyes.

"I'm sorry about that," he said, and she knew he meant it.

"We should go to the police," Josie blurted out.

"And in another city you would," Roy King answered calmly. "But here, we do things our own way. Underneath it all, this is still a frontier town."

"You let them get away with it. Why would you do that? A man was murdered!"

Her father got up from his desk, emptying an ashtray filled with cigarette butts in a waste can, and then walked over to Josie and put his arm around her.

"Don't touch me!" she said, wriggling away

He backed off and sat in the chair next to her, leaning in and studying her pale face.

"I'm going to tell you things that I never want you to repeat," Roy said. He looked beat. His shirt was wrinkled and his jacket was slung over the back of the chair. It had been a long night for both of them.

Josie looked at him, dumbfounded. What could he possibly say? It was the first and last conversation they would ever have about the incident.

"There are people we work with, who control things," he said. "Silent partners. We have obligations to meet."

"So that means it's okay to murder someone?" she asked sarcastically.

She knew she was on shaky ground. No one in the family challenged her father in this way.

"Look, I didn't kill the guy." Her father threw up his hands. "And these people, they don't like their business disrupted. They get very upset if that happens. Which is why no one should know what you might or might not have seen tonight."

"I *know* what I saw."

"And I feel badly about that. But this is what I've decided. Tomorrow morning, Moe will pick you up and take you to the airport. I'm arranging for you to spend some time in LA with your Aunt Helen. This is for your own good."

"You're trying to get rid of me? I'm in the way now?"

"You know that's not true." His voice was calm, but it had the ring of finality. "Anyway. End of discussion. I'm calling my friend who's on the board of USC and we'll get you in there in the fall. We know you have the grades."

"So I'm supposed to just go to LA and not come home?" Josie was incredulous.

Her father shook his head. "Not for a while. I want to keep you safe."

"It's not my fault! Why am I the one being punished?"

"Jesus, Josie, let it go." He stared her down. "You don't know *anything*. I want you to forget about tonight. Erase it from your mind."

As if she could. His nonchalance was crushing. He was exiling her like a medieval tyrant.

"What if I don't want to go? What if I *won't* go?" she said defiantly, knowing her pleadings were futile.

"You're going. Don't you understand?"

Josie shuddered. At this moment, she hated him. She could see dust motes swirling around and the heavy, wood-paneled walls were closing in on her. It was difficult to breathe, hard to swallow. She felt like she was being buried alive.

"What the hell were you doing up there anyway?"

Chapter 44

Frank hesitated at the entrance of the Jackpot. He was pale and perspiring. He pulled a handkerchief from his pocket and wiped his forehead, then looked over his shoulder to see if anyone was following him. This whole goddamn nightmare was making him sick.

He passed the strikers, avoiding eye contact, and thought about the casino—*his* casino, a business he inherited from his father. Now their employees were striking out front, and the back rooms were run by a shadow operation. A throwback to the hidden Vegas of days gone by. The Vegas of brutal beatings, shakedowns and murder. A time when no one was safe. And here he was, Roy King's son, presiding over a skim that dwarfed anything his father had ever done.

This shit show of a setup had been constructed right in front of his face as the payback for his gambling debts ballooning out of control. The few times he had questioned Lionel, the conversation went south almost immediately. He thought about the old saying "if a camel gets his nose in the tent, look out, the rest of him is sure to follow."

Now Josie had been in the one room he had carefully kept hidden—the cash room, which was probably empty by now, the funds disbursed to offshore bank accounts, where they'd scrub their cash and wire it under phony names and shell corporations to dozens of tax havens around the world. Untraceable. Jesus, Lionel had to know about Josie. The more he thought about it, the angrier he got.

"You're late. Where were you?" Lionel was standing outside Frank's door when he arrived.

"You're not my fucking boss," Frank growled, slamming the door in Lionel's face. He had no idea what to do next.

Lionel gave Frank a few minutes to cool down, then opened the door.

"You want to talk about your sister's little field trip last night?" he asked.

"Get out," Frank said, his head down, shuffling papers on his desk.

"I've got news for you. You don't give *me* orders."

"Bullshit. You want to talk about our agreement? Let's talk about our agreement."

"I don't want to talk about our agreement. I want to talk about your sister."

"Leave her out of this," Frank spat.

"This sneaky shit your sister's pulling will get ugly fast." Lionel walked in and closed the door behind him. "Her face came up on the security cam the minute she tried to open the file drawer. Now I have to call New York, and they're *not* going to be happy. You people are such amateurs, it's pathetic."

"You don't have to call anyone. I'll talk to her."

Lionel crossed his arms over his chest, but he relented. It wouldn't help him to have New York know there'd been a security breach on his watch.

"Make sure it fucking sticks when you do."

"What are you going to do, shoot me?" Frank scoffed.

"Don't tempt me," Lionel spat back. "You're a bunch of fucking hicks and you don't know who you're dealing with."

Frank leaned back in his chair. "Let me tell you something, Lionel. I may be a 'hick' but the judges and the sheriff in this town are hicks too and I've known every one of them since I was a kid."

"Threaten someone else," Lionel said, his voice deadly calm. "You're in way too deep. You inherited everything, you pampered, entitled piece of shit. You had it all and you blew it. I clawed my way up, crawling over bodies you can't even imagine. And if you fuck this up for me, I'll crush you without even blinking an eye. So shut up and do your job."

The two men stared each other down, until Frank turned away. Lionel casually lit up a cigarette and headed out the door. Frank waited until he was sure he was gone, then he grabbed his briefcase and rushed out. He had to talk to Josie.

Frank knew his office was bugged, but he was fairly certain they hadn't gotten to his house. He had it swept regularly just to make sure.

His home was on an exclusive golf course—a mansion that locals called "Little Versailles." The exterior was an unlikely combination of Southern plantation and French chateau. Frank's wife, Sue, liked to throw lavish charity events in her own mini Hall of Mirrors. The Greek revival entry with its white-columned portico looked especially out of place among the single-story mid-century homes and palm trees that lined both sides of their street.

Sue's weekly mahjong game was in full swing when Frank appeared in the hallway. He gave her a quick wave and disappeared into his office. Sue was momentarily surprised that he was home in the middle of the day, but she almost had all fourteen tiles into four sets. All she needed was the chow. Frank could do whatever he wanted in the meantime.

Frank was jumpy as he dialed Josie's number.

"Lionel knows you were in the security room," he blurted out when she answered.

"What?" Josie dropped her keys on the table by the front door.

"Apparently, you set off some kind of alarm with the file cabinet. He has you on video."

"Shit," she replied.

"Jesus, Josie. You've really done it now. You have to back off. Our asses are all on the line."

"*I've* really done it? *You* started this, Frank. If you'd come clean in the beginning, maybe we wouldn't be in this position."

"And how the fuck do you think you would have been helpful? You don't know shit."

"I know we need to get these guys out and take our casino back."

"Oh, what a great idea!" he said sarcastically. "I would've never thought of that. Lionel's just the tip of the iceberg. How did you get in the room in the first place?"

Josie thought for a minute. There was a short silence between them. She could hear the tension in Frank's voice. Should she trust her brother, despite everything?

"I have to call you back," she said curtly.

Josie called Moe and told him about the money, the art, everything. She added she had inadvertently set off an alarm and that Lionel knew she was in the room.

"Goddamn it! I told you not to touch anything," Moe barked. She decided she'd wait to tell him about the trash from the wastebaskets.

"How do we dig ourselves out of this?" she asked, fighting the urge to grab Billie and keep on driving away from all this madness.

"It's not gonna be easy."

"I didn't say it would be easy. We're in a fuckload of trouble here, aren't we?"

"Definitely," Moe agreed. There was a long silence on the other end of the line. "But I have some ideas. I'll call you tomorrow."

Chapter 45

In the middle of all this chaos, Josie was guilty as hell about Billie.

"Sam, what can I do? I've spent my life trying to create a normal home for Billie. Now I might be dragging her back into the same cesspool we grew up in."

"Don't be so dramatic. You didn't have it so bad." She could hear him inhaling God knows what.

"Oh yeah? Witnessing a murder and then getting exiled? It feels like the hand of Roy King is reaching out to fuck things up for another generation."

"Look, all we know is Frank is skimming and we shook him up. Nothing's going to happen in the next few days. Don't get all paranoid. Let's wait and talk to Moe."

What choice did she have? For the moment she was out of ideas. She agonized over it for days. And now it was Friday. Billie was arriving in exactly one hour.

As they piled Billie's duffels into the back of the car, Josie noticed that her daughter was wearing blush and lip gloss. She was endearingly awkward, in the way that young colts are initially hampered by their anatomy—limbs too long for their immature bodies. But even now Josie could see that in a few years, with her long legs, patrician nose and deep blue eyes, she would be beautiful.

When did this happen? Josie wondered. She wasn't aware of how quickly her daughter was growing up.

Josie had planned to take Billie to the Jackpot Grill for dinner, but her daughter had already invited Cassie to sleep over that night.

"I was going to take you out." Josie was disappointed. "Okay. Never mind."

Once they got home, Josie pulled out the two shopping bags filled with stolen cosmetics and set them down in front of her daughter. Billie glanced at her mother, then turned her head and looked out the window.

"Look at me, please," Josie said, slightly annoyed.

"It's only nail polish, Mom. What's the big deal?"

"That's not the point. It's stealing. It's a crime. Not an extracurricular activity. Just tell me you won't do it anymore."

"I won't do it anymore," Billie said, rolling her eyes and repeating her mother's words in a monotone.

Her daughter did agree that she and Cassie would find other ways to spend their time. The doorbell rang before Josie could say much else.

Flora, Cassie's mother, was standing by the front door, holding a poinsettia wrapped in gold foil and Cassie's overnight bag.

"I can't thank you enough for getting me in with the Jackpot," Flora said, taking both of Josie's hands in hers. "They even gave me a raise."

Josie knew she was lucky to be in the position to help Flora, but she had an ulterior motive. If Josie had to work late, which was pretty common in the casino business, having a neighbor who could look after Billie would help her enormously.

After Flora left, the girls spent a half hour in the bathroom, applying green clay masks to their faces and braiding their hair. Josie could hear them laughing. She renewed her pledge to make sure her daughter had a normal life.

Even if Josie didn't.

Chapter 46

As the girls watched a movie in the living room, Josie was finishing up a cigarette outside on the porch when Moe called.

"I talked to a couple of my guys on the inside. They're going to try to find out who's involved and how the setup works."

"Do you have any ideas?" Josie asked as she walked farther out on the lawn.

"We'll find out. But I don't want you going to the office until we have a plan. Let's talk when we know more."

Josie had a hard time sleeping after Moe's call. She was uncomfortably aware of the trove of trash from the security room that she had hidden downstairs in the closet. She finally threw off the bedcovers, put on her robe and wandered down to the kitchen to have a second go at it. The contents of the bag were now whittled down to just notes and papers. There had to be something she could use. It was like doing a crossword puzzle. The second and third go-around, you always come up with another clue. That's just the way the brain works. It took patience and time. Most people give up too soon.

Josie organized all the notes that had numbers on them. A few of them looked sequenced, like a bank account. Others could be fragments of wire transfer records or shreds of computer printouts. Someone else might not recognize this, but her old accounting skills were flooding back. It was the notes with names that convinced her she had to tell Moe what she found in the trash. It wasn't exactly a mountain of evidence, but it might just help with his sources.

At 2 a.m. her eyes were heavy and her head was swimming. Jesus, she thought, she had to stop. Josie returned the bag to the bottom of the closet, checked on the girls and went back to bed.

She slept in the next morning. Sunlight streamed through the blinds and hit her face full-on, and she could hear the girls' voices in Billie's room. She picked up her cell from her bedside table, put on her robe and walked outside past the patio. Then she called Moe.

"Hey Moe. I have a confession to make."

"Yeah?"

"Remember when you told me not to touch anything?"

Moe sighed. "I'm not getting a good feeling about this."

"Well, I emptied all the trash cans in the room and found a few things that might be helpful," she confessed.

"Very entrepreneurial of you. Stupid, but entrepreneurial. What've you got?"

"The numbers are just fragments, but the names might mean something."

Josie read the names to Moe, who said he recognized a couple of them. He needed more time to put it together. It was Saturday, and his inside guys weren't working. They'd talk on Monday.

As she hung up, she noticed that there were three missed calls and several voicemails from Rob. When had she last talked to him? She couldn't even remember. She dialed his cell, thinking she'd leave a message, but he picked up immediately.

"Hey Rob. It's Josie."

"Josie who?"

"Very funny."

"Not really. Are you ignoring me?"

"Are you free tonight?" Josie asked.

"Are you asking me out?" He sounded surprised but pleased.

"I believe I am." Why not, she thought. It was Saturday night and Billie would be at Cassie's. "I have to warn you, I'm sort of a wreck."

"Okay, I'll cancel the acrobats. Dinner's at my place at eight."

Chapter 47

When Josie strolled into Rob's penthouse, he put his arms around her. "Can't you at least lie and tell me you missed me?"

"I missed you," she repeated dutifully.

"I meant with feeling. God, Josie, your shoulders are tight. You need a massage."

"I need a new life," she admitted, but she smiled.

"How many do we get?"

"I don't know but the one I have is seriously messed up."

After dinner and a bottle of Chateau Margaux, Josie and Rob sat by the fireplace in the living room.

"So, history question. My father used to say that the seventies marked the end of the mob era in Vegas. Is that true?" Josie asked, staring into the flames.

"How far into the weeds do you want to get here?"

"Very, very far. I know what I know, but I suspect I don't know everything."

"Okay. Most people don't know this, but the biggest reason for the mob getting out of Vegas was the change of the laws regarding corporate ownership. Two bankers in the late sixties knew that they had to get rid of the mob if the town was going to grow. They petitioned the state legislature up in Carson City to allow corporate ownership of the casinos."

"Because before that, only individuals could be licensed to own a casino. Like my father."

"Yep. The new law brought in public corporations. That meant the SEC, full disclosure and government oversight."

"Not the mob's cup of tea."

"Not at all," Rob agreed.

"So. Theoretically"—Josie kept her gaze on the fire—"if someone wanted to get rid of a mob guy in their casino—not that there are any still around—how would they do it?"

"Theoretically?" he asked. She knows, he thought.

"Yes, of course theoretically," she replied. He knows, she thought.

"Well, the best way would be to let the mob get rid of him themselves. Then you're out of it."

"Right. The mob retirement plan." She smiled. He smiled.

"Reckonings." Rob stretched his arms, laying one along her shoulders. "Like Willie Bioff, RICO snitch, got into his truck, turned the key and boom! Dynamite wired to his starter."

"Al Bramlet, tough union boss, found in the desert with three bullets to the heart," Josie threw in.

"Gus Greenbaum and his wife, Bess. Double-crossed the mob. Both their throats were slit."

"Even though it was reported they died of natural causes," Josie added.

The game between the two of them had begun. Vegas bedtime stories. Both Josie and Rob knew these lurid tales by heart. Josie was raised on these stories as other people were raised on Brothers Grimm and the Bible.

"How about glamorous Johnny Roselli, testified before Congress, found floating off Miami."

"Or Tony 'The Ant' Spilotro, mob hit man, one-way ticket to Chicago."

Now they were rolling. One-upmanship.

"Don't forget Lefty Rosenthal," Josie said.

"Who could forget Lefty Rosenthal?" he replied. "Botched hit at Tony Roma's. Bombed his Cadillac but the steel plate under the floorboard saved him."

"I've always liked Cadillacs." Josie smiled.

"Yes. Very nice car. And Jerry Delman."

"Who?"

"Gotcha," Rob said, grinning from ear to ear. He paused and looked at her. "You're flirting with me, Josie King," he said with delight.

"Yes," she replied, delighted as well. "I can match you. But I'll give you this one."

She looked at him for a moment. And then said, "I happen to find you very handsome."

"Take off your clothes," he said.

"You first."

The next morning, they had breakfast on the terrace. They could have been an ordinary couple enjoying the morning after. He asked about her brothers. Whether Frank was coming around with the union demands. She could talk about the union until she was blue in the face but what she could use right now was someone she could trust, besides Sam and Moe. It would be nice to be able to confide in Rob, ask for his advice, but that wasn't in the cards.

Family casinos are insular. They don't share information with competing businesses. From the time the old pioneers rode their horses down Fremont Street, it was a race to see who could reel in the customers, who could create the Number One Joint. The place in the sun where tourists would want to stay inside and lose their money, then come back and lose it again. There wasn't a lot of camaraderie.

So instead of unburdening herself, Josie floated a few innocuous updates regarding the union. Over breakfast she mentioned Billie and her light-fingered new friend.

"I'd like to meet her sometime," Rob said casually. A nice, normal suggestion. Josie sipped her cappuccino. He looked at her for a response but she said nothing.

"You're a difficult woman to read," he said.

"You think so? I'm just so overwhelmed at the moment."

"I've tried to show you that you can trust me, Josie."

"Yes. But you're still a competitor."

"This isn't Ali-Frazier. I'm here if you need me."

"I know. I believe you."

Chapter 48

When Billie woke up the next morning, it took her a few minutes to remember where she was. Cassie's house was dead quiet. Sealed-up boxes were scattered around the bedroom, which still had bare walls and no curtains or shades. The house was about half the size of Billie's, with two small bedrooms, which shared a bath. Cassie was still asleep, curled up with a teddy bear tucked under her chin, so Billie walked quietly into the bathroom to wash her face.

It was not the most inviting place. No towels, an almost empty toilet paper roll, and a crusty nub of soap in the stall shower. On the floor in a box were dozens of miniature bottles of bath gel, shampoo, conditioner, and body lotion, all of them with a fancy Caesars Palace label. Hanging on the back of the bathroom door were two white terry cloth robes with the initials "CP" in gold on the front pocket. Cassie's mom had obviously cleaned out the place when she quit.

Billie crawled back into bed until she heard noises from downstairs in the kitchen. Cassie's mom fixed bacon and eggs, and then suggested the girls go "play outside," like they were five-year-olds. They decided to walk over to the Boulevard Mall, even though it was freezing. They put on their parkas and wool hats, stuffed a few dollars in their pockets and headed toward Maryland Parkway. Cassie told her that in the summer, when it was really hot, they could fry eggs on the neighbor's metal garbage can lids. People hated it because their whole driveway smelled like rotten eggs.

They hit Target first. Cassie came alive in the store, darting from aisle to aisle. They looked at pj's, jeans, T-shirts and dresses. Billie warned Cassie that they couldn't shoplift anymore because her mother "went psycho" when she found the shopping bags from their last trip. She had promised not to do it again. But Cassie lifted a lacy camisole and slipped it in her backpack. Billie didn't say anything. Cassie was kind of touchy and Billie didn't want to argue.

As soon as they walked out of Target and into the parking lot, they noticed a white van with what looked like the mall insignia on the door. The man behind the wheel was wearing a baseball hat and mirrored sunglasses. When they turned the corner, he did too. It happened a few more times and Billie got nervous. This was no coincidence.

"You got us busted," she told Cassie, trying not to look back at the van. "I think a security guard is following us."

Cassie shrugged and looked at Billie with a half-amused expression.

"You're paranoid," she said. "Nobody saw me do anything. And anyway, those mall cops are really lame."

The girls ducked into a fabric store and waited a few minutes. But when they went back outside, the van was idling on the corner, the driver staring straight at them.

"Let's walk faster," Billie said, panicking.

"Let's run," Cassie answered in a shaky voice. She was now just as scared as Billie.

They passed a dirt lot where an ice-cold wind blew sand in Billie's face. She looked back over her shoulder. The van was still following them, so they cut across a construction site to the next street over and started running. They raced through someone's backyard and decided to hide in a carport. Cassie sat down next to Billie and opened her backpack to look over her stash. They were both out of breath and Billie was sweating, even though it was freezing.

Up to this point, nothing even remotely this scary had ever happened to Billie. God, she thought, she couldn't trust Cassie for shit. That girl had a *big* problem.

"Let's split up," Billie proposed, thinking that they'd waited long enough in the carport. Also, she didn't want to get caught with Cassie.

"Fine, if that's what you want," Cassie said, annoyed.

But the white van was waiting just outside the carport. The driver rolled down his window and motioned for them to approach. The girls stared at each other.

"Hey, Billie," the man said politely. "I'm sorry if I scared you. I have a message from your mother. It'll just take a minute."

He was big and heavy, with a fat, red face and bad skin, and his scraggly hair stuck out from his black baseball hat. Something about him reminded her of the guys hanging around outside the casino who always creeped her out.

"What is it?" she asked, fighting the urge to run. Why would a mall cop know her name? Or her mom?

"Which way are you going?" he asked her. His arm was resting outside the window and he flicked his cigarette butt toward the curb. "How about a lift?"

Billie hesitated just long enough. Another man slid open the side door with a thud, grabbed her under her armpits and threw her into the back of the van. It was dead dark, no windows, and the carpet stank of mildew. Billie screamed as loud as she could, kicking and scratching as he held her down. She could feel his skin under her nails. But he overpowered her, slapping a piece of silver electrical tape across her mouth, blindfolding her eyes and zip-tying her hands and feet.

"Well, well, well," he said, pleased. "Look who we have here."

Billie's heart was pounding, it was hard to breathe and she felt like she might pass out. She could hear Cassie screaming on the corner as they drove away.

Chapter 49

Josie got the call as she was pulling into her garage. She had left Rob's place around noon and was looking forward to taking Billie to lunch. But Flora's voice was high-pitched and terrified. She could hear Cassie crying in the background.

"Billie's gone! Someone took her!"

"What?" Josie said, turning off her car radio. She wasn't sure she'd heard Flora correctly.

"She's gone!" Flora shouted. "Where are you?"

"I'm home!"

Josie rushed into the house, running up to Billie's room to see if she was there.

"Billie? Are you here? Billie?" she called out louder.

She checked the bathroom, her bedroom, the spare room and the closets. She ran back downstairs to look in the kitchen and on the back porch and patio, still calling her daughter's name. Billie was not upstairs. Not downstairs. Not outside. Nowhere.

Stay calm, she thought to herself. There must be some logical explanation. Maybe Sam had picked her up? But Josie instinctively knew that wasn't the case.

By the time she'd made a second run through all the rooms, Cassie and Flora were standing at her front door. Flora had her arms protectively around Cassie, who, through bursts of half-finished sentences and tears, told her what happened. She was shivering and biting her lips, hanging on to her mother for dear life.

"This man, this security cop, was following us."

"Why would he be following you?" Josie interrupted impatiently.

"I don't know," Cassie said, flushing and lowering her eyes.

Josie knew the girl was lying, the little thief.

"Anyways," Cassie went on, sobbing and gulping breaths, "we were scared and ran and then the man shoved her in a white van and drove off."

Every mother's worst nightmare. She was about to call the police when her cell phone rang. There was a strange silence on the line, but she could hear breathing. Then a muffled voice repeated what sounded like a script from a police procedural.

"We have your daughter. If you want her back alive, no cops and do exactly as we say."

"I want to talk to her." Josie took a deep breath, trying to control her tone. She struggled not to sink into hysteria.

"She's okay," was the monotone response.

"I want to talk to her! Right now! Put her on the line." Josie's voice sounded tough, but her hands were shaking. Her mind was going a mile a minute.

The line went dead for a second. The guy had a low, gravelly voice, and her fear turned to anger.

"Stop fucking with me," Josie said with fury. "You hear me?"

He finally came back on the line. There was the sound of static and then muted conversations.

"Mommy, do what they say. They aren't . . ." Billie's voice was faint, but Josie could hear her crying.

"Are you hurt?" Josie asked, but her daughter was gone.

"Fifty grand. All in hundreds," a calm voice ordered. That was the clincher—his disembodied, atonal voice. As if her daughter's life was of no great importance.

He told her to leave the cash in a white Honda parked at an abandoned trailer park north of town. Josie imagined Billie somewhere, blindfolded, gagged and paralyzed with fear, and the thought sent her reeling with rage. Then she heard more voices but couldn't make out what they were saying.

"No deal until she tells me she's safe and unharmed. And what's my guarantee I'll get my daughter back after I give you the cash?"

"There are no guarantees in life. You're gonna have to trust us. Make the drop in two hours. Instructions where to pick up your package will be in the car. And no cops," he repeated, and then the line went dead.

Josie stood there a moment, trying to compose herself. "Goddamn it!" she shouted. This was all her fault. Moe had warned her. She immediately called Sam.

She had to catch her breath and calm the furious thudding in her chest, as if she had run twenty miles in a marathon. Sam picked up right away.

"These fucking monsters took my kid!"

"Wait a minute. Slow down," Sam said.

She managed to explain what happened and spoke the word that had haunted her since Flora's frantic phone call: *Kidnapped.*

Chapter 50

Sam's pickup peeled around the corner to Josie's house and screeched to a halt. His Browning rifle was in the back seat and his face was red with rage.

"Jesus. Get in!" he said, the engine still running. Josie threw an empty duffel in the back seat and slammed the door shut.

"Drive," she said.

Sam floored it, picking up speed as they headed to the bank. They sat silently, their fear amplified by the knowledge that Billie's life depended on it. They turned into the parking lot and Josie ran in with the duffel and withdrew fifty grand in hundreds from her account. The teller barely raised an eyebrow. This was Vegas. The bank was used to dealing in cash.

They blasted north on US-95, weaving through lanes of traffic toward the trailer park. The angry glare from the sun was blinding. They flew down the freeway to the designated exit, cutting off cars as Sam swerved off the ramp.

"When we get there, you sit tight and I'll take the cash to the car," Sam said as they neared the drop-off spot.

"What if they think you're undercover? They said no cops. I should go alone."

"I don't know. It's dangerous."

"I don't want to take any chances. Stay back. I can do it." A cold sweat broke out all over her body.

"Here, take my other gun," Sam said, pulling a 9mm Glock out of his glove compartment. It was surprisingly heavy and cold as ice.

"It's loaded. Be careful."

Josie shoved the gun in her coat pocket and grabbed the duffel. She walked slowly toward the white Honda, looking over her shoulder to see if anyone was watching. She opened the trunk and dumped in the cash. On the front seat she found a small piece of paper typed with these words:

"McCarran Airport, parking lot C. Space 143. Red Chevy."

The nightmare wasn't over. After the drop, they had to find Billie and hope to God she wasn't hurt. They jumped back on the freeway, turning hard through the traffic. She felt sick to her stomach.

The airport was fourteen miles away. They raced back down the highway in silence, past the Strip to McCarran. Lot C was the last building past the terminal. The least crowded. They pulled into the parking structure, not knowing what they'd find. It was Sunday afternoon and the lot was half-empty. They circled up to level 4 and searched for space 143. And there, parked between two trucks, was the car—the red Chevy, right where they said it would be. Sam pulled in behind it. Josie grabbed the gun and leapt out.

Oh God, she thought. Please let her be safe. She called her daughter's name.

"Billie? Billie? Shit! Where are you?"

Billie wasn't inside the car. Sam flung open the trunk. Empty. Josie's eyes filled with tears of fury. Sam slammed the trunk down.

"Goddamn it!" he said in a rage. "They fucked us!"

He kicked the fender of the empty Chevy, then out of his peripheral vision he noticed a white van pulling out of a space at the end of the row.

"What the . . ." he yelled as he aimed his gun at the escaping van.

"Stop! You motherfuckers," he yelled, racing toward it.

The van suddenly accelerated, its brakes screeching as it backed out. Sam was closing in, running with a speed and ferocity that was almost inhuman. He was barreling toward the van, closing the gap between them.

It all happened in a split second. The first bullet fired from the van hit a parked car a few inches from Sam's face. The alarm shrieked, and shattered glass flew out of the car and just missed his eye. Sam tumbled to the side and tried to roll behind a truck, but he couldn't move fast enough. Josie screamed in panic as the second bullet hit the ground behind him and the third ricocheted off the wall as Sam crawled behind a car. If he stood up, he'd be an easy target.

Josie charged toward the van, muscles tightening, trying to avoid the barrage of bullets. She flattened her body against a truck but then had to risk it. There would never be a better chance. She jumped out, aiming her gun at the man in the passenger seat, and fired off four bullets in a row, shattering the window. A spray of blood hit the side of the van as it sped down the ramp.

Josie and Sam jumped back in the truck and followed the van. It careened down the spiral ramp ahead of them, rocking back and forth, toward the exit of the parking structure. Sam's truck barely negotiated the tight curves, as he and Josie both ignored the ear-piercing, scraping sound of the fender dragging along the walls. Sparks bounced off the tire rims and they almost flew off the ramp, but Sam kept going. Adrenaline surged through his veins, his eyes darting back and forth, trying to keep the van in his line of vision.

"Jesus! Can't you go any faster?" Josie asked, grabbing the "oh shit" handle over the passenger door and holding on with a vengeance.

"If I go any faster we'll roll over. Do you think you killed him?" Sam asked.

"I hope so."

When they reached the bottom of the ramp, there were four possible exits—the I-215 to the south and north; the tunnel that circled back to the terminals; and the left lane, which fed onto Paradise Road. No sign of the van. They were stunned. Gone. The van had completely disappeared.

"I'm calling the police," Josie said, her head pounding.

They both froze as her cell phone rang. She struggled to grab it from her purse and gripped it with both hands. A jolt of fear rushed through her body as she heard the same disembodied voice. Something inside Josie snapped.

"Give me my child!" she screamed.

"We will. A little change of plans. First, you have to drop off another fifty in the same spot as before. You have two hours."

"I need to talk to her," Josie pleaded, squeezing the phone. Dirty fucking monsters, she thought. The next time she'd kill them.

"She's busy. And don't call the cops," the voice said, "or you'll never see your daughter again."

As Sam and Josie pulled out of the lot, both of them kept a firm grip on their guns. Josie thought they should call the cops. But Sam was adamant. "Bad idea!" he shouted.

He reminded her of a kidnapping of a casino kid during their own childhood. The parents called in the feds and they bungled the whole operation. The FBI tracked the perps to the hiding place where the young girl, bound and blindfolded, was being held for ransom. The agents opened fire and the girl was shot and killed. Josie remembered her. She had sat next to her in math class. "Okay, okay," she agreed. "No cops."

With time running out, Josie and Sam sped back to the bank to get more cash. Josie had obviously hit one of the kidnappers and they were probably desperate at this point. She walked back to the same teller, a full-figured matron who had given her the first fifty grand. This time the woman called the branch manager, who took one look at Josie and approved the withdrawal. He remembered Roy King's daughter from years ago. She hastily piled the rest of the cash into a garbage bag and then recoiled at the sound of her cell ringing. It was a number she didn't recognize. Her hand gripped the phone tightly as she answered.

"Am I speaking to Josie King?" The voice was deep and official, and there was a siren in the background.

"Yes, who is this?" Josie asked carefully, her pulse quickening.

"Detective Morris, ma'am. Las Vegas Police Department."

Josie closed her eyes and dropped the cash bag on the floor, a million terrifying thoughts flooding her mind.

"We have your daughter. She's unharmed."

"Thank God," she sobbed, sinking to her knees. "Where is she?"

"She's at the station. Someone saw her waving down cars near the off-ramp of the I-215 and called it in."

Chapter 51

Lionel watched a white van pull up to his Pahrump house and park on the rutted driveway. The gravel was so coarse he could hear stones popping like gunfire under the wheels. The wind was roaring across the highway and the driver had a hard time opening his door.

The first guy to appear was six foot something and heavyset, with a beer belly and greasy hair that kept blowing in his eyes. He was buttoning a sport coat that looked too tight for him. Probably swiped it at Target, Lionel thought. The second guy was younger, bulging with gym rat muscles. There were visible red, angry scratches on his face and neck, and a small diamond stud in each earlobe. He was cradling his left arm, which was wrapped in a blood-soaked towel. He pulled a small zip out of his pocket with a dime's worth of weed.

"Put that shit away until after," the big guy said, grabbing the bag and stuffing it back in his partner's pocket.

"This fucking arm is killing me. I need a fucking doctor."

"Jesus. I told you. Right after we get the cash. You already made me dump the kid on the freeway and lose the second fifty."

"She wasn't worth me bleeding to death."

They walked up to Lionel's small frame house, which was surrounded by overgrown bushes, weeds and dirt. Streaks of rust stained the siding, and the roof was scattered with broken tiles.

"What's with the arm?" Lionel asked, inspecting the bloody towel with distaste. The injured man's face was pale and sweaty.

"The bitch shot me."

"Why were you anywhere near her? You were supposed to just drop the kid at the airport and disappear."

Lionel looked at the driver. A nasty, two-bit Neanderthal, he thought.

"They came at us with guns. We had to defend ourselves," the big guy protested.

"You think I'm stupid?" Lionel said, frowning. He looked away for a minute to give them time to figure out they screwed up royally. "Why did they come at you with guns if you left the kid in the car like I told you?"

"We thought we'd get you more money," the younger one admitted. He was shifting his weight from one leg to another like he wanted this shit to be over.

"Aren't you two the generous ones," Lionel said, giving them a dead smile. "And what's with the scratches? I told you not to hurt her."

"We didn't. She put up a fight."

"The whole point was just to scare her, you morons. You have the cash?"

Jesus Christ, these guys were pathetic, Lionel thought. He knew the younger one was smoking meth—he could smell it on his clothes. Couple of kiss-my-ass losers.

"What now?" asked the bigger one as he handed Lionel the bag of cash.

Lionel's voice dropped a notch, conveying the importance of what he was about to tell them.

"There's a box of cash buried out back. Help me dig it up and I'll give you a cut as your fee."

"How much?" the crackhead asked.

"Another five grand."

"How about six?"

"Deal," Lionel said shortly.

Lionel went into the garage and brought out two shovels. He led them out back to a deserted area behind the old chicken shed. Wasps and rats had taken over, their nests everywhere. Nobody ventured out there anymore.

"You guys start," Lionel said, scratching out an X with his boot on the ground.

The wiry guy picked up the shovel and winced. "You know I can't dig with my arm."

"Oh yeah. Use the other one."

Lionel stood there for a moment to make sure they were digging. Then he walked away, pulling out his cell and making a call. A half hour later, he returned. Sweat soaked the big guy's shirt. He had pulled his jacket off and thrown it on the ground.

"You sure this is the spot?" he asked, looking down into the hole.

"Yeah," Lionel answered. "That's the lid of the box right there. See it?"

As they both bent over to look in the hole, Lionel popped the big one twice in the head, his body falling with a thud into the hole. The other man twisted around, dropped his shovel and started running. "Oh shit, oh shit!"

Lionel squinted, slowly and deliberately aiming his gun at the guy's back. As the bullet tore into his spine, the man dropped to the ground. Lionel calmly walked over to him, pressed the gun barrel to his forehead and squeezed the trigger. Then he jammed the gun back into his waistband.

He wheeled a dolly from his carport and started moving the body. Blood seeped in a long, thick trail across the gravel and bits of brain matter clotted a few spots on the dirt, which Lionel covered over with his boot. When he rolled him over into the hole, he noticed the dead man had a wad of cash in his back pocket, which Lionel assumed was lifted from the ransom money. He pulled it out, and the weed too. No sense wasting it.

Lionel was sweating and out of breath. Shit. Life can be tough, Lionel thought, pressing the bag of ransom money under one arm and walking to his vault in the backyard. He almost felt sorry for them. He lifted up the bulletproof hatch and climbed down the ladder into the cavernous bunker. He couldn't use any of his regular guys for this job. It wasn't an authorized hit. And New York wouldn't like him kidnapping a twelve-year-old. But it was the only way to keep the King family in line. A one-shot deal. When you think about it, it was a good tactic.

Lionel glanced around the dank underground shelter—fourteen feet below the surface. No one could ever find this place. It was built initially as a bomb shelter, constructed of solid steel when all the anti-commie chickenshits were convinced that Russia was going to nuke them. Someone could live here for months—the whole reason Lionel had bought the house in the first place.

He sat down at the Formica table next to the small kitchenette and rolled his head in a circle, working out a crick in his neck. The room was cold, fifty degrees with a concrete floor, so he lit the alcohol-burning stove and made himself comfortable. The low temperature and dry air was actually good for the art, which was stacked against the wall.

Lionel had once tried spending the night here on the bunk beds, but the mattress was lumpy and there wasn't enough room to stretch out his legs. He made a mental note to bring down some throw rugs next time. Something that would go well with the Renoirs and Manets, when he eventually unwrapped them.

He adjusted the row of rifles hanging on the wall, and then stuffed the cash into one of the twenty boxes sitting in the corner. He was going to give these guys ten grand—that was the deal—but the punks pissed him off. And he didn't like leaving loose ends.

Lionel took his time reorganizing the shelf of canned soups and bottled water. Then he checked over a box filled with files that could bring down the whole New York operation if it ever got into the wrong hands—wire transfer records, offshore account numbers, names of shell companies and a few other things that would make them shit a brick if they knew he had them in his possession. Insurance. What wasn't noted in the files was what Lionel had taken for himself. That, no one would ever know about.

When he climbed back up the ladder hours later, Lionel noticed the white van still sitting in his driveway. Damn. The guys picked it up under an assumed name from a rent-a-wreck off the Strip. It stank of weed. The keys were still in the ignition, so he drove the van into his garage and closed the door.

He removed the license plates and put them in his car. He'd throw them in a garbage dumpster south of Pahrump. He wiped down the seats and steering wheel with some old bleach he had in the house, and then poured the rest on the floor of the back of the van. This would have to do until he could get some new plates and drive the piece of junk to California to dump it.

For the first time today, he thought about Josie. She must have gone fucking nuts. Who knew the bitch could shoot? Now maybe she'd mind her own business and stop creeping around. She got exactly what she deserved.

Chapter 52

From the moment Josie brought her daughter home, she was consumed with thoughts of revenge. This was her punishment for breaking into the room. Frank told her that Lionel knew and there would be trouble. But she never dreamed he would go to this extreme. She tried to tamp down her fury as Billie was introduced to the FBI agents in charge of the investigation.

Her head was throbbing, her fist clenched, but Josie's mind was alive with payback.

"We're just glad you're safe now," the young female agent began. "Billie, we understand you've been through a terrible experience."

"Yes. I was kidnapped," Billie replied, searching her mother's face to see if that was the right answer. Josie was sitting on the living room couch with her daughter, who was squeezing her hand so tight Josie's fingers were numb. There were visible bruises on Billie's wrists.

It was all Josie could do not to call Frank and tell him to take Lionel out to the desert and bury him alive. She looked at Sam, who was pacing up and down the hall. His face was bright red, his nostrils flared. Josie had never seen him this angry.

The thirtysomething detective, who was dressed like a bank executive in a navy suit, smiled sympathetically at Billie and took out a pad and pencil from her jacket pocket. She was accompanied by an older woman who told Josie she specialized in forensic interviewing of children. She seemed kind and gentle, and had taken Josie aside to tell her that sometimes officers made the victim feel guilty about what happened to them. Her protocol was to focus on the offender's wrongdoing, while getting the information they needed to apprehend them. She gently told Billie that she would need time to recover from the trauma, which sometimes comes several weeks or even months after the actual incident.

"It's like whiplash," the officer said. "You don't always feel it right away."

Both agents had shown up a few hours after the police had contacted them from the hospital. She and Sam had taken Billie there from the station to make sure she was okay. The nurse asked Billie if she had been assaulted. Billie shook her head, no. Thank God, Josie thought. They eventually took skin samples from under Billie's nails after she told them she had scratched one of the assailants.

"He was trying to put a gag on me, but I got him first and it made him mad," Billie told one of the nurses, who replied, "Good for you."

The agents asked her daughter multiple questions. Josie hated the intrusion, but they had a job to do and a limited time to do it. "Can you describe the men?" "Were they carrying a weapon?" "What kind of car?" "What were they wearing?" "Hair? Body type? Glasses? Mustache? Beard?" "What did they say to you?" "Did they hurt you?"

Then they asked her to relay in her own words exactly what happened. Billie went into her version of the abduction, including the gun fight. She knew one of the kidnappers had been hit because he started cursing like crazy and his partner told him to "suck it up." Then she veered off track, blaming Cassie for everything. Tears welled up in her eyes as she told them that if Cassie hadn't been shoplifting, they both would have realized the van was creepy and called for help.

Josie was horrified. Her daughter blamed herself and Cassie for the kidnapping. She held Billie tightly in her arms and heard her muffled sobbing against her chest.

"My sweetheart," she said, lifting her daughter's chin and looking into her eyes, "whatever happened with you and Cassie had *nothing* to do with shoplifting. Absolutely nothing. We're going to find the bad men who did this. *They* are the ones who will be punished. *They're* the ones at fault. You understand?"

After the interview, Billie went to her room to change into her pajamas, and Sam cornered Josie in the kitchen. He took a swig from a bottle of Maker's Mark, lit up a cigarette and motioned for her to step outside.

"Let's not pretend we don't know who did this. This is Frank's fault too. I've had enough," Sam said, stubbing out his cigarette, grabbing his gun and heading for the door.

"I've got a better idea," Josie said. "Sit down."

Chapter 53

Josie's initial instinct was to leave the kidnapping to the authorities. To let them handle it. But then she thought about the bruises on Billie's arm, the terror her daughter must have felt, blindfolded and tied up in the back of the van. Or the way they tried to fuck her over with the second drop, using her daughter as bait. Her father used to say that you're either "at the table or on the menu." Josie was going to be at the table.

"So what's the big idea?" Sam asked.

"The best way to get rid of a guy like Lionel is to have the mob eliminate him themselves," Josie said, remembering her conversation with Rob.

"How do we do that?" Sam countered, fingering his pistol. "Let me just shoot the bastard, okay?"

"Sam, forget the gun and start using your head."

The conversation was interrupted when Frank appeared at the door, saying he had cut his meeting short with the gaming board in Carson City, and flew back the minute he heard about Billie. His pilot made it in less than an hour.

"Where is she?" he asked, following Josie out to the patio and taking in Sam's stony expression.

"Well, if it isn't the devil at our doorstep," Sam said.

"What!" he snapped, glaring at Sam. "You think this is *my* fault?"

"Yeah. You're the front man, right? You did nothing as these fucking guys took over."

"So typical. Blaming me for everything," Frank said. "Why does this family always make me feel like shit?"

"Just stop. Both of you. I'm thinking," Josie said.

She proceeded to think out loud. "Lionel is basically just the bagman," she began. "He oversees the skim and keeps Frank in line. That's his job. But what if Lionel fucked up? In his line of work, there are two ways he could do that: He could either get caught helping himself to something off the top—shortchanging his partners—or he could cooperate with the feds. Both offenses get five sticks of dynamite wired to his starter. And send a warning to the rest of the gang.

"So," she continued, "let's get Lionel to fuck up."

"How you gonna pull that off? We don't have the feds on payroll anymore," Frank said. But he was listening in spite of himself.

"I don't know yet," Josie said quietly. They sat in silence.

"So what do I do in the meantime?" Frank asked.

Josie looked at him, still furious. "Do what you always do around Lionel. Kiss his ass."

After Frank left, Sam pulled out a bottle of Valium and offered one to Josie. She swallowed it without water and gave him a hug. Then she went upstairs and checked on Billie, who was sleeping. Josie stripped off her clothes and turned the shower dial all the way to the right—so hot that the spray stung her face. Steam clouded the glass door and she couldn't see or hear anything except the rush of thunder in her ears. She was dog-tired, trying to clear her mind of all the images swarming around and concentrate on one thing. Revenge.

For the first time, she understood her father. To him, retribution was a fundamental human need. One could not exist in this world unless the person who threatened you was eliminated. Her father knew that. Now she did too.

She turned off the water and put on a robe. Her cheeks were bright red from the steam. She finally started to relax but then she had to endure a hostile conversation with Stuart, who would arrive in Vegas the next afternoon. He insisted on immediately taking Billie back to

LA. On the phone, he flew into one of his rages and accused her of being reckless with Billie's safety. Vegas was no place for a kid, he said. A bunch of lowlife criminals living there. And Josie was in the middle of it.

"I'm picking her up tomorrow morning and the deal is off. I'm going for full custody. You think I'd let her stay there now? Not for all the dirty money in your casino."

Josie let him rant and rave for a few more minutes, then she hung up on him. Billie would go with him the next day, stay for the rest of the semester and then move back with her permanently as planned. No one is going to take my daughter away from me, she thought. Not even her father.

She remembered being exiled by her father. And now she could understand his decision. He wanted her safe. But she stayed away too long and paid too high a price. She was determined not to do that with Billie. She would secure her daughter's safety above all. She'd be damned before she let Stuart get full custody.

Later that evening, Josie padded into Billie's room and stretched out on the bed next to her daughter. She could feel her warm, moist breath on her neck. In and out, in and out, the innocent sleep of a child. Nature's healing. Billie didn't stir the rest of the night, but Josie lay there wide awake, every thought like a dagger as she stared into the dark.

Chapter 54

Stuart arrived in Vegas at 5 p.m. the next night. He was greeted at the airport by Moe and one of his security guys in dark suits, who told him they were sent from the casino to drive him to Josie's house.

They were polite and treated him like a VIP. Fuck it! Stuart thought. He deserved it. After all, he was the father of a King grandchild. He was escorted to a shiny black Lincoln Town Car, the kind usually reserved for whales. When Moe climbed into the back seat with him, Stuart was a little surprised.

"Here you go," Moe said, handing him a thick manila envelope. "Don't open it now. You can count it later."

"What the fuck?" Stuart said, confused, tossing the envelope back to him.

"Well. It was either that, or . . . you know."

"No, I don't know. What are you talking about?"

"C'mon. Let's not pretend you don't understand. You've been kind of a prick to Josie, right?"

"Look, I'm not going to be threatened—"

"You catch on quick." Moe shoved the envelope back in Stuart's lap. "This is because you enjoy feeling like a big shot and bullying your ex. And you know what Josie found out? You naughty boy, you withdrew money from your client's escrow account to pay for that fancy vacation last year to Maui."

"That's bullshit. How would you know that?"

He tossed a xeroxed copy of the bank transfer on Stuart's lap. "Just a suggestion. You need a better cybersecurity system."

Damp circles were forming under Stuart's armpits as he closed his eyes and leaned back into the seat.

"So what are we talking about here?" Stuart asked.

"You're okay with a little extortion, right?"

Stuart looked at him in silence and then sighed. "How much?"

"Three hundred grand to start. And more if you play nice."

Stuart considered this. "How nice?"

"The kid goes home with you temporarily and then moves back here in January when the semester is over. Just like you agreed."

"Four hundred," Stuart countered.

"So, the eunuch has balls after all." Moe chuckled but his eyes stayed fixed on Stuart's face. "That's it for now, asshole. Take it or take it."

Chapter 55

Christmas came and went with little fanfare. For the next ten days, Josie went into the office as usual. From all outward appearances, the trauma was past and her routine had returned. Her daughter was safely back in LA. It had been agreed that once Billie moved back to Vegas, Stuart would have reasonable visitation rights and some vacations with her.

But meanwhile, Josie's days were uneventful. She scheduled daily (very expensive) phone conferences with the DC attorneys, and endured long, contentious meetings with the union. She prepared documents for the upcoming settlement, and tried to appear as though she had moved on from the terror that had upended her life.

Lionel was watching and listening, of *that* she was certain. And she was watching him too. Her first morning back in the office after Billie had left for LA, Lionel approached her and expressed his sympathies.

"Must have been a terrible shock," he said, feigning concern.

"Yes, it was." Josie busied herself with the papers on her desk, not wanting to look up for fear he'd read the rage in her eyes.

"Hopefully we'll catch the bastards who did it. Let me know if I can do anything."

"Oh, I will," Josie said as he left. Enjoy your last few days, you fucking thug, she thought.

Later that morning, Cindy poked her head into Josie's office and nodded toward the door. She walked out first, and Josie followed a few minutes later. They took the elevator down to the gambling floor.

"We need to talk," Cindy said, looking at her with tired eyes. They kept moving through the floor until they were at the far end, behind a bank of noisy slots.

"Smile and laugh as though we're telling funny jokes," Cindy said, glancing up at the cameras. The slots were clanging away.

"I knew your father so well. Anyone who hurt his grandchild would have 'been found floating,' as he liked to say. Smile while I'm talking to you," Cindy reminded her, motioning for a cocktail waitress. "Hey Patty, can you get us a couple of coffees?"

Cindy turned to Josie. "Now, we're simply two colleagues on a break having a laugh."

She nodded toward a man who Josie recognized—one of Lionel's thugs, the same creep she had noticed her first day of work.

"Let's move," Cindy said, slinging an arm around Josie's shoulder. Both women smiled and took their coffees to the bar lounge, where horse races thundered away on five large screens. Josie grabbed a small table under one of the speakers and sat down.

"I know Lionel was involved," Josie whispered, the screen illuminating her face. "This was his warning."

"You're not wrong," Cindy said, taking pains to look as cheerful and chatty as a woman at the local bingo club. "He's dangerous."

"What else do you know?"

"Every few weeks he leaves the office late at night with boxes. He says he's taking work home, but he gets one of his guys to help him. The boxes are heavy. And paperwork is not part of Lionel's job anyway."

Josie had seen those exact boxes and knew they were filled with mountains of cash.

"So, you think Lionel is skimming the skimmers?" Josie murmured.

"I do believe that's what is going on."

"When does he move the boxes?"

"It varies. But it's usually before the regular shipments go out around the fifteenth of every month. And always in the middle of the night. I'm sure your brother doesn't know Lionel is double-dealing."

"So that would be next week sometime. Can you call me if you hear it's going down?"

"I'll try but I'm not here in the middle of the night."

"I want him dead," Josie said, her teeth clenched in a false grin.

Cindy gave her a genuine smile of approval. "You *are* your father's daughter."

Chapter 56

Josie immediately spotted the feds parked across the street as she pulled up to her house. FBI agent Gavin was sitting in the front seat of his government-issue sedan, checking his phone. He and his partner were about as inconspicuous as two gunners in an armored tank. She pulled into her driveway, sat there for a moment thinking, then walked over to their car.

"Waiting for me?" she asked.

"How'd you guess?" Gavin said, opening the driver's side window and exhaling a stream of smoke from his cigarette. He was juggling an open can of Sprite between his knees and there was a bag of pork rinds on the dashboard. The other guy had a military haircut and cold blue eyes. Josie could see his pistol wedged into the waistband of his jeans.

"Well, it's obvious I missed happy hour, so what do you want?" Josie asked, leaning into the window on Gavin's side.

"You ready to make a deal? We need your help, and it's obvious you need our protection. How's your daughter, by the way?"

"As you well know, she's back in LA. But this isn't about her, is it?"

"We're looking for the usual—you know what I mean. Offshore bank accounts, wire transfers, money-laundering schemes, shell companies, names of their partners—anything that would help us put them away."

"And my brother. Is he looking at hard time?" Josie asked.

"We can arrange something."

"I'll bet. Let me think about it. Don't call me. I'll call you. And if you follow me again, no deal."

Josie watched as the agents started up their car, then disappeared around the corner. When they were out of sight, she walked into her kitchen, picked out a nice Chablis and a wedge of Brie and headed over to Flora's house. Josie knew that Cassie was still upset because Billie refused to speak to her after the kidnapping. Her daughter had totally ignored all of Cassie's calls, and when Cassie came to see her to say goodbye, Billie wouldn't even come out of her room. She didn't know that the kidnapping had nothing to do with the girl's shoplifting, and Josie hadn't wanted to tell her until after the danger had passed. When Billie came back to visit, she would try to get the girls together.

Flora gave her a big hug and seemed happy to see her. Cassie was upstairs, but she called down to say hello as well.

"I'm sorry about Billie's behavior," Josie said. "I'm sure, in time, she'll come around."

"Oh God. Don't be sorry. Jesus. After all you've been through? Cigarette?" Flora asked, as she led Josie to the small living room couch, which was covered with a basket of folded laundry, her knitting needles, balls of tangled wool and a box of clipped coupons from the local paper.

Josie plucked a cigarette from the pack and sat down, pushing the clothes basket aside. "Why would they take Billie?" Flora asked. "It doesn't make sense."

"Well, the cops think it was for the ransom. But I'm pretty sure I know who did it."

"Did you tell them?"

"I can't prove anything, and these people are tough. They're professionals."

"I'm not understanding. I mean, why would they do this to you? To your family?"

"It's about the casino. And honestly, I could use your help."

Josie explained that she needed Flora to switch to the graveyard shift just for the following week. Flora could make up some plausible excuse about needing to take care of an elderly relative during the day, and then take the night shift, which cleaned the executive suites. She was to call Josie the minute she noticed anyone taking things in or out of the offices, no matter what the hour or what they were moving. Josie had purchased two burner phones, one for herself and one for Flora.

"To be safe, from now on, we can't talk at my house or on my phone," Josie said. "I'm convinced they're listening, and they might even be following me." Josie nodded at the burner. "Call on this phone and don't say your name."

"Should I be scared?" Flora asked, tucking the burner into her laundry basket.

"Probably. I am," Josie said honestly. "You don't have to do this, you know."

"I want to help. I mean, after all you've done." Flora looked away from Josie and out her living room window. "I've been through much worse in my life."

Josie understood, and she didn't pry for details. Vegas was not an easy town to make a decent living. She was sure that Flora's childhood dreams did not include cleaning other people's dirty hotel rooms. Josie knew what some of these rooms looked like after people checked out. Once a housekeeper told her that she opened the door to the hotel room and just started crying. People can be such pigs.

Josie left Flora's house deep in thought, with renewed conviction. One step at a time. This was war.

Chapter 57

Josie arrived home to find Sunny sitting in her living room, surrounded by piles of designer dresses that still had price tags attached. She was dressed in her riding clothes but had made herself comfortable on the couch, slipping off her boots, untucking her white blouse. She was talking on her cell to Trent about a two-year-old filly from Smithwood Farms who was coming up for auction that month. Apparently, their trainer had a problem with the horse's hind legs.

Sunny had been on a buying trip to New York when the kidnapping took place. She rushed home when she heard and then offered to keep Josie company after Billie went back to LA. Josie appreciated having someone else in the house but was too exhausted after work to sit and chat. Still, she tried to be polite. Tonight, Sunny had packed a few things from the new evening wear collection in her trunk. It was destined for the casino shop the next day, but Sunny figured she would bring in a few pieces to distract her sister for a while.

"Pick one out. Keep them all. I don't care," Sunny said, giving Josie a hug. Each dress had to be worth at least two grand, some even more.

Josie glanced at the clothes spread out on a chair. Everything was black and wildly expensive. The tags said Chanel, Dior, Lanvin, Armani and Dolce & Gabbana.

"Please, Sunny," Josie said, "I'm grateful, really I am. But I'm just not in the mood."

"Of course, I understand. What's going on? Are they any closer to finding the kidnappers?"

"Not really," Josie said, looking away.

"But what did they say?"

"Not much. It's really been a slow investigation," she said, hoping to shut down the conversation.

Josie knew that her house was bugged, and she wasn't about to reveal anything. Also, *anything* she told Sunny was repeated immediately to Trent. Even if Sunny promised not to tell him, she told him anyway. It was one of *those* marriages. Josie didn't know if Sunny was as devoted to Trent as she used to be, considering her extracurricular activities, but she couldn't trust her sister with any information. No matter how many fucking dresses she gave her from New York. It was sad, really. They could pretend they were close, but they never confided in each other, even when the situation was dire.

"Why don't we offer a reward?" Sunny asked. "For Christ's sake, it's been two weeks and they have nothing?"

"We might . . ." Josie said vaguely, but then was cut off by the doorbell.

Josie opened the door to find Rob holding two large brown bags that smelled like a Chinese restaurant.

He stepped inside, and couldn't help but notice the array of gowns draped over the living room furniture.

"You don't have to get all dressed up for me," he joked, giving her a quick kiss on the cheek.

"I didn't know you were dropping by."

Sunny stood by the couch, looking perplexed.

"I'm not staying," Rob told her. "I just thought you might want some food from China Mama's, our new place downstairs."

"Are fortune cookies included?" Josie asked.

"Yep. But I already read yours. An irresistible man will be coming into your life."

Josie laughed despite herself. "Sunny, meet Rob McCarthy."

Josie took the bags from his hand and went to the kitchen.

There was enough food for an army. She'd have leftovers for days. Sunny followed her to the kitchen.

"So?" she asked quietly.

"So nothing," Josie answered. "Just a friend."

"Well, I'm going home to my 'friend' and leaving you alone with yours."

Sunny put the dresses back in their wardrobe bags, intentionally leaving the black velvet Dolce with a deep V-neck and a slit up one side. Maybe Josie would look at it later.

"How are you, really?" Rob asked, after Sunny was gone.

"It's been a rough few weeks," Josie said, cutting him off. "I could use some air."

She took his hand and led him outside.

"Okay, then." He popped an egg roll in his mouth and followed her into the yard.

"We can't talk in the house," she whispered.

"Shit. That too?"

"Yes, I'm sure of it."

They stood there without speaking for a few awkward minutes.

"If you really want to know," she said, "I never dreamed it would come to this. Going after my child. Good God. It's all my fault."

"How is that your fault, Josie? In what way?"

"You tell me," she said, studying his face. It was obvious he knew something dodgy was happening at the Jackpot, but she was not about to give him details—certainly not about the secret room. The fact was, she poked the bear. And the bear struck back.

"I think I might have some information . . ." he began. "In reference to your 'theoretical' questions the other night."

Josie folded her arms. "I'm listening . . ."

"You know the Five Families in New York still exist, right? They don't have the power they had years ago. Too many of the bosses went to jail—along with some guys lower on the ladder who would've taken over. The FBI has tried to completely shut them down, but they're still alive and well. They're into drug dealing, loan sharking, extortion . . . all the nice things they used to do. But they're much more willing to cooperate with the feds. The RICO laws have made it easier to get convictions because, essentially, the mob has become a cage full of canaries. And this is where you fit in."

"I do?"

"Yes. One of them sang—a Staten Island boy. Gambassi's right-hand guy."

"And . . ." Josie prompted.

"And he confirmed what you already know."

"Which is?"

"These are your guys. The Gambassi family. The boss was gunned down about five years ago outside a christening in Brooklyn, but his nephew Bobby took over. Bobby is the one who's calling the shots. He'd been groomed by the old man, but if you saw him walking down the street, you wouldn't look twice. Went to a good college, lives in a nice house, refined tastes, but he's a cold-blooded killer."

"So how did they become my problem?" Josie asked.

"They can smell an opening—and your brother gave them a big one."

Now she understood how the feds knew so much. One of Gambassi's guys had spilled the whole operation, and they were just waiting to get enough evidence to indict. And this wasn't just about skimming at the Jackpot. This was about trying to bring down the whole family.

"I won't ask you how you got all this information."

"And I wouldn't tell you."

The words "refined tastes" stuck in her mind. She'd be willing to bet that Bobby Gambassi was an art collector, which would explain the paintings wrapped and labeled in the secret room. There were some things that Rob didn't need to know.

Josie shivered. Rob wrapped his jacket around her shoulders.

"My father taught us that family was sacred," Josie said. "He wanted us to stick together. It was an 'us against the world' mentality. But in reality, the unit is only as strong as the members. And we have a few weak links. Doesn't every family?"

"I wouldn't know. I'm an only child."

"Lucky you."

"Not really." Rob's face was thoughtful. "All the pressure was on me to succeed. At everything."

"Well, I think you nailed that."

"I was always jealous of big families."

"Ah, the fantasy of the big, happy family. I don't think it exists."

"Don't burst my bubble." He laughed as they walked back into the house.

It was Rob's first time at her place. He looked around and spotted the black dress draped over the sofa. He fingered the velvet and ran his hand down the slit in the skirt. Then he looked at the price tag.

"Tell you what. Why don't you put this on?" Rob whispered in her ear. "Then I can take it off you."

Chapter 58

The week after the kidnapping Flora was standing at the entrance to the Jackpot's executive suite, leaning on her trolley. She slipped out her security card and pressed it to the controlled access point. The door unlocked with a click. She rolled her cart inside, leaned over and placed the bright yellow "Housekeeper in Service" sign on the floor.

The place was dead quiet at midnight, as it had been the last two nights. Flora switched on the lights and looked around. She couldn't believe she put up with the graveyard shift all these years. Eight to four was a gift, and she'd always be grateful to Josie for helping her get back to a normal life. Flora didn't mind doing her a favor; she owed Josie, and Cassie owed Billie.

Flora was emptying the trash cans in the front office when she heard deep male voices in the hallway. One of them moved her sign, and then called out, "Hello? Anybody here?"

"Housekeeping," Flora responded.

She peeked her head out and saw two men walking toward the back office. One was tall and heavyset, wearing a suit with an open shirt and a gold chain. He seemed like he was in a hurry, his expression tense and hard. The other guy was younger and kept his head down as he wheeled an empty dolly across the hall.

"Lionel Barrick, head of security," he barked at Flora, his eyes flicking over her. "We're doing some work here. Why don't you come back later?"

"Okay. No problem, Mr. Barrick," Flora said, happy to leave. This guy seemed too keyed-up, and she had no desire to be alone in a room with him.

Flora pushed her cart back outside the suite, walked past the elevators and called Josie.

"Head of security just came in and kicked me out," she whispered, describing the two men, and adding that one of them was pushing a dolly.

That was all Josie needed to hear. She threw on her sweats, grabbed her pistol and jumped in a Honda sedan she had rented for this very purpose.

Josie hoped her hunch was correct. Cindy had told her that this was the week the transfer usually happened. Why else would Lionel bring a dolly to the suite in the middle of the night? He had to be taking boxes out. She raced out of her driveway, and arrived outside the Jackpot's executive garage in ten minutes flat. She parked the Honda and waited for Lionel to pull out onto the street.

Josie thought maybe she made a mistake not asking Sam to come with her, but there wasn't time. This whole thing might be a bad idea. She felt a headache forming in her right temple but the moment of indecision passed as Lionel pulled out of the garage.

He was hunched over the wheel of a Ford Ranger, and he made a quick U-turn on Fourth. Josie stayed about three cars back, her hands gripping the steering wheel so tight she had cramps in her fingers. It was dark, and the oncoming headlights of passing cars temporarily blinded her. The good thing about Vegas was that the roads were busy 24/7. The city that never sleeps. Slim chance he'd notice her.

Lionel was moving along with the traffic. At one point he signaled with his left blinker and stopped at a 7-Eleven. Josie pulled into the gas station next door and waited. She watched him come out with a six-pack and light up a cigarette. Then he got back in his car and headed down Las Vegas Boulevard. Josie eased between two trucks as he jumped on the interstate and drove toward US-95 North.

She hunkered down, always making sure she was at least a car or two behind him. Where the hell was he going? He was driving too fast and, at one point, she watched him drift perilously close to the shoulder, then whip back into his lane. This is good, she thought. He's tired. He won't be that focused on surrounding cars.

She turned the radio on briefly, flipping the dial from a late-night jazz station to the Christian radio hour featuring someone reading an essay called "Why I'm Lost." Too much noise. She turned it off and cracked the window to let cold air blast her face. It was now nearly 3 a.m.

As they neared the Nevada Test Site, she remembered her second-grade field trip to Yucca Flats, where thousands of nuclear explosions had been detonated on the open desert floor, as if the desert were some worthless wasteland. She had been to many strange places, but none as eerie as this otherworldly setting.

Her father used to tell her that in the fifties, it was a big attraction for the tourists to stand on the roof of the Jackpot and watch the mushroom cloud blossom in the sky. They would sip mimosas as explosions vaporized huge craters in the earth, peeled paint off buildings and turned sand into glass. The winds carried lethal doses of radioactive fallout to small towns in Utah, whose unsuspecting citizens would later see cancer clusters in their children and their children's children.

The miles flew by. Josie hoped Lionel would get to where he was going before sunrise. As he veered toward the 160 East, it suddenly occurred to her that the only place he could be going was Pahrump—a dead-end town that wouldn't arouse any suspicion from New York.

He pulled off the 160 onto Carpenter Canyon Road, the only car taking that exit, so Josie stayed on the highway and sped right past him. She took the next off-ramp, made an abrupt U-turn, and headed back to Lionel's exit. Now what? There were no cars in either direction. She turned north hoping that was the route he took. After a few minutes, she spotted his truck moving toward the mountains. She slowed down and pulled off the shoulder. A few yards ahead was the entrance to what used to be a park. The wooden gate was hanging off its hinges near a sign pointing toward the grave of an Indian warrior. There was also a rusted-out metal swing set and slide that looked like it hadn't been used for years.

After Lionel disappeared from view, she headed back on the road. The houses were spaced far apart and she was guessing he was going to one of them. She passed an old barn where a mangy horse stood by a fence, and a rotting mattress had been left in a ditch by the road. A few of the houses had off-road vehicles parked in the front yard.

Josie slowly drove up the road toward the Spring Mountain Range finding nothing. She went all the way to the foothills, then circled back. And there it was—Lionel's truck—partially hidden by a tin shed and parked next to a small white-framed house.

Josie pulled in behind an abandoned horse trailer. Satisfied that she couldn't be seen, she turned off the motor and waited.

She was lucky she found the trailer to hide behind because the entire area was flat as hell, with scrub brush, low chamisa and tumbleweeds. The wind had kicked up, and there was dust and rubble everywhere—a barren wilderness, a no-way-out kind of place.

As the clouds lifted and the sky turned pink, she heard echoes of guns firing at the local Pahrump firing range. Exhausted, she rubbed her eyes, put on her sunglasses, pulled the seat back and settled in. Now she would wait. But she didn't want to get too comfortable and fall asleep, so she rifled through her purse for a pack of cigarettes. Sometimes she just liked to smell them. She didn't dare turn on the radio.

She sat there as the sun rose in the sky. The thought occurred to her that this was the world her father lived in before she was sent away. He had to deal with these people. And sometimes there was only one way to deal with them.

She glanced up at the house. Still no action. She pulled out her phone and called Sam.

"Hey, I just wanted you to know where I am in case I never come back."

"Josie?" Sam said. She could tell she woke him up—his voice was faint and scratchy.

"Can you hear me?" Josie asked. Then the line went dead. "Hello? Are you there?"

Shit. No reception. She was on her own. She knew she couldn't stay here forever. What if Lionel saw her? A few moments later, Josie watched as Lionel's door opened. He took a dolly out of the garage and proceeded to load it with boxes from his truck. Then he wheeled it around the yard and seemed to disappear into a giant hole. Josie took it all in. He repeated this several times and then lifted two brown-paper-covered frames from the front seat of his truck, carefully carrying them down the rabbit hole.

He surfaced one more time, holding a can of beer in one hand and a set of keys in the other. He bent over and it looked like he was locking something up. Then he retrieved the dolly and wheeled it to the garage. Josie held her breath and slumped down in the seat as he finally got in his truck, closed the door and drove right past her hiding spot.

Josie sat there, motionless, until his car was out of sight. She was hungry, thirsty and terrified. She wanted to see where Lionel stashed the boxes, but her instincts told her she should get the hell out of there. She looked up and down the road, seeing nothing. Then she made her move.

She threw her pistol in her coat pocket, scrambled out of the car, then walked through the scrub brush to the side of the house where Lionel had disappeared. Nothing looked out of the ordinary. Yet something was here. And then she saw the glint of metal reflecting the rising sun's rays. There was a partially concealed round steel hatch in the ground. She tugged on it, but it didn't budge.

No matter. Her plan had worked. She felt the flush of victory. The son of a bitch had a buried vault in Pahrump.

Chapter 59

Before Josie got on the interstate, she decided to stop somewhere and rest. Even after she left Lionel's place and everything had gone as planned, she struggled with this overwhelming sense of dread. She kept checking her rearview mirror, almost as if she were steeling herself for some sort of ambush. She just couldn't shake the jitters.

The wind had picked up, but the morning was clear and cold. The desert shimmered with early morning dew. The beauty of the hostile environment—one she'd always loved—calmed her nerves. She took a right, down Pahrump Valley Boulevard and pulled into the Roadhouse Casino, "Open 24/7."

In a way, she loved these small-town ma-and-pa joints. This one was painted bright red and surrounded by tall palm trees planted in the cement parking lot. It was a welcome oasis in the middle of nowhere—like stepping back in time. Her father had started out in a place like this on Fremont Street. These neighborhood businesses still did well, offering just the basics—gambling, air-conditioning and cheap food.

She scanned the area for Lionel's truck. No sign of it. The parking lot was pretty empty—it was just after 8 a.m. As she entered the casino, a cloud of cigarette smoke wafted toward her, along with the jarring noise of the slots. Even at this hour, the locals sat under the glowing lights giving it "one last try," before they headed for the breakfast buffet.

Josie stopped in the bathroom, glanced in the mirror, wet a paper towel with cold water and pressed it against her face. Jesus, she looked beat. Her eyes were bloodshot, and her hair was tangled in a messy ponytail. The seat of her sweatpants was damp, and there were sand burrs stuck to her shoes and socks. She rummaged through her purse for her lipstick. A plan slowly hatched in her brain. Rob had said, let the mob get rid of its own, and now she could clearly see how to do that. It was clean and it just might work. Finally she had some ammunition. She ordered a black coffee to go and walked back to the car.

Before she left, Josie tried Sam once more and he picked up right away. She knew she had to proceed carefully, deciding who she should talk to and who she shouldn't. Everything had to fall into place or the plan would collapse.

"Where are you?" he asked.

"Can you meet me in a few hours at the ranch?" she answered evasively.

"Josie, what's going on?"

"Just stay there, okay?"

She got back on the road and dialed Moe. Turned out he had some information. A name she'd retrieved from the trash can in the locked room was a "made" man from New York. Part of the Gambassi family.

"That makes sense." Moe just validated what Rob had told her.

"Do I need to remind you that you're playing with fire?"

"I'm well aware," she told him. "Can you meet me at the ranch later today?"

As she neared Vegas, Josie heard an enormous boom like a clap of thunder. Her car windows rattled as a pair of silver fighter jets from Nellis Air Force Base streaked against the sky, breaking the sound barrier. Another pair of jets followed, the shock waves hitting her Honda like supersonic bullets. All things considered, she hoped this wasn't prophetic.

Chapter 60

Josie spent the rest of the drive with her car windows open, sipping her coffee and switching the dial from Jesus Radio to KXNT, the local news station. She let the wind blow her hair, hoping the chilly breeze would keep her awake. It had been a long time since she'd pulled an all-nighter, and she still had a full day ahead of her. Sam had told her that nicotine pills jolt the brain like a hit of cocaine, so she stopped at a twenty-four-hour pharmacy and bought a bottle that was behind a locked glass cabinet. She popped two pills, then grabbed another coffee to go.

Josie's scalp started prickling, a side effect of the nicotine, and the coffee put her on high alert. She had finally figured out how to get rid of Lionel, but there were still a few loose ends. If she was to make this work, she had to move fast. She called Flora right after her conversation with Sam and Moe, and asked if she could meet her in an hour.

They met at one of those old-time coffee shops you hardly see anymore. It was about a mile off Fremont Street, in a strip mall with a nail salon on one side and a pawnshop on the other. Half the restaurant was occupied by a row of torn red plastic booths, the other half by a cracked, yellow-tinged Formica counter that had seen better days. On the wall were framed signed photos of a few dead Vegas lounge performers. A waitress with a weathered face and a smoker's cough handed Josie a menu. Flora was already seated in the booth.

They spent a few minutes catching up and then Josie got to the point.

"Would you mind staying on graveyard?"

Flora hesitated a moment. She hated that shift.

"How much longer?" she asked.

"Not that long," Josie reassured her. "I hate to ask, but it's important."

"Same as before? I call you if there's action in the suite?"

"That's it."

"Should I bring my gun?"

"You have a gun?" Josie asked, surprised.

"Of course. I have a 38."

"Special?"

"Yep. It's the best gun for women. Less kick."

"To be honest, you're not going to need it. Just act completely normal and get out of there as soon as you see the men arrive."

"Got it," Flora said as she pulled her gun out of her purse. "See. It has a pink handle."

After the meeting, Josie drove directly to the ranch, where Sam and Moe were waiting. They were sitting outside near the barn, drinking Sam's three-hundred-dollar bottle of French burgundy and swapping tales about the good old days.

Moe seemed a little overwhelmed by the whole scene—he hadn't been at the ranch since the place had been renovated. He glanced at the black jet helicopter, the huge, rock-lined pool with the waterfall gently cascading down one side, the ten-foot equestrian sculptures and the corral where a few rodeo horses were being exercised by a uniformed trainer. An enormous Christmas wreath with a red bow still hung on the barn door. Twinkly lights were threaded through the trees and were shining on the driveway.

Sam wasn't hungover, and there was no sign of Crystal. Josie didn't dare ask him where she was, hoping Crystal had moved out.

Josie's plan was dangerous. She couldn't tell them exactly what night it would happen, and she wasn't even sure it would work. They'd have to get pictures of Lionel moving the stolen boxes of cash and send the photos to New York. Let the mob get rid of the mob. That was her mantra now. Lionel was greedy and Josie would figure out a way to get him back to Pahrump. They'd all have to be ready as soon as Flora called her from the suite.

Sam told Josie that her plan was bat-shit crazy, but he was all in. Moe was more circumspect.

"There's a million things that can go wrong," he warned.

"I know," Josie said with a smile. "But there's a couple million reasons for you to help us out, if you get my drift."

Chapter 61

Growing up, it was an unspoken rule in the King household that whatever happened at the ranch was never discussed outside the ranch. Lying was a part of their culture. It was a matter of self-preservation.

Josie called Lionel at ten the next morning. They hadn't said two civil words since the kidnapping. Now, though, what she really wanted to do was blow his head off and bury him in the desert but she made her voice sound calm and confident.

"We need to talk," Josie told him.

"Yeah?" His voice was even and disinterested.

"I want to discuss some ground rules." Josie could picture him sitting at his desk, his big, ugly face unsmiling. "I'll be at the saloon next door at three."

"What if I'm busy?" Now Lionel sounded irritated.

"Wait at the booth in the back. I have something you'll want to hear."

"I'm not going to some fucking bar. Just tell me now."

"Lionel, we do it my way or no info. Trust me, you're going to want to hear it. It's about New York."

There was a brief silence. She could tell he was mulling it over. He was trying to figure out her angle. He knew she had been in the security room. Maybe she found something. Maybe not.

"I'll give you fifteen minutes," he conceded.

"That's all I need," Josie agreed.

The Pioneer saloon was dark and mostly empty. There were a couple of women sitting at the bar, nursing cocktails, and a few guys playing pool in the back. The music, which was normally blaring, was turned to country. Some faux spruce garlands hung from the rafters, a leftover attempt at Christmas cheer.

Josie took a seat in one of the back booths. Lionel was late, of course. He still thought he had the power, and he was reminding her of it by making her wait. He found Josie in the booth drinking a beer and slid in across from her.

"This place is fucking dead. Maybe the health department found rat droppings in the kitchen," Lionel said.

"I'll tell you what they didn't find. Bugs." She slid a Corona over to his side of the table. "I ordered you a beer."

"What's so important?" he asked, taking a swig off the head of the beer and slouching back in the seat. Okay, he thought. So she knows about the bugs. Who gives a fuck.

"One of my contacts told me something that might interest you," Josie began.

"Get to the point," he snapped.

"Okay. You know that room where you keep all your souvenirs . . ."

"I'm listening," Lionel said, his expression changing ever so slightly.

"How long do you think you and Frank can keep this up before someone from New York starts taking their own inventory?"

"I don't know what the fuck you're talking about." But his eyes narrowed and she could almost see the wheels begin to turn in his head.

"I happen to have a source who tells me New York is sending out another guy to replace you."

"That's bullshit," he scoffed. "If I were you, I'd keep my head down and stop this crap right now."

"Okay," Josie said, finishing her beer and casually motioning for the check. No reaction, no hysterics. She was actually quite good at it.

"And if this is true, why would you care?" Lionel said, staring her straight in the eyes.

"Because Frank is my brother, and if this shit gets serious, I don't want him to blow up in his car. You get it?"

Lionel stood up, finished his beer and slammed the bottle on the table. Josie could tell she had gotten to him. If she was right, his next move would be to haul more boxes to the vault. He wouldn't wait until the fifteenth to make his move. And neither would she.

Chapter 62

Josie's burner phone woke her around 2 a.m. Lionel must be moving boxes. She slipped out of bed, trying not to wake Rob, who had dropped by with dinner from Desperados' Michelin-starred Italian restaurant. He joked that he could bring take-out from three more of his restaurants. It was his culinary bargaining chip. Her head was resting on his chest, and their legs were intertwined. It was the first night in a long time she had actually fallen asleep early. For the last several nights, she had lain awake expecting this call.

The plan was for Josie to contact Sam and he would call Moe. They agreed to meet on the corner of Mesquite and Las Vegas Boulevard, near the on-ramp of US-95. She hadn't considered the consequences of Rob sleeping over, or what he would say when she dashed out in the middle of the night.

"Hey, baby," she whispered. "I have to do a thing."

"What? Now?" His voice was groggy with sleep.

"Yes. Sorry. Go back to sleep. Just lock the door when you leave."

"You're joking," he mumbled, but he rolled over and fell right back to sleep.

Josie put on her jeans and sweatshirt, and then grabbed the backpack hanging on a hook by the front door. She had packed an old Nikon with a zoom lens, along with a few bottles of water. She also pulled on her hiking boots and grabbed gardening gloves and bolt cutters. She walked outside and called Sam, who sounded out of it, as usual, and

Josie was concerned he wouldn't make it. She had planned ahead for this, and threw two cans of Red Bull in her backpack. "Red Bull Gives You Wings" was the company slogan, and that's what she needed. The massive jolt of caffeine would wake him the fuck up. Just before she left, she loaded her pistol and placed it in the backpack as well.

Josie and Sam parked their cars in an empty lot and jumped into Moe's tank of a truck. He mostly used it to haul logs from the forest to heat his house, and there were wood shavings and brush all over the front and rear seats. It was freezing, and Josie put on another layer of fleece. The two men wore parkas and knit hats.

"What's the address?" Moe asked. Josie noticed the gun in his waistband. A couple of shotguns lay across the back seat.

"I don't know, but I remember the exit and I'll recognize the house."

There wasn't much conversation. Moe asked what they'd do if it was a false alarm and Lionel didn't show. Did she have a plan B?

"He'll show," said Josie confidently. "He's got the boxes. Where else is he gonna go?"

"Okay, what if he's already there? How are you going to get the photos without him seeing you?" asked Sam, finishing off a Red Bull and crushing the can with his fist.

"It's not rocket science. We park the truck. I've got a zoom lens and we take pictures," she said as she pulled her camera out of her backpack.

Moe glanced at her camera.

"What is this shit?" He frowned.

"It's a Nikon."

"And you'll get a nice picture of nothing at night. I brought my own equipment—thirty-five-millimeter, telephoto lens, high-speed film and tripod. We'll pick the spot, I'll set up my remote, dial the shutter speed to, say, two seconds. And we're good to go."

"I don't think we need a tripod," said Josie.

"You want photos you can use or a blurry mess?" Moe insisted. "I just tweak my camera settings, adjust the shutter speed. I won't bore you with the five-hundred rule."

“Jesus. Why don’t we just fucking shoot him?” Sam blurted, only half-joking.

“Because we’re not murderers,” Josie told him dryly. She was fairly sure she meant it.

They hit the 160 East around 3 a.m., driving through the outskirts of Pahrump. Everything was pitch-black, no streetlights, and Josie squinted through the window searching for the road that Lionel had taken. As they swept around a curve, she finally spotted the turnoff coming up on the right—Carpenter Canyon Road.

They traveled down the dusty road for a while, and then pulled up behind the abandoned horse trailer. Just like last time, Lionel’s truck was half-hidden behind the shed.

“Bingo. He’s here. I knew it,” Josie said, grabbing her gun from her backpack and putting it in her pocket.

Moe calmly collected his gear and zipped up his parka. Then he pulled a shotgun from the back seat. Crickets chirped outside and a crescent moon shone dimly through the night clouds.

“So where is the vault, exactly?” Moe whispered to Josie.

“I have to point it out.” She pulled out her small flashlight. “Follow me. But we can’t get too close and let’s hope he hasn’t already made the transfer.”

“Gimme that! No flashlight.” Moe shook his head.

“I’ll cover the back,” Sam said, as if he were part of a SWAT team.

“Stay in the driver’s seat,” Moe ordered.

“But—” Sam protested.

Moe cut him off: “Don’t talk. Don’t think. Just do what the fuck I tell you. Are we clear?”

“What is this, Hitler Youth?” Sam muttered as he turned back to the truck.

It was freezing as Moe trudged behind Josie with his equipment. She stopped a few yards past the trailer, and they both looked toward the house. One of the porch lights was on as well as a lamp in the front room.

"This is the best angle," she whispered.

Moe set the camera on the tripod and lay the shotgun at his feet.

"I don't see any action," he said softly as he moved the dials around on the lens and connected the remote to the shutter. Then he backed up into the bushes next to Josie.

"He may already be in the vault or the garage. That's where he keeps the dolly."

They stood there like sentries in the dark, but heard nothing. Then there was the sound of a car door slamming shut. The metallic noise echoed through the yard. Josie felt a surge of adrenaline and instinctively reached for her gun.

"There he goes," Moe said, watching Lionel leave the truck with the dolly stacked with two boxes. Click. Click. Click.

"He's moving toward the vault—can you get that?" Josie asked.

"Yeah. Got it." Click. Click. Click.

"Zoom in so we know it's him."

"It's him all right." Click. Click. Click. "Clear as day."

They watched as the dim figure rolled the boxes across the grass. Lionel stopped over the vault, opened the hatch, unloaded the boxes and disappeared with them, one by one. Click. Click. Click.

"Down the rabbit hole!" Josie whispered.

"Motherfucker," Moe said quietly, with a hint of admiration. "Great way to hide your stolen shit. How the hell did he ever find this place?"

"What's going on?" Sam asked, getting out of the truck and walking toward them. "Do you have him?"

"Shhh!" Josie said. "I think so."

Suddenly the perimeter security lights flashed on. Moe, Sam and Josie jumped behind the trailer. There was only one way out, and for a minute they thought they'd been made. They stood stock-still and listened, attuned to every sound. Moe crept out to retrieve his shotgun and tripod. But then a car with brights roared up the driveway, the thick gravel shooting from under its wheels. A guy got out, holding a high-powered flashlight, and they heard him call Lionel's name. Lionel climbed out of the vault, empty-handed, to greet him.

The two exchanged a few words, and the new guy picked up the dolly and wheeled it back to the truck. More boxes appeared. Jesus, thought Josie. Lionel was a greedy son of a bitch. There were twice as many boxes as last time.

The men disappeared into the hole for what seemed like hours. Sam climbed back into the truck, and Josie could see him take a swig from a flask and then light up. Moe walked over, reached inside the window and pinched out the cigarette.

"No smoking!"

Josie was bone-tired and her toes were frozen, but then she had a thought. What if they waited until both men left and then tried to get into the vault? She hadn't had much luck before, but now they had the means to see what was inside. They were so close.

"Looks like they're hibernating down there. Got enough?" Sam asked Josie.

"No, I need shots of what's inside."

"It's fucking freezing out here," Sam said.

"Josie's right. We need more evidence," Moe agreed.

"Yeah. So he's rolling boxes. So what?" Josie added. "He could talk his way out of it."

"Okay." Sam relented. "Fine by me. Let's throw the motherfucker under the bus."

Chapter 63

They didn't have to wait long. The hatch opened after about fifteen minutes, and Lionel and his sidekick climbed out and wheeled the empty dolly back to the garage. Josie could just about make out the figure of Lionel handing the guy something in a paper bag. He went back to lock the metal hatch. Josie watched him stretch, rolling his neck and shoulders back and forth. Moving those heavy boxes was hard work. He looked around casually one more time and got in his truck. The two vehicles followed each other out of the driveway and disappeared into the dark. Josie shook Sam awake. He mumbled and closed his eyes again. She shined the flashlight right in his face.

"We're on," she said. "Let's see what Lionel has stashed."

"Jesus! Get that thing out of my face. Is he gone?"

"Just."

Sam took one more slug from his flask, grabbed his gun and climbed out of the car. He headed for the yard, but Moe stepped in front of him.

"Let's wait a little longer," Moe said, "in case he forgot his toothbrush and comes back."

Moe put his camera in a bag and slung it over his shoulder. It was almost dawn when they finally made their move. They walked toward the house through the scrub so as not to trigger the security lights or camera in the driveway. Then Moe took his shotgun and blew them out just for good measure.

They circled back to the side yard and stood over the vault. Sam pulled out his .44 Magnum and aimed at the lock. At last he was wide awake, Josie thought.

"This baby could blow a man's head off," he boasted as he blasted the lock twice. The crack of the bullet echoed across the highway. One of the pins on the lock was blown upward, and the bottom half was dented, but the lock was still frozen shut.

"What the fuck?" Sam cursed. Moe just stood there and smiled.

"Allow me," he said, aiming his 12-gauge shotgun at close range. The lock blew apart, sending pieces flying twenty feet away.

"Wait here," Moe said. "Sure as hell there's a camera down there." He pulled a black wool ski mask down over his face, took a pair of bolt cutters from Josie and disappeared down the hole. They waited a few minutes until he called up, "All clear."

Josie and Sam climbed down the steep, wobbly ladder, fourteen feet below the surface, passing a sticky, black blotch of mold on the wall. Everything smelled musty and earthy, like an unmarked grave.

"Holy shit, this is a bomb shelter," Josie said, glancing around at the galley kitchen, bunk beds with bare mattresses and shelves of canned goods and bottled water.

"You could live down here during a nuclear war," Sam said.

"Or a mob war," Moe added, nodding at the rifles lined up on the wall.

"Where's the camera?" Sam asked.

"There were two, one on the wall and another on the ceiling," Moe said.

Sam looked up and saw the cameras with the cables cut and wires dangling.

All Josie could see were boxes and more boxes, stacked on top of each other, filling up half the room.

"Hand me a knife," she said.

Sam rifled through the kitchen drawers, pulling out a box cutter. Moe pulled the top box off the stack and set it on the floor. It was sealed tightly, closed with clear plastic packing tape. Josie opened it, but she already knew what was inside. Cash and lots of it. All hundreds in neatly bundled stacks. The "soft count," as they called it, pilfered from *her* casino and stolen from the mob. A nice little retirement package for Lionel. Secret, anonymous and ripe for the taking. Set up a shell company, an offshore account and he was set for life.

"Jesus!" Sam said, stunned. "Stealing from the Gambassis? That takes balls. How much you figure is here? Millions?"

"I don't know," Josie answered, opening the box wide, showing all the cash. "Moe, grab your camera. Can you shoot this? Open the other one and get it also."

"Do you want me to shoot the whole shebang?"

"Just a couple boxes, that's enough."

Sam opened a small package on the kitchen table.

"Ten large—in chips," he said. "This guy stole whatever wasn't glued down."

As Moe was clicking away, Josie pulled out a large package wrapped in brown paper that was leaning against the far wall. She tore open the top, enough to see that it was an oil painting. And not just any oil painting. It looked impressionistic, with visible, messy brushstrokes and a thick, gorgeous palette of colors that reflected the light. She couldn't tell who the artist was, but curiosity washed over her. She could hardly contain herself—she tore off the paper and gasped. It was a fucking Renoir. But this was one she'd never seen before. The ornate gold frame was carved in wood and the edges were covered with soft padded corner protectors.

Lionel was probably getting ready to move the art to storage at a free port or some offshore tax haven, and then anonymously sell it for millions to a private dealer. It was ideal. No paper trail, no title history. The perfect storm for money laundering. Josie noticed a fake shipping invoice attached to the back of the painting, declaring that the contents of the package were worth a hundred dollars. She fought the urge to tear open all five paintings in the vault. But she regained her composure and looked at Sam.

"Get the dolly," she said.

"What do you want?" Sam asked, surprised.

"I want to take all of it."

"Shit. All of it?"

"All of it. It's ours. He stole it from us. The boxes. The art. All of it."

Chapter 64

For the next few hours, Moe, Sam and Josie carefully hauled boxes up the ladder and stacked them on the dolly. Moe's truck was getting filled to the brim, and they were constantly readjusting the placement so everything would fit. None of them could figure out where to put the paintings so they wouldn't get damaged. Josie couldn't decide whether to take them to her house or give them to Sam for safekeeping. Sam was grumpy, his flask was empty and Moe was still skeptical about the whole operation.

"This wasn't the plan," Moe kept repeating. "The mob doesn't like their shit stolen."

He was standing at the base of the ladder, handing boxes up to Sam, who in turn handed them to Josie.

"This is *our* money," Josie insisted, pulling up a box from the vault. Her arms ached as she pushed it on the grass, sliding it next to other boxes that had already been retrieved. "New York doesn't even know what's here," she added, sweating under her fleece. "And if they did, Lionel would be dead."

They finally decided to put the art in the back seat, with Sam holding the paintings steady so they didn't knock against each other. On the drive back, the physical tension of the day began to ease, although the urgency of getting the photos to New York made Josie anxious. Moe told Josie that first thing in the morning, he would send the pictures to an associate from New Jersey who owed him big-time.

That man had the right connections, and Moe trusted him to pass along the files.

"Only send pictures of two boxes, okay? No more," Josie said pointedly.

Moe looked at her for a moment, immediately realizing what she wanted. "I got it."

Sam lit up a Marlboro, but Josie immediately told him to snuff it out or he'd ruin the paintings. He pulled the tab on the last Red Bull and then said he needed to stop "to take a leak." Moe idled on the shoulder for a few minutes while Sam jumped out. He seemed to take a long time.

"What are you doing?" Josie shouted. "We happen to be in a hurry here."

"Keep your shirt on. I'm just having a smoke."

"Jesus, Sam, what's the matter with you? We aren't in the clear yet. I have a candy bar in the car."

"Don't talk to me like you're trying to bribe a kindergartener," he snapped, squatting down so he was out of the wind, puffing away at a joint. "I'm having a smoke so just wait the fuck until I'm done."

Josie could push her brother just so far, and that was it. It had always been that way. She gave up and sat there annoyed, while Moe shrugged. He looked every bit of his age, a long way from the college grad who first started working for her father and climbed his way to the top of the organization. When Moe was running things, he commanded respect, not fear. That was a tricky thing to achieve in his line of business. But he did it nonetheless.

While Sam was finishing his smoke, Josie turned to Moe.

"I've been thinking. I can take the art to the ranch because it needs to be climate-controlled, but can we store the boxes at your place?" she asked, knowing that it might put Moe at risk.

He looked at her, surprised.

"Why not the ranch? You have more than one vault there," he asked.

"I don't want the money anywhere near the ranch. That's the first place someone would look. No one would suspect you have anything to do with this and no one can get to your place easily."

"You trust me?" Moe asked with a wink. "I could run off tomorrow and take it all with me."

"But you won't." Josie dropped her hand over his. "I may not trust many people, but the Kings have always trusted you."

Chapter 65

It was nearly noon and the winds were starting to come up from the north. Gusts up to 55 miles per hour were predicted later in the day, which could most certainly knock down utility poles. Josie feared there would be power outages in the central corridor around US-95, making it difficult to get home.

Josie got out of the truck, bracing against a roaring wind. She felt a huge gust moving directly toward her that threw her off balance. Dust particles clung to her eyelashes and hair. She leaned into the wind as she opened her car door. Moe and Sam carefully transferred the paintings into her back seat. She hoped the gusts didn't get any stronger. At 40 miles per hour, you could still walk, but at fifty it was almost impossible.

Sam and Moe drove up to the cabin to unload the boxes and Josie headed to the ranch. She hadn't been in her father's vault since she was a child, and at that time, he had used it to store his silver bricks and firearms. It wasn't a large space, but it would easily hold the five paintings. The wind pummeled her car back and forth across the road and, at one point, she had to take a detour to avoid a stretch where an old, thirty-foot-tall mesquite had crashed across an intersection. The gray-green foliage was blown everywhere, and the dark trunk was shredded clean in half. She could see some downed power lines near the tree and executed a sharp U-turn.

A wall of thick dust covered her windshield, and she could hear the paintings slide around in the back. Oh God, she thought. If something happened to the art she'd never forgive herself. She was dead tired and couldn't see where the hell she was going. She had no choice but to pull off the road onto the shoulder until the storm subsided.

When the wind finally died down, Josie turned on the windshield wipers to clean the dust off the glass and headed for the ranch. Sam would be another few hours, at least, by the time he and Moe unloaded the truck. She'd have to put the paintings in the vault by herself.

A man in the guardhouse waved Josie through the entrance to the ranch. He was smoking a cigarette and watching a security screen that was turned to a local basketball game.

"Hey Josie," he said, barely looking up.

"Hey Paul, how's the team doing?" she asked.

"Might make the finals this year."

"I'll keep my fingers crossed. Just dropping off a few things."

"Need some help?"

"I'm fine," Josie said, driving down the road to the barn.

The horse trainers usually left at noon, so hopefully the place would be empty by now. She pulled up to the parking area next to the barn door. One of the stable assistants was still sweeping the stalls, but everyone else had left. Sam's dog, Rex, bounded up to her and jumped on her legs. She stroked his snout and looked around for a stick to throw. A good way to kill time until the guy left. Fifteen minutes later, he loaded up his truck and finished for the day.

Josie walked to the back of the barn and approached the small storeroom door. She entered the combination, remembered from childhood—817# (her mother's birthday)—the lock clicked and she pushed the door open. Inside the nondescript room were cans of paint, a few brooms, mops and, behind a shelf next to the wall, a small metal door in the floor that led to her father's vault. She leaned over and inputted the second, much longer, passcode, hoping that it had not changed. She was relieved to hear solid steel bolts unlock.

Josie pulled the thick steel plate door open and climbed down the ladder through the foundation.

It had been twenty-five years since she'd been in this room. When she was nine years old her father burst into her bedroom in the early morning hours of Christmas Eve and told her to get up and put on her robe.

"Follow me," he said gruffly, without explanation. Sam, Frank and Sunny were all gathered at the bottom of the stairs in their pajamas, looking around in panic. Their father led them into the underground tunnel, which connected the house to the barn.

"It's a bomb," Sam whispered to Josie, grabbing her hand. "I heard Dad say that . . ."

"Daddy, is that right? Is there a bomb?" Josie asked.

"We're not sure what it is, Josie. We're just being extra careful," her father said evenly. "Sam, keep your mouth shut."

"Who's after us? Where's the bomb?" Frank asked, his eyes darting from side to side and his clammy hand holding on to Josie's.

"You too, Frank. Just be quiet." Their father's voice echoed in the tunnel.

They reached the vault and climbed down the ladder.

"Stay here until it's safe," he said, cutting off any more discussion.

There was an ominous thud of the metal door as their father left them in total darkness. They were huddled together, as if in some deserted cave. Frank fiddled with the camp light but for some reason it wasn't going on. Despite the fact that she was with her brothers and sister, she was scared. Nothing made sense. She was dizzy, disoriented and thought she heard an alarm going off. Then she closed her eyes and felt faint. When she opened them, Sunny was slumped next to her, like a rag doll. She grabbed Josie's hand, then clutched her tighter.

"Don't let go," she sobbed in sheer terror. "We're all going to die."

"You have to be quiet," Josie said, shocked at her older sister's hysteria. Sunny was crying so hard she could barely speak.

Frank was sitting in the corner, his arms hugging his knees.

"I think it's some dick who has a hard-on for Dad. We could be here for hours," Sam said, baiting Frank, who was wheezing and coughing.

"Jesus, get me outta here," Frank pleaded. He was drenched in sweat and his whole body was trembling. He stood up, stumbled to the door and started kicking it in a rage.

"What the fuck are you doing?" Sam asked. "You want to get us all killed?"

"Open the goddamn door!" Frank shouted, ignoring Sam and pounding on it with his fists.

"What's the matter, pussy? You afraid of the dark?"

Frank whipped around and tackled Sam. The two scuffled on the ground like wild animals, Frank yanking Sam's hair and kicking him wildly.

At that moment, the vault door opened and light streamed in from above.

"Get up," their father ordered. "Knock it off."

Later on, they found out that one of their father's enemies had tried to fly his private plane to Vegas to bomb the Kings' house but was arrested at the last minute by local cops. The attack was in retaliation for the execution of the man's brother, who had been found dead with his mistress at a local motel. The man blamed the murder on Roy King, even though he was never charged.

Josie flipped on the lights in the vault and breathed deeply, blotting out her childhood memories. She had mastered that in the years she had been away. After their incident, her father had installed battery-powered bunker lights with globe fixtures that lit the area.

She went out to the car and carried the largest painting into the vault. If she stacked the five paintings carefully, they would all just fit into the space. She went back and forth five times. At one point, she was tempted to look at the other paintings, but that would involve unwrapping them and she didn't have the energy to wrap them back up. She slammed the vault shut, now filled with a fortune in stolen masterpieces.

Her anxiety increased, gathering momentum. Don't run, she said to herself as she walked briskly to the car, the wind whipping her hair into knots. Don't run. She looked around, but no one was there.

Chapter 66

Josie knew what the mob would do when they found out about the boxes. At 7 a.m., she got out of bed, put on her robe and walked outside to the patio. Then she called Moe on her cell. He told her that he had sent the pictures off to New York and there was no way to trace it back. The deed was done and now they'd have to wait.

"How long?" Josie asked.

"Depends on how pissed off they are," Moe answered. "My guess? It won't be long before Lionel gets a phone call."

Josie was relieved it would be over soon. The longer this thing dragged out, the more jeopardy there was for everyone involved.

"I'd like to come over and look at the spoils of war," she said, trying to sound as casual as possible. "Let's count the money."

Moe thought it a bit premature, but who was he to question the boss's daughter?

Josie headed northwest on US-95 toward Mount Charleston. She threw her parka and snow boots in the car, along with a thermos of coffee. The temperature had dipped into the teens. The sun was a cool disc in the sky, blanketed by clouds and half-blurred from view. She had a strong sense of being alone, wintry deadness in every direction.

Josie looked out the window and thought about her father. The way Roy King had lived was still painful to her. And yet she saw no other road forward—this landscape and this world now belonged to her.

At one point, she checked her phone and realized that Rob had left her several messages. He reminded her that this was the third time she had ditched him in the middle of the night. "Call me," he added offhandedly. He knew something was up. What to tell him?

She gripped the wheel with increasing intensity, her eyes straying toward the side of the road. A light fog cast shadows on the windshield, and she hoped it wouldn't turn to snow. In the distance, she noticed a car speeding behind her, and wondered if anyone could be following her. It was possible. In the old days, Roy King picked up an FBI tail every time he left the ranch. Josie doubled back, flipping a U-turn and getting off the highway.

She parked behind a sign advertising the Las Vegas Paiute Resort—three golf courses and a clubhouse—on a sliver of the tribe's ancestral land returned to them by the US government. This, in exchange for white settlers taking their territory, selling their children into slavery and forcing them into labor on their own land.

She sat there for a while and watched the traffic stream by on the highway. Satisfied that she hadn't been followed, she got back on US-95 North and made the final trek to Moe's house. He had recently cleared the road, and she was able to pull up to the house. Of course, he was standing at the door as she walked up, having seen her on one of his nine thousand security cameras. He looked as tired as she felt. There were pouches under his eyes and white stubble on his chin. He and Sam had stacked the boxes in the back storeroom. There were close to twenty altogether.

"So. Do you want to count *all* of them?" Moe asked. There was an awkward pause as Josie realized how long that would actually take. His voice was scratchy but cordial. He'd do it, but he wouldn't be happy about it. He rubbed his arm against his forehead, and then threaded his huge fingers through his hair.

"Let's count one and then multiply," Josie said, looking at the high stack of boxes. "They all seem to be around the same size. I just want an idea of how much he's stolen from us."

"And from the mob," Moe reminded her.

"That too."

He lifted a box from the top of a pile and tore off the packing tape. Josie blinked and felt a surge of excitement in her stomach.

"How did Lionel ever pull this off?" she asked.

Moe didn't answer. Sometimes he knew a lot more than he'd tell her. They began carefully laying out stacks of hundreds on the table then slowly counted each stack. They were all the same—a hundred bills in each stack. And there were one hundred stacks.

"Jesus Christ, each box has a million dollars in cash!" said Josie. They looked at each other, stunned.

"Twenty fucking million dollars? We're in deep shit," said Moe.

"I don't think so. No one knows the full extent of this except Lionel. And he's about to get recalled."

"That's a nice way of putting it."

"Clipped. Whacked. Popped. Hit. Burned. Whatever you want to call it."

Josie felt no guilt over Lionel's fate, but still her hands were sweating and there was a prickly sensation at the back of her neck. Taking all the boxes was a rash, impulsive action based on nothing but hubris and a sense that whatever was in those boxes was hers. But now what?

"Do you have anything to drink?" she asked.

"Whiskey? That's all I got at the moment."

"I'll take it."

Moe patted her gently on the shoulder. He offered her a Marlboro from his shirt pocket, and then went into the kitchen to get the bottle.

Josie needed a plan to deal with this, but first she had to make sure the whole Lionel issue was resolved. Once he found out the money was gone, he was going to be one angry motherfucker, and he might come after them before the mob got to him.

Josie lit up her cigarette and gazed around the storeroom. The smoke swirled in thick clouds above her head. It was then she noticed one more box, smaller than the others, that was tightly sealed and had a list of different dates scribbled on top in black marker.

She opened it. It was filled with files, each dated and numbered. She glanced into one of the folders and—Jesus Christ—it contained detailed financial information, including computer printouts, numbered bank accounts, wire transfer dates, payoffs to customs agents, names of shell companies and where they were chartered. There was also a file of what looked like tax returns. More damning were names of the Gambassi operatives around the world.

When Moe returned with the bottle and two glasses, Josie hastily closed the box and pressed the tape across the top, covering the dates.

"I'm going to take this one with me," she said, mustering up a last bit of composure and downing the glass of whiskey. "Just a bunch of office records."

"No problem. I'll put it in your car. What do you want to do with the cash?"

Josie thought about it for a minute. "Give me a few days."

"Okay, but no longer. I'm like a sitting fucking duck up here."

Josie drove back down the hill with what looked to be highly incriminating documents that could put away the capos of one of the most powerful mob families in the country. She sat in silence thinking about the significance of what she had just seen. This could be the most valuable box of all.

Chapter 67

The day after they emptied Lionel's vault, Josie lugged the box of files up the stairs to her bedroom and locked the door. She peered out the window, making sure no one was hanging around outside or parked by her house. Then she closed the shades and carefully pulled the files out, one by one, spreading them across her bed.

Each one was a study in evasion. There was a shred of legitimacy in each of the transactions—ideal ways for the mob to engage in the dark art of money laundering. Records from different banks in Geneva, The Bahamas and Antigua. Free-port storage facilities invoices. Shipping receipts from Costa Rica to the US by way of Mexico. Sotheby's certifications from London art auctions. Receipts from private art galleries in New York and London, wire transfer documents, numbered bank accounts around the world, various real estate transactions that dumped a shitload of cash into circulation through offshore shell corporations. Stock manipulation. A list of all-cash businesses that fed the beast. Enough ammunition here to shut down the entire New York mob.

Jesus. This would be like handing the FBI a Christmas gift. Based on this information, they could indict the whole damn operation and Agent Gavin could take an early retirement. This was definitely Lionel's insurance policy. If anyone came after him, he could use this information to cut a deal with the feds or buy his way out of the mob. And now *she* had it. The question was, what to do with all of it—the cash, the art and the files.

Give the information to the feds and she would be a marked woman. No witness protection program could hide her forever. Even if the top bosses wound up in prison, they would eventually come after her. Did she really want to spend the rest of her life somewhere like Peoria, living under an assumed name without Billie, constantly looking over her shoulder? Josie recalled one witness, the former sister-in-law of a local politician, who sang to the feds and four days later was found dead in her hotel room from an overdose of heroin. A sad end to a woman who was never known to take more than an aspirin. No. Josie would not be calling the feds.

Then there was the cash. Based on the photos Moe had sent them, New York only knew about two boxes of skim—$2 million. The others were Lionel's—and now Josie's—little secret. Whether or not anyone else knew about the art was up in the air.

Josie sat on the edge of her bed, trying to think. In her mind, she was still overwhelmed with all that green—the color of greed, envy, jealousy, sickness, mold and unripe fruit. But it was also the color of growth, potential and preservation. What to do with the sudden windfall was just one of her many problems at the moment. She would like to take her time, be patient, but the house was on fire.

The most immediate thing to do was to make copies of the documents and hide the copies and the originals in two separate secure locations. The safest way to make this happen was to drive to the ranch and lock herself in her father's office.

She carefully put all the files back into the box and carried it to her car, placing everything in her trunk before she opened the garage door. On the way to the ranch, she called Sam, telling him she needed to use their father's office to go over some of his tax documents.

"Really? After everything we've been through, that's what you're doing?"

"It's important."

"Aren't you exhausted?"

"Yes, I'm going to get this done and then crash," she said, grateful that Sam wasn't asking detailed questions. All you had to do with Sam was mention taxes and his eyes rolled back in his head. And hopefully, by this time, he would be conveniently lubricated by alcohol.

"Okay, but stop by and say hello. Crystal and I will be in the media room."

"You didn't mention anything to her, did you?" she asked, disappointed that Crystal was still around.

"I may be a drunk, but I'm not an idiot. And we *do* need to talk about the boxes."

"I agree. How about tomorrow?"

"Where's Frank?"

"Cindy says he's downstairs in the casino monitoring the slot zombies. Completely fucking out to lunch."

Josie entered her father's office carrying the box in her arms and set it on his desk. She threw her coat on the chair, locked the door and pulled the blinds down. The air was stuffy, and everything smelled stale. It felt like nobody had been there since the funeral, and his desk was still just as he left it. She didn't want to think about what she had done on this very desk with Rob. She opened the wood-paneled doors flush to the wall, revealing her father's printer and file cabinets. On top of the largest one, there was a small bronze statue commemorating Roy King, United Way's "Man of the Year."

The first file had ten pieces of paper stapled together. She copied the document and then re-stapled it. There were at least fifty files in the box, and she meticulously copied each document. There were also random pieces of paper with names and numbers handwritten on them. Those she had to feed separately into the printer. She copied everything.

Halfway through this process, the door to the office rattled. Josie panicked, then heard scratching as well. Shit, it was Rex. She ignored the dog at first, but he kept scratching. At this rate, the copying would take a few hours, so she ran to the door and let him in. As soon as she closed the door, the dog wanted out, so she shoved him out again and locked the door. Why was it Rex always had his nose in everything?

When she was finished, she packed the originals into a leather duffel she'd found at the bottom of the closet. She placed the copies back in the original box. Then she carried the duffel to her car and locked it in the trunk. She walked back into the house to retrieve the box of copies, and found Sam standing by the office door.

"What's going on, Josie? I don't buy this tax bullshit."

"What would you say if I told you it's better that you don't know?"

"I'd say you don't trust me."

It was at this moment that Crystal came around the corner, wearing tight-fitting velvet sweats embellished with rhinestones and a pair of flip-flops. Her toes were bright orange.

"Hey Josie," she said, giving her a peck on the cheek. She smelled of weed and Chanel perfume.

"Sweetie, can you go back to the media room and get me my drink?" Sam asked, giving her a pat on the rear. "And put Rex out. He's a pain in the ass."

They watched her reluctantly walk to the end of the hall. She would be back in about sixty seconds.

"We can't talk now," Josie said, glancing in Crystal's direction.

Sam nodded. "She's not as stupid as she looks."

"I'll call you later, okay?" Josie said, forcing a smile.

She walked back into her father's office, picked up the box and headed for her car. Her back was aching as she slid the box on the front seat next to her and pulled up to the barn. It was close to five o'clock, and all the help had left by now. All those years she'd avoided the vault and now she'd been there twice in two days. Her father's presence loomed over her. The vault was his plan B, in case his fire walls were penetrated and the world erupted into violence. And it wasn't a nuclear war he feared when he built the thing in the first place.

Josie carried the box to the back of the barn, entered the code on the small storeroom door, walked in and closed the door behind her. She leaned over the in-ground floor vault and entered the second code. She pulled open the door and climbed down the ladder, carefully balancing the box on her hip. This is how people break their necks, she thought. Finally, she placed the box on the shelf behind the paintings. God only knew the value of what she was hiding here. Then she climbed out, slammed the vault with a thunk and locked the storeroom door.

As she drove back down the long, tree-lined driveway with Sunrise Mountain turning purple at dusk, she noticed a few bighorn sheep grazing against the splendid landscape.

Josie thought that if she ever lived long enough to enjoy her golden years, they would be here at the ranch, where the natural world sustained her. She could envision her father, shaking his head and smiling. The family comes first, Josie, he would say. Protect the family.

Chapter 68

Valley Bank of Nevada was downtown on Fourth Street, a block from the Jackpot. This was where all the casinos did their banking. Valley was initially the only bank in town that would lend money to the gaming industry back when the big national banks didn't want to "dirty their hands." By the time the big banks found out that the business was legal and lucrative, it was too late. The old guard remained loyal to Valley Bank.

Josie's father had banked here. In fact, in the early days, he had been chairman of the board. The family's safety-deposit boxes were here, and many of the employees had known Josie since she was a child.

At 9 a.m., Josie parked in the lot, grabbed the duffel from the passenger seat and carried it over her shoulder, past the security guard at the entrance. No one even looked twice. Vegas banks were used to people coming in with duffels filled with God knows what. Cash, jewelry, silver dollars. They didn't ask a lot of questions.

After Josie registered for a new box, she entered one of the private, electronically monitored rooms and looked over the original documents one more time—fifty files that could poison anyone who came in contact with them. Lock them up, she thought, placing them in the extra-wide secure box. Then she shoved the rolling drawer back into the wall, like a corpse in the morgue. She'd keep one key and give the other to Sam.

When Josie got back in her car she called Cindy, telling her she had some business to take care of and wasn't coming into the office until tomorrow.

"Is Frank in?" Josie asked. She still wasn't sure when she should tell him about Lionel's vault.

"No one's here at the moment. Frank is downstairs with the construction crew and Lionel went to New York for a few days."

"Why did he do that?" Josie tried to sound casual.

"I don't know. He got a phone call this morning and took off."

Josie breathed a sigh of relief. Lionel was gone. *Gone gone gone.* She would have liked to have seen the look on his face when he got the call. The thought of it was exquisite. Perhaps her father had ordered her home for a reason.

She hung up with Cindy and dialed Moe.

"Lionel's gone," she announced.

"I guess they got the photos," Moe replied. She heard the click of a lighter as he lit a Marlboro.

"Cindy said he went back to New York. You think we're good?"

"Don't celebrate yet. Sit tight for a few days. We don't know what they'll do."

Chapter 69

Lionel had been meticulous. The house, the dead-end town, the vault. How was it possible for New York to discover what he'd been planning ever so carefully, step by step? But something was off—he could feel it in his bones. Just when he had perfected every little detail and was confident his covert operation was running smoothly, there was a breach somewhere. Josie had something to do with it. He knew it. So it was time. He had planned for this as well. He would take off with his winnings while he still could. A good gambler knew when to hold 'em, and when to fold 'em.

After the call, Lionel kept his cool, telling Cindy that he was catching a flight to New York in the afternoon. Let them all think that's what he was doing—taking a meeting, updating the bosses, discussing financials, whatever. He wasn't sure of New York's intentions, but a wrong move could be fatal. He would not make that mistake. He was tired of the game anyway. He wanted out.

Lionel had chartered a Cessna Citation at the North Las Vegas private terminal, which was scheduled to depart at midnight for Antigua. He had rented a high-security storage space at the free port and would transfer the cash upon his arrival. He had exactly one day to cram everything in his truck and then torch the property. The two bodies in the backyard would rot until the next owner bulldozed the area. By then they'd be dust, and he'd be long gone.

He went home to pack up his things and then downed a few Oxys.

He couldn't get help this time, and his back was shit. He'd save the rest for the flight. Booze made the pills stronger, and he'd have a nice rest on the way to the Caribbean.

As Lionel was driving to Pahrump, he felt confident he had thought of everything. A few months ago he had put a down payment on a remote, beachfront house on one of the Leeward Islands. He let his mind drift to the life he would have in the near future. The place sat on a wide, sandy shoreline, and he'd spend his days lolling in the salty breeze or dozing on a braided rope hammock. The real estate agent said that there were no paved roads. The only access was by four-wheel-drive vehicle, and it was impossible to arrive by boat because of the perilous barrier reefs. Wild horses were the only thing that roamed the area—way the fuck better than the coyotes here. He thought of New York—what they'd think when they found out he went AWOL. They could all kiss his ass.

Chapter 70

As Lionel's car sped down US-95 toward Pahrump, Josie sat in her house with a growing sense of dread. She had an overwhelming feeling that what had seemed like a good plan had taken a turn.

She had accomplished what she wanted, but why didn't she feel safe? Maybe Moe was right. There could be repercussions. Stealing from Lionel's vault was not a free ride. Even though it was *her family's* money. She could picture his cold, predatory eyes when he realized he'd been had. She sat motionless on the couch staring out the window with a vague sense of unease. I'm trapped, she thought. I should have never come home.

The sky took on that sludgy color it gets before a storm. A faint view of the Spring Mountains was in the distance. They glistened in the summer, but now they seemed ominous. The crags of whitened rock looked like shrouded figures, standing guard in the middle of the Mojave Desert. Outside, the wind was picking up and there were a few minutes of hard rain. Josie made a cup of hot tea and tried to tamp down the heavy feeling of anxiety that swept over her from nowhere.

A stack of unopened mail was piled up on the kitchen counter, along with rolled-up past issues of the *Las Vegas Sun*. She looked out at the geological wonderland near the Spring Mountains. She had hiked there a few years ago, passing relics of petrified trees that dated back over a hundred million years. A local legend described a spirit world where souls of the dead could communicate with the living. Perhaps her father was all around her. She wished she could talk to him now.

She dialed Rob, but only got his voicemail. There was the crack of thunder, then the lights went dead and the alarm went off, shrill shrieks in the darkness. She reset the alarm. There was a battery backup, but any heavy gust of wind set off the window breaks. After a few minutes, the lights flickered back on, the refrigerator motor started up and all the clocks flashed the incorrect time.

Josie drifted off to sleep but woke with a start when her cell phone rang. No one on the other end, just an eerie silence. She had slept most of the afternoon. It was close to seven. She stripped down and stepped into the shower stall, closing her eyes as the hot, steamy water rushed over her head and down her body. Time flew by. How long had it been? Twenty, thirty minutes? Afterward, she leaned against the cool tile and closed her eyes. That's when she heard something. Where was it coming from? Maybe it was a branch that fell against the house, or the old pipes banging out heat, or some kind of animal skittering over the pitched-roof tiles.

She cracked open the bedroom curtains and looked outside. The street was dark and empty and the wind was winding down. The traffic light at the end of the road was blinking, the cars slowly moving through the intersection. She glanced around and saw only the neighbors' cars parked in their driveway. But she thought she saw something moving in the shadows. She wrapped her robe tighter around her waist and walked out of the bathroom. There it was again. She couldn't put her finger on it. Something was off. This was not nothing.

Now she was on high alert, conscious of every sound. The noise was on the other side of the wall, in another room, maybe, maybe not. But it was definitely there.

She felt a spike of panic, went to her closet gun safe and took out her new Glock. She worked the slide to load a cartridge into the chamber. The slide wasn't as buttery as her old Glock, but it would do. The barrel smelled like powder solvent from its last cleaning. She used to complain about the ammonia smell but now it felt comforting. She was still able to take her gun apart and put it back together with her eyes closed. She quietly padded to the top of the stairs, her hair dripping on the carpet.

The house was now quiet in a way that made it all seem like nothing. Was it possible she was imagining the noise downstairs? Then she heard it again. Footsteps on her front porch. She aimed her gun at the front door and cocked it. Then she heard a knock.

"Josie, I just want to talk. Open the door."

She could barely hear the voice, but it was unmistakable. It was Lionel.

"Who is it?" she asked. She knew very well who it was. Shit! Where was her cell? By the bed?

"It's Lionel. I think you know why I'm here. Let me in."

She knew this man would come for her. She just didn't realize it would be so soon.

"Hold on a minute," she shouted, stalling, as she raced around the bedroom trying to find her phone. Where the hell was it? She frantically looked in a few places, pulling off the covers, throwing the pillows on the floor, kneeling down and looking under the bed. For Christ's sake, it was nowhere! And the fucking landline was in the kitchen near the back door. No way she was going down there. She punched in the silent alarm code on the security panel next to her bedroom door.

"Jesus, Josie. I'm not going to hurt you," Lionel said as he rattled the outside door.

Adrenaline surged through her body, and she could hear herself breathing. Water trickled down her neck and across her chest. She walked barefoot to the top of the stairs, her eyes not leaving her target, still aiming her pistol at the door.

"I want to make a deal," he said.

"You're not in a position to deal, are you?" she asked.

"Sure I am. I know who has the money and the art. And my employers do not. Unless I call them and inform them of this fact."

"I don't know what you're talking about," Josie said, moving a few steps farther down the stairs.

"Funny. Because when I discovered that someone had broken into my vault and emptied it, I thought, who in the world could have done this? The cameras were shot out. But then I looked at my security monitor and scrolled back a few days. Imagine my surprise that it was Josie King casing the joint. Now, hypothetically, if someone, like Josie King, discovered a vault of cash and art and took off with it, where would she put it?"

"I don't know, Lionel. That's *your* specialty."

"Let's stop the bullshit. You keep half and I'll keep my mouth shut."

"And then you'll disappear, right?"

"Right," he agreed.

"What about Frank?" Josie asked, stalling.

"What about him? He's up to his ass in debt. He's the gift that keeps on giving."

"No deal." Josie moved one more step down the stairs. There was silence, then the sound of sirens.

"Shit! Did you call the cops?" Lionel began pounding on the door. "Stupid cunt! Did you really think I wouldn't figure out who took my shit? You think you can destroy me?"

If there was any doubt Lionel meant business, it was dispelled by the crack of a bullet in the door lock as he burst through the front door. The security alarm went off, a high-pitched scream instilling maximum panic, as Josie ran upstairs and locked herself in the bedroom. She should have blown his fucking head off when she had the chance. She backed up to the opposite wall, facing the door, keeping her finger on the trigger.

There was the heavy tread of footsteps on the bare boards of the stairs. More than one person. She heard Lionel scrambling, shouting to no effect. Two men said something in low tones; she couldn't hear the words.

"You don't want me. You want the woman upstairs, she's the one who—"

Josie heard the sound of three muffled shots, and then a body crashing on the stairs.

She looked out the window and saw the sweaty faces of the two men from the casino who Cindy had pointed out. Lionel's men. They had removed their wool masks and their faces were shiny as they wrapped Lionel's body in a plastic tarp and threw it into the trunk of their black Lincoln Town Car. They were clearly professionals—button men. In and out in thirty seconds. The alarm was still shrieking as the car peeled away from the curb.

Josie collapsed on the bed, her heart thumping, and then felt something dig into her hip. The goddamn phone was in her robe pocket the whole time. The police arrived minutes later. Every neighbor she had never met was standing outside their house, watching the action. A fire engine pulled up shortly afterward, lights flashing. Someone shouted, "Police!" and then a uniformed cop kicked in her bedroom door and found her sitting on the bed, staring straight ahead, still gripping the gun.

"Miss? You're safe. Miss? Would you mind lowering your weapon?"

Chapter 71

Lionel, in his desperate attempt to save himself, had said just enough before he got whacked on her staircase. She was next. And it wouldn't take long. She was sure of it.

She had watched the hit men carry off Lionel's body as if he were a dead buck with a big rack. Their hunt was successful, but they weren't done. One night they'd put on their masks and gloves, maybe break a few windows, make it look like a robbery gone wrong. Or kidnap her and drag her to the desert, shoot her in the head and leave her for the vultures.

The police investigation went downhill fast. She couldn't let them know what really happened. If she told them it was a mob hit, it would lead right back to the Jackpot.

She had to hold it together. They found no fingerprints, no security camera footage, no missing items. The young, uniformed officer looked perplexed. He was a skinny kid who kept fingering his Motorola walkie-talkie, which was squawking static updates. The older cop was more skeptical. Josie could tell he'd been around.

Both officers were geared to the hilt, fitted out with so much equipment that Josie doubted they could even sit down. The older one wore mirrored wraparound sunglasses, which he pushed up on his head as he reached for a small notebook. She imagined them getting dressed in the morning, checking off the list of essentials—gun on one side, holstered Taser on the other, handcuffs dangling off their thick, black leather belt, large brass Metropolitan Police badge and shiny, lace-up duty boots.

"People assume that because we run a casino, we have suitcases of cash sitting around the house," Josie offered.

"So why did one of them shoot the other?" the younger cop asked.

"How should I know? When one of them shot out the front door, I ran upstairs and locked myself in the bedroom. And then I heard more shots—"

"You mean to tell me," the older officer interrupted, "they come in, they take nothing and all of a sudden they start shooting each other? I'm sorry. That doesn't make sense."

"I agree," Josie said.

"Did you recognize any of them?"

"No, I was locked in my room," she lied.

"And you can't think of anyone who would want to cause you harm. After all, you're Roy King's daughter and that puts you at some kind of risk, correct?"

"Correct," Josie said. "But this is just plain weird."

"I still don't get why they'd come here and shoot each other," the younger cop persisted.

"These sort of guys don't need a reason to shoot someone," Josie replied.

"What?" the older cop asked. He had finally caught something that made an impression. "What 'sort of guys' are we talking about?"

"I just meant in theory . . ." Josie explained, her voice trailing off. The two cops exchanged glances.

"So, 'in theory,'" the older cop repeated sarcastically, "who are 'these sort of guys' who don't need a reason to shoot each other?"

"In theory, they're the kind of guys who blow their neighbor's head off because their dog shit on his lawn. I'm sure you know the type. Potheads. Psychos. Druggies. Ex-husbands."

"You think this is funny?" the older cop asked.

"Do I look like I'm laughing?" Josie replied, feeling her cheeks sting. She adjusted her robe, ran her fingers through her damp hair and looked at the unholy mess around her. There were splatters of blood on the wall, sticky red footprints on the hardwood stairs and an empty shell embedded in her welcome mat. Her front door was hanging on one hinge, and wood splinters littered the entryway.

"These men broke into my home and tried to kill me. This interview is over. I'll have my lawyer call you in the morning. The house was rented in the name of a trust. I assume you will respect that and not reveal my name to the press."

"Of course, we always try to respect the privacy of our citizens."

Josie gave it a few hours before they leaked it.

"Please secure the front door when you're finished," she told the younger officer.

"Will do," he said, as crime scene investigators wearing gloves, goggles, booties and jumpsuits entered the house and began gathering and analyzing physical evidence.

Josie went back upstairs, closed her bedroom door and changed into sweats. She had to think clearly and come up with a plan. It wouldn't take long for the mob to figure out that she knew where their money was hidden. Otherwise, why would Lionel have been at her door? And who knows how long those guys had been sitting in front of her house? Maybe they heard every word. How much did they know?

She looked at her gun, still sitting on her bedside table. Sam's housewarming present had turned out to be more valuable than she ever imagined. She could shoot to kill and she would have. She was capable of defending herself. She reached in her purse and took the last cigarette out of the pack. Her hands were shaking as she lit up.

Chapter 72

What were her options here? Her car was off-limits. If it wasn't bugged by now, the Mercedes with its LA plates was easily identifiable. She'd need to use another car. She opened her purse and slipped her pistol inside along with the backup magazine. Then she walked down the stairs, carefully stepping around the investigators who were taking blood samples from the wall. She assumed that they were all watching her as she opened the connecting door to her garage. She stepped inside, then circled back out the side door and through her yard to Flora's house. Flora was in the kitchen when Josie knocked on the window.

"My God, Josie. What happened?"

"It was a break-in. I'm okay but I can't sleep there tonight. My car is dead. Can I borrow yours? I'll get it back to you in the morning."

She jumped into Flora's Honda Civic, which was littered with takeout bags, empty plastic cups with lipstick-stained straws sticking out of the lids and a ziplock bag filled with hotel amenities. The gas gauge showed less than a quarter tank. Josie pulled out of Flora's driveway and glanced in both directions, making sure no one was following her. The street was still filled with police cars and other official vehicles. She didn't think the gunmen were operating with backup, but she couldn't be too careful.

She turned abruptly left at the corner, the opposite direction of where she was headed. The traffic signal was still blinking erratically from the power outage. She stopped briefly at the intersection and then jumped on the I-215, flooring the gas pedal until she was well past her neighborhood. The freeway paralleled the Strip and, as she drove past all the resort hotels, she breathed a sigh of relief. She was sure that no one had followed her—a diversion that would have made her father proud.

Her first call was to Sam. She left a message saying she was okay. If he was on a bender, he wouldn't pick up until tomorrow anyway. Her next call was to Rob. At this point, he was safer than anyone in her family, and no one would connect the dots if she stayed at his place.

"Are you alone?" Josie asked.

"No. I'm in the middle of the casino. Where are you?"

"On my way over."

"You okay? Your voice sounds strange."

"I'm fine."

"How far out are you?"

"Ten minutes."

"Meet you at valet."

"I'm driving a green Honda Civic with half a fender."

Chapter 73

I have no right to complain, Josie thought. I caused all this. It would be like an arsonist whining about getting burned. She thought about the carnage she had left behind. And what could happen in the future. A shiver of dread passed through her. She needed to get a grip.

Josie's next call was to Moe.

"Lionel's dead," she said.

"What?" he replied. He was sitting on the living room couch watching the last quarter of the UNLV basketball game. "How do you know?"

"Just a hunch. He was carried out of my house in a plastic tarp and thrown in the trunk of a car."

She heard Moe's sharp intake of breath. "Jesus! Are you all right?"

"He came over with a gun, Moe, and wanted to make a 'deal.' Obviously, he'd been to the vault."

"Did you kill—"

"No," she interrupted. She explained, beat by beat, what happened.

"Get the hell out of there."

"I'm in the car. I'll be okay tonight. Call you tomorrow."

Two minutes later, she pulled into Rob's hotel and gave the car to the valet.

Josie entered his suite with an agenda. Time was of the essence. It was inevitable that New York would come around to her.

Maybe she was taking a chance telling Rob everything. Her father had always warned her, "Be careful who you trust. And even then, don't trust them too much." He had a very small circle of people he relied on, and most of them, like Moe, worked for him. Josie didn't have that luxury. She thought about Rob. He had clawed his way to the top. He had planned every step of his success, anticipated every hurdle. He must have faced this type of enemy. Perhaps he cared enough about her to help. If she was honest with herself, she still had some misgivings. But she had no choice.

They sat across from each other on the couch.

"Take off your shirt," Josie said.

Rob looked at her and a small smile spread across his face. Without a word, he twisted off his gold cuff links, and carefully unbuttoned his custom-made white shirt. Josie looked at his bare chest with no expression.

"Good. No wire."

"Are you joking?" His smile vanished. Her expression gave it away—he knew she wasn't.

She began her saga—the missteps, blind alleys, betrayals and the final scene erupting into violence. Rob buttoned his shirt up and stared at her with an intensity that was unnerving. As he interrupted to tell the chef to put dinner on hold, he turned back to her, saying, "Sorry." He was cool and composed, as if she were relating the details of a petty family squabble.

"As far as I can see, you have one card left to play," he said. "I can call Mel Davis."

Josie stood up and walked to the window, staring out at the glittering lights of the town that had repelled, sustained and consumed her. She hadn't talked to Davis since the funeral but he had told her to call if she needed anything. And she thought he meant it.

Josie watched as Rob picked up the phone.

"Hand it to me. I'll talk to him."

"Okay," Rob said. "It's your call."

It was hard to imagine that she would ever be in this position, making an emergency call to Mel Davis. But this was quite possibly her last chance to get out of this fucking mess. Mel answered on the first ring.

"Mr. Davis. I hope I'm not disturbing you. It's Josie King."

"Josie?" He sounded surprised but then recovered. "Always a pleasure."

"Thank you. I'll get right to the point. I'd like to ask a favor."

"Anything, sweetheart."

"I know this is short notice, but could you meet with me tomorrow? I wouldn't ask if there wasn't some urgency."

"How about ten? You got a pen? I'll give you my address."

"I know where you live. I can't thank—"

"Stop. Your father would do the same for me. See you tomorrow."

Josie walked out onto the terrace. Her face was pale, and she was shivering. She looked out into the darkness as though hypnotized. The neon glitter of the Strip was like a veil obscuring things, hiding a world around her that was falling apart. Rob followed and wrapped his arms around her. She leaned into him.

"I'm here for you." He spoke gently, pulling her in. "You can do this."

Chapter 74

The Davis estate was located on 150 acres on the outskirts of the Red Rock Conservation Area, about twenty-five miles west of the Las Vegas Strip. Josie sped by the vibrant crimson rock formations, the sky-high sand dunes and deep gorges. The area was known for eight-hundred-year-old prehistoric petroglyphs carved on the canyon walls. Legend had it that winter was the storytelling season, and tales about spirits and coyotes and giants were passed on to future generations. But Josie's mind wasn't on historical legends. Her mind was on her meeting with another legend, closer to home.

When she brought Sam up to date, he suggested that she tread carefully. Despite never being indicted for anything—and the feds tried for decades—Davis was known to be a powerful figure in the world of organized crime. He would probably be ten steps ahead of whatever she had to say. And though he was theoretically retired from that life, he was still one of the most respected and successful gangsters in history.

As she drove through Davis's impressive wrought-iron gates, Josie noted his extensive gardens, with some of the largest ponderosa pines she'd ever seen. She pulled into the cobblestone motor court in her black rental; Rob had a couple of his guys return Flora's car. The house itself was designed like an Italian villa, with a koi pond, reflecting pools, a fifty-foot-long swimming pool and two tennis courts. There was even a private nine-hole golf course, which her father had mentioned to her. Roy King didn't give a shit about golf, but he knew enough to be impressed that it was a Robert Trent Jones–designed course.

Josie was ushered into the marble-tiled entryway by a fifty-something woman who was dressed like an old-school librarian: low silver bun and sensible heels. Josie was wearing one of the four outfits Rob had sent up from his designer boutique—a white silk Chanel blouse, navy pencil skirt with a matching jacket and slingback kitten heels. No one would ever suspect the bloody mess she had lived through the night before.

The long hall to Davis's office had a beamed ceiling and carved mahogany-paneled walls. He was standing in front of the arched limestone window, wearing gray slacks and a baby blue cashmere sweater that matched his eyes. The slanted light washed down his face like a benediction. He turned when Josie entered the room. She had no idea what to expect when she asked this man for help. Davis looked at her, a note of concern in his voice.

"Josie, come in. Are you okay?"

"Not really. It's kind of you to see me," Josie said.

"Of course." He motioned for her to sit in one of the leather armchairs in front of his desk.

A housekeeper appeared from the hallway carrying a tray with two crystal glasses of orange juice and a silver thermos of coffee.

"Try some juice," he said, handing Josie a glass. "From our trees. Every damn morning I'm supposed to drink a full glass of this shit."

Josie sipped hers, as Davis downed it in one round, like medicine, and placed it on the side table.

"Now, how can I help?"

Josie paused before answering.

"I'm not sure where to start."

Sensing that this was difficult, Davis walked around his desk and sat down in the chair next to her.

"I can only imagine what life was like for you growing up. No mother, and a father who was otherwise occupied. Now, my daughter, my only child, was coddled to death by my wife. They're still thick as thieves, those two."

"Well, we had our own world out there on the ranch," Josie said, giving him a half-smile.

"It was a different time."

Mel poured himself some coffee, leaned back in his chair and waited for her to begin.

Sitting there on this sunlit morning, looking out the window, Josie could barely see where the hills began and Mel Davis's property ended. She had always thought of her homecoming as something forced and unpleasant, but now she felt oddly comfortable. The ghosts of the past were returning, and she realized she had come here for not only advice but maybe some compassion from someone who might understand.

"I guess you could say this whole thing started with Frank," Josie began. "I can't blame him for all of it. He lived in a world where doors opened on command. He learned the trade from our father, but he is also a reckless gambler. From what I've heard, he'd lose five million in one casino, and then move on to other casinos, winning a million here and a million there. His lucky streak ran out permanently when he made a deal with the devil, and they took over the Jackpot. My brother Sam hasn't been much help either."

"I heard Sam's about to get his gaming license suspended permanently," Davis said. "Sad news. Your father once told me he was the best in the business."

"My father had high hopes for Sam," Josie said. "But Frank was the go-to guy. He was dedicated, a hard worker, but he's had a gambling addiction that he can't control."

"It's no secret what's going on at your casino," Davis interrupted. "And it is very disappointing. Your father and I worked hard to bring respectability to this town. To clean it up. And ever since those two bankers went to Carson City and changed the law, allowing corporations to run casinos, we pretty much succeeded. Then someone like your brother comes along and threatens to bring us back to the dark days."

"No one has been able to control him, Mr. Davis."

Josie proceeded to tell Davis everything: the violence, the FBI, New York, the secret room, the vault and Lionel's execution. The only information she held back as she did with Rob, was that she was secretly sitting on the cash, the art and the incriminating files in her safety-deposit box.

"I'm impressed. Truly I am. But you know these things are like Whac-a-Mole. You smash one punk down, and another appears in his place."

"Which is why I'm here. I want to cut off the head. I want my casino back. In the old days, you were the person everyone turned to in a crisis."

"That was a long time ago. I will tell you that I'm no angel . . ." he began.

Josie remembered her father saying these very words—the hymn of a long line of distinguished killers.

"But I'm just a simple businessman now." Mel smiled serenely. "A member of the chamber of commerce. My contacts in that world are dead and buried."

"I appreciate your honesty, Mr. Davis," Josie said, although she didn't believe him.

Davis stood up and poured himself another cup of coffee.

"You still have your dad's car collection?" he asked, changing the subject. "That was really something."

Josie was disappointed. She rubbed her temples and sighed. She had come here as a last resort. She was led to believe that Davis had the ability and the guts to do things other people couldn't. And she knew he was still the most powerful man in the state. She realized that she had to do something. She had one round left in the chamber. One ace in the hole. She had to give up her personal insurance. No one knew about the files except Lionel. But she had no choice.

"What if I told you that I could give you something that could make New York fall to its knees—the Holy Grail of mob indictments?"

Davis went still and cocked his head.

"What New York family are we talking about?" he asked, his voice a bit sharper now.

"Gambassi."

"I knew the old man. I hear the nephew took over after the capo was hit. What's going on here?"

Josie took a deep breath and then described, in detail, the files she had found in Lionel's vault. Numbered bank accounts, private business communications, false social security numbers, records of large cash transactions, names of shell companies and their operators, wire transfer receipts, records from Antigua, The Bahamas and Geneva, free-port storage facilities and more. Enough proof to bring down the whole organization.

Davis fixed his eyes on Josie. The gentle, fatherly affect was gone, replaced with a sly and almost predatory expression. When he spoke there was a note of admiration in his voice that hadn't been there before. She looked like a pigeon, he thought, but she was really a shark. She had outwitted them all.

"Your father may be gone but his soul rests with you, my dear. This is the mob's greatest fear. It's the nightmare that always kills them. You can talk about murder, drugs and whores 'til the cows come home. But it's the money laundering and tax evasion that always throws them in the slammer. If you have their paper trail, you have them by the balls."

He asked Josie where the files were being held. She hesitated a minute and then told him. He suggested she give the second key to her father's attorney, Theo Goldman. He also suggested that after she gave him a copy of the files, she make an additional copy and move that to a second safety-deposit box at a different location.

"I assume you don't want to make a deal with the feds?" he asked.

"For some odd reason, I don't believe they'll keep their word." Josie cracked a smile.

Davis barked a laugh. "Now why would you think that?"

"Many of us remember them from the bad old days," Josie told him, her skin prickling at the memories of the wiretaps and harassment she'd seen. "Anyway, I grew up in this town and I'd like to stay here."

"Got it. So. Once you give me this ammunition, I'd be happy to make a few calls." Mel Davis leaned back in his chair and made a steeple with his fingers. "Just to be clear. What is the goal here?"

Josie leaned forward and met his eyes. "To get them the fuck out of my casino."

Chapter 75

On the way home, Josie veered off the highway onto a rocky dirt road bordered by ancient junipers and the charred remains of a controlled burn. It was a long detour but it gave her time to think.

The meeting with Davis had lifted Josie's spirits. In a lifetime spent trying to chase away the demons of her past, it was ironic that turning to this man—the embodiment of all she had fled—was the one thing that filled her with hope.

Now, at least, there might be a way out. She would give Davis the documents from Lionel's vault that afternoon, then hole up at the ranch with Sam until he called. Josie decided to hire a few extra security guards until the situation was resolved.

After she briefed Sam, they played blackjack and stayed up half the night, drinking bottles of vintage French wine that had slightly turned. Josie took the first sip and thought it tasted a bit vinegary. She swirled the liquid in her glass. The color didn't seem quite right. They drank it anyway. They talked about the days when they were kids, when Sam would bring girls back to the ranch, take them to the wine cellar and impress the hell out of them by introducing them to the world of fine wine.

"This one," he said, holding up a bottle with bold-faced French words, "would get me to first base."

"Cheap date."

"But *this* one," he said, holding up another with an ornate, yellowed label and a picture of a pastoral French vineyard, "was a sure thing."

The next day, there was a bitter southwest wind. Josie got out of bed at dawn, layered on a parka and long underwear and peeked into Sam's bedroom. He wouldn't be sober until noon, she estimated, so she put a leash on Rex and set out on her own.

When she hit the beginning of the first trail, she unleashed the dog and watched him bound ahead of her into the brush. She called him a few times to make sure he didn't wander off, and when he came right back, she forged ahead, taking a series of switchbacks and narrow trails in the canyon to reach her special spot, Cathedral Rock.

Whatever happened next, one thing was certain—her relationship with Frank would never be the same. She thought back to an early spring morning when she was nine. The ranch hands had passed on a rumor that a herd of wild mustangs normally in Tonopah had roamed farther south, close to the Kings' ranch. They told Sam that the horses could be viewed at a distance in a nearby canyon, so the next morning Sam woke Josie, Sunny and Frank and they all set out for the spot where they could catch a glimpse of the wild horses.

Even though Josie was much younger, she was the leader: She knew the desert better than any of them, and if she followed the right trail, she figured she could get them there by noon. She took binoculars in her backpack and a single bottle of water. The others brought nothing.

The winter frost was over, and there was a peace in the horsetail grass as bright yellow buds of western wallflower and Indian paintbrush cropped up among the piñon and juniper. Wildflowers were starting to bloom, and ants crawled over their shoes scavenging for dead insects.

The four of them hiked through the broken-down fences and gates that allowed cattle to descend into the canyon to graze. The trail got more difficult. It was eroded and rocky in places, as it hadn't rained in seventy days. But as the morning wore on, they noticed that the cool air had changed and grown muggy, thickening with the threat of storms. It was then Josie decided to go off trail, avoiding the rocks and gutted dirt and weaving through the brush and fallen dead trees. Roots and stumps caused them all to trip and stumble, and a few times they had to climb over boulders blocking the way. Josie was a little turned around but didn't mention that to the others. At one point, she asked Sam if he had a compass.

"Even if I had one, I wouldn't know how to use it. Are we lost?"

"I don't think so. I can figure it out," Josie said unconvincingly.

Just as they reached a peak that Josie didn't recognize, an unexpected, violent thunderstorm tore through the area. It was nearly fifteen miles in diameter and lasted what seemed like hours. The sky turned a violet-gray, and then unleashed a torrent of rain. The four started running for shelter. They finally crouched down and huddled in a circle, away from the tall trees. Bolts of lightning struck just inches from where they were sitting. The winds battered them harder than the rain, and suddenly, Frank was caught by a gust and disappeared down a deep ravine.

They stared at each other in shock. There was an ominous silence. Sam stood up first and peered over the edge of what turned out to be a rocky cliff. Frank was at the bottom, his leg twisted underneath him. He was motionless for a moment, and then they heard him scream.

"Are you all right?" Sam shouted down to him.

"Do I look the fuck all right? I think I broke something. Get me out of here."

"I can't," Sam hollered back. "Can you stand up?"

Frank rolled over and screamed again in pain.

"We need to get Dad." Sunny's voice was high and thin with panic.

"But we went off trail. He'll kill me," Josie protested.

"No shit," Sam replied. "I'll go with you. Sunny, you stay here."

"Why me?" she shrieked. "Don't leave me here alone!"

"You talk to Frank, okay? Keep him calm. We won't be long," Sam said.

Josie gave Sunny her water bottle, and ran with Sam back through the desert. She can't remember to this day how she found her way back to the ranch. Her father grabbed a couple of ranch hands and they piled into his four-wheel-drive vehicle. When they got there, Sunny had somehow hiked down the ravine and was holding Frank's head in her lap. Their hands were intertwined and she was giving him sips of water. They looked almost saintly, there in the hazy twilight.

Josie thought about the old western saying "When you're riding ahead of the herd, look back every now and then to make sure they're still with you." Josie knew after her meeting with Mel, her family as it was would no longer be with her.

Chapter 76

Forty-eight hours later, Josie got the call from Mel Davis. The meeting was set for the next day and Davis's assistant had also summoned Frank and Sam. In this town, when Mel Davis summoned, you showed up. It was a matter of respect.

Josie had been in some difficult situations with her brothers, but nothing compared to this. It was a miracle there wasn't a shoot-out. The one thing they agreed on was not to tell Sunny what was going on. They couldn't trust Trent and Sunny would tell him everything.

Josie was the only one who knew the agenda. She sat in Mel's office with her hands clasped tightly in her lap. Frank was on edge, shifting in his seat. Sam nervously adjusted his sport coat and smoothed out his tie while they all sat in silence and awaited Davis's arrival. Somewhat to Josie's surprise, Sam was clean-shaven, and sober.

Mel finally walked in a half hour late, trailed by his assistant and apologizing for the delay.

"It's good to see you all together," he said, reaching out a hand to Frank, then Sam, and giving Josie a warm smile and a kiss on the cheek. He settled behind his desk and poured himself a cup of coffee.

"You know," he began, "your father and I had a lot in common. We loved what we did. We loved this town. And we loved our families. What could be more important?"

The three of them looked at him and smiled stiffly. Sam nodded agreeably, seeming to relax a bit, while Josie focused straight ahead, not looking at either one of her brothers. She wished there had been another way. She wished she had a family that hadn't forced her hand. But she was where she was. And nothing could turn this train around.

"So, I'll get right to it," Mel said. "You all know the current circumstances of the Jackpot. I've made a few calls. There are some silent partners who have been involved in the operation of your business in order to safeguard their investment. As you might know, Frank made a deal with them to help repay his gambling debts. At one point, he owed over a hundred million dollars."

Josie and Sam both gasped.

"Jesus Christ! A hundred million dollars? What the fuck, Frank!" Sam yelled.

They knew Frank had been reckless, but they had no idea he had been *this* reckless. He had hidden it well. Casino owners are prohibited by law from gambling in their own establishments but that didn't stop Frank from gambling at tribal casinos on the East Coast, even getting them to sign NDAs. But failure to pay casino markers is a crime, and criminal activity cancels out the NDAs.

"With all due respect, Mr. Davis," challenged Frank, "there's no reason for you to get involved in our family issues. My debts are now nowhere near that amount, and I'm working it out with our New York lenders."

"It's true. Your debts have been partially repaid through the casino, and you currently owe around thirty mill, give or take a few."

"See?" Frank said to Josie and Sam. "I told you."

"When I referred to paybacks," Mel continued smoothly, "I was referring to the skimming that is currently taking place at your casino. That's an illegal practice that has the FBI interested and threatens the very existence of your family business."

"What is this?" Frank turned on Josie in a fury. "How much have you told him?"

"Are you fucking kidding me?" Sam said, shooting him a hostile stare. "Your goon Lionel kidnapped Billie and almost killed Josie. And the whole time he's been stealing from you, right under your nose, you dumbass."

"Who told you that?" Frank asked, shocked.

"While you were jerking off in Connecticut, your trusted advisor was fucking you over big-time," Sam said.

"Bullshit! I would have known," Frank shot back.

"Grow up! You're fucking pathetic," Sam snapped. "You've put us all in danger, not to mention almost shutting down our *family* business. It's not your fucking empire."

"Spare me your lectures," Frank said hotly. He stood up and buttoned his suit jacket. "I'm outta here."

"Sit down, Frank," Davis ordered. There was no mistaking the quiet authority in his voice.

A security guard in a navy blazer and tan pants appeared out of nowhere and stood silently in the doorway. Defeated, Frank sat down.

"You've been a selfish loser all your life. Even Dad thought you were a dick," Sam spat out.

"You can't talk to me that way," Frank said.

"I can talk to you any way I want . . ."

"Silence, please. I spoke with your lenders yesterday, Frank," Davis said, his eyes meeting Josie's. "They seemed amenable to forgiving the balance of the debt. They would be willing to withdraw from your casino."

"In exchange for what?" Frank snarled. It was the smartest thing he'd said all day, Josie thought.

"In exchange for several things. But in your case, son, you have to retire. Today."

"What? Why would I agree to that?"

"Because you have no choice. You're tapped out. Unless you'd prefer to end up in jail. The FBI is one step away from an indictment and if they get it, you'll be arrested."

Frank sat still for a moment, the color draining from his face. He was clearly stunned.

"You're done, Frank," Josie said. "You're out of the casino business."

Shocked, he turned on Josie. "Is that what you think? You can pretend you're going legit. But guess what? That's not the world we live in. There is no 'clean' and I don't answer to you."

"You do now," Josie said decisively. "I got you out of trouble. This is the price you're paying. You're welcome."

Frank glared at her as the reality set in.

"I'm calling my lawyer."

"You can call him," Davis said mildly, "but I already talked to Theo Goldman, and he agreed. It's the only way out."

Goldman was the best criminal defense attorney in town, which was why Roy King had him on retainer for decades. If he thought the only way for Frank to stay out of jail was to retire, no respectable lawyer would tell Frank anything different.

"We're trying to protect you here." Davis was starting to sound impatient.

"Well, it sure the fuck doesn't feel like it. More like a railroading," Frank countered. But his shoulders slumped like he was accepting defeat.

For a moment, Josie felt a wave of sorrow at her brother's obvious pain and humiliation. Frank headed for the door, and at a nod from Davis, the security guard stepped aside to let him pass. Frank left without looking back, his heavy footsteps echoing down the hall.

There was a brief silence.

"Would you mind excusing us?" Davis said, turning to Sam. He had been blunt and merciless with Frank, but now his voice softened. "Josie has asked me to help her with some accounting issues."

Sam glanced briefly at the security guard still standing at the door. "Sure," he said, standing up. "Thank you, Mr. Davis."

He extended his arm across the desk and shook Davis's hand. Always the charmer, Josie thought, watching Sam nod at the guard and slip out the door. Davis waited until the guard left and the door shut behind him. He removed his glasses and wiped them with his silk handkerchief. Then he leaned forward in his chair and set his elbows on the desk.

"I spoke with Bobby Gambassi yesterday and informed him of your desire to run the casino without his organization's interference. He checked with his operation to see where they stood financially. Turns out, the entire principal of the debt has been repaid, and the casino was working now to pay down interest. I suggested that since the original loan had been paid off, it was relatively easy to forgive the rest of the interest and conclude their business operations." Davis paused and looked at her. "Are you with me?" he asked.

"Yes, sir. I'm an accountant by trade, although this is outside my usual expertise."

"So I will go on. The beneficial owner in this case—the person who actually controls the business and receives its profits—has been compromised. The sheer volume and size of these transactions, although raising suspicion, have not yet led to indictments. This leads me to believe the feds do not have the proof they need to proceed. The offers of immunity from the agent you spoke with was simply fishing. I explained to Gambassi we needed to shut down any illegal activity as soon as possible to avoid further government involvement."

"What was his reaction?"

"Of course, he hated losing such a lucrative income stream . . ."

"But you made them an offer they couldn't refuse," Josie said with a knowing smile.

"This isn't Hollywood. It would be more accurate to say that we came to an understanding based on the financial evidence you and I now hold. Unlike his uncle, Bobby thinks of himself as a businessman. He sees himself moving entirely into legitimate enterprises. His wife joined one of those fancy New York museum boards. And his daughter is an equestrian, for Christ's sake."

"So I'm safe?"

"Yes. In addition to the man's social ambitions, your files were very persuasive."

"My father used to say that some people are not your friends. They're just scared to be your enemy."

Davis picked up a glass globe paperweight and tossed it back and forth between his palms. Josie could tell he wasn't finished. He pushed his chair back from the desk and walked to the window. He was wearing black snakeskin cowboy boots with snip toe design, a feature her father always liked because they looked sleek and elegant.

"In our day, your father and I found that civilization had a pretty thin skin covering it. It's best to be nobody's fool. There *are* a few conditions."

"I thought there might be. What do they want?"

Mel gazed out the window. "They have proof that two boxes that belong to them are now in someone's possession at the Jackpot. I assume these are filled with cash? They would like these boxes returned to them."

So much for going legitimate, Josie thought. Luckily, they had only seen photos of two boxes.

"Gambassi also specifically requested that a Renoir painting be immediately returned. He gave me the name of a company that specializes in transporting fine art—evidently they work for The Met and the Getty."

"That's it?" Josie asked. "We give them back the cash and the painting, and they agree to sever all relationships in our casino, front *and* back of the house?"

"That's the deal," Davis said.

"Everyone disappears?" Josie confirmed.

"One hundred percent," Davis agreed. "So I take it you know where these items can be found?"

"I do."

Davis nodded at his security guard, who disappeared down the hall.

"The files should stay where they are," he continued. "As insurance. I also told Gambassi that if anything should happen to you, the files would be sent, intact, to *The New York Times* and the Associated Press."

"I understand." Josie stood up, shoulders back, somehow managing to stay calm. "I can't thank you enough, Mr. Davis."

"I'm sure your father never imagined that you'd be the one taking over the casino." Mel turned away from the window and pinned her with a sharp-eyed stare. "His two sons and heirs, sidetracked, and the baby of the family steps up. I'm not a literary man, but this is almost Shakespearean. Roy King led his organization with courage and compassion, and I'm certain you'll do the same. This was an unexpected coup on your part. And not easy.

"Congratulations, my dear."

Chapter 77

Josie drove slowly out the gates of Mel Davis's massive estate. She should have been elated, but it was a hollow victory. She heard a few cracks of dry thunder off in the distance and felt another one of her headaches coming on. A tight band of pressure turned into a throbbing pain behind her left ear. She took one hand off the wheel and began massaging her temple.

Driving through the desert—the desert she belonged to—she thought back to the days when they were all so young and the animosity, violence and corruption hadn't yet affected their lives. She heard another crack of thunder, but this one was cloud to ground, much closer, more threatening. Two decades had passed and yet, in her bleak mood, the memory of one day long ago entered her consciousness and made her yearn for the time when they were truly a family.

When she was twelve, she made a secret pact with her sister and two brothers. At that time, Frank owned a baby-blue convertible Chevy, and they drove for miles out in the Nevada desert, past the glitzy hotels, past the suburbs, which rolled out like tumbleweeds, past the Paiute reservation and then through the nothingness of US-95 North to the 159.

The wind from the desert picked up as they neared Red Rock Canyon. Josie used to hate the wind. She remembered trying to hike, fighting the hot, dusty winds that blew across the Mojave Desert, sand pelleting her face. Everything rumbled and hissed like angry spirits on the rampage. Legend had it that the wind was a powerful god, an air spirit who carried messages. Sometimes Josie listened to the howling and was convinced this was true.

They parked near the entrance of the canyon, where the scenery was stark and elemental. They descended through the bright, red canyon walls, noticing a few desert bighorn sheep grazing on the mountainside. There were stands of barrel cactus blooming with bright, unexpected orange blossoms and dried-out chamisas as they hiked through the Joshua trees down a ridge to a secluded spot. Then Sam pulled out a hunting knife attached to his belt, and they all held out their arms. He made a narrow slit on their palms and blood rushed down into the sand and pooled beneath their feet. They pressed their arms together in silence.

The children told no one. There was no one to tell. Certainly not the powerful, smiling man, the killer who was their father. Or their mother, who had died years earlier. They grew up knowing that in the casino world of cards and dice, prostitutes and payoffs, there were some things you could talk about, and other things you couldn't. It was just one of those facts of life that was understood. But then their father, like an aging emperor, grew tired and weak, and he looked to his children to take his place. They had pressed their hot blood into each other in a silent vow, but in the end, it didn't matter. They were never blood brothers again.

Josie turned on her windshield wipers and drove back to town through the gathering storm. Her family, as she once knew it, was lost forever. They did love each other. Maybe they still could. But the reprieve she had been hoping for never happened. There was no more to be said. Her own role in the matter, and all its consequences, clearly led to this moment. Not simply a breach, but a catastrophic break. She thought about the way things used to be and quietly said goodbye.

Chapter 78

ONE YEAR LATER

On her one-year anniversary as chairman of the Jackpot, Josie made a last attempt to reach out to Frank. He had not spoken to her since the day he stormed out of Davis's office. He told her they were done. But she knew with families, you were never truly done. She might try again next year.

Billie was living with her now at the ranch, and her school was just fifteen minutes away. Times had changed. The building boom had reached almost to Lake Mead. Suburbs had encroached on the desert, and the community of Green Valley with its restaurants, shops and theaters was nearby. The ranch was alive again with kids. Billie had friends, activities and parties. Josie made sure Billie did not suffer the cold isolation that Josie felt as a child. Sam stayed with them every so often, now that he had moved to a ranch in Wyoming. Three costly stints in rehab later, Josie was relieved that Sam had finally seemed to have gotten himself straight. He might fall off the wagon, but he would never again live in Las Vegas.

Josie drove through the desert to the casino. She pulled into the first spot in the executive parking lot, the one labeled "Jackpot 1," and was greeted by the security guard.

"Good morning, Ms. King," he said, opening the iron gate and then ushering her into the casino.

Josie walked through the gaming floor, like her father had done for so many years, asking a pit boss if his daughter won the school soccer match, checking in with one of the dealers who had recently returned from sick leave, grasping the hand of a waitress and giving her a friendly smile. One of the first things she did, upon becoming chairman, was settle the strike with the Culinary Union Local 226, negotiating pension benefits and wage adjustments. She also instituted the Roy King Scholarship Fund, guaranteeing college tuition at UNLV for all of her employees' children.

Sunny's boutique was still dark, but Josie rapped lightly on the glass to see if she was there. No answer. The two of them were back to normal, after a rough patch that lasted several months. The details of the Davis meetings were never fully disclosed, and Sunny, egged on by her husband, was stunned and aggrieved that she had been left out of the discussion. Frank's attempts to explain his actions fell on deaf ears. Sunny eventually decided she didn't want to know more, and became estranged from Frank as well. Eddie the pit boss still visited Sunny at the boutique occasionally, but Josie got the sense that Sunny had cooled toward him.

Josie reached her office, the office her father had occupied for more than four decades. Moe was already there waiting for her. He had been promoted to chief operating officer. He was clean-shaven and wearing a black silk suit and crisp white-on-white shirt—a far cry from the retired mountain man she saw standing on his porch a year ago. Moe was holding a bottle of champagne and he handed her a glass.

"Isn't it a little early for this?" Josie asked.

"It's a celebration. I just returned the last box to the counting room."

Josie sat down at her desk and took a tiny sip. So now it was finished. Twenty boxes gone and accounted for. Two back to New York. Two to Moe. Six returned to the counting room to be recycled back onto the casino floor. And ten flown by private jet to Josie's numbered offshore account in the Cayman Islands. Lucky Luciano once said that there was no such thing as good money or bad money. There was just money. But perhaps it could be used for something good.

Josie leaned back in her chair and glanced at the glorious Harry Jackson cowboy sculpture that Rob had given her for her birthday. He knew it reminded her of her father. When he first gave it to her, they sat down on his couch and stared in silence at the sculpture. And then they went to bed.

In the last year, their relationship had subtly shifted. She was now his equal, and in some ways, that made her even more appealing. The white-hot attraction was still there. But they lived apart as lovers and competitors, occasionally flying out for a weekend to Monte Carlo or Deauville. Rob was researching European gambling operations, always searching for the next new thing.

After work, Josie parked near the barn, where a stable man was riding a palomino—one of her favorites. She still boarded a number of rodeo horses, who were trained and exercised daily, and on some weekends, she and Billie rode out in the desert. As she walked past the back storage area, she thought about the four impressionistic paintings previously locked in the underground vault. The paintings still had the invoices taped to the back, with the name of the private London dealer. Their value far exceeded what was in the twenty boxes. Josie had told no one about these. And she didn't intend to. She had moved them to a climate-controlled offshore facility and at some point she would decide what to do with them.

Once in a while, she still had the urge to get up at dawn, pull on her boots and venture deep into the desert to her special spot. She'd settle down, take off her hat and turn her face toward the mountains. Every so often, she thought she saw her father. Like a desert mirage, the light rays bending his image, floating in the distance, rising up from the sand and walking toward her.

Somewhere deep inside her, a thought would creep into her head. She heard it as a whisper. She heard it as a warning.

I'm no angel.

Acknowledgments

Foremost, we are deeply grateful to our brilliant agent, Molly Friedrich, for her many years of encouragement and unwavering support. It made all the difference.

We would also like to acknowledge Lucy Carson, whose excellent advice and editorial skills were enormously helpful throughout this process.

In addition, we are indebted to our formidable agent at WME, Hilary Zaitz Michael, who was an extraordinary champion of our work. We were incredibly fortunate to have her in our corner.

Finally, we were privileged to work with our editor at William Morrow, Rachel Kahan, whose expertise, wisdom, and thoughtful insights made the novel better. She was instrumental in bringing *The Kings of Vegas* to publication.

About the Authors

Karen Mack has cowritten four novels with Jennifer Kaufman, including the national bestsellers *Literacy and Longing in L.A.* and *Freud's Mistress*. She is also a Golden Globe and Emmy Award–winning film and television producer. Mack was raised in Las Vegas, Nevada, where her family has lived for generations.

Jennifer Kaufman is an award-winning journalist and bestselling novelist. Kaufman cowrote four novels with Karen Mack, including the national bestsellers *Literacy and Longing in L.A.* and *Freud's Mistress*.